ROCK BOTTOM

EMILY GOODWIN

Rock Bottom
A Dawson Family Novel
Copyright 2020
Emily Goodwin
Cover photography by Sara Eirew
Editing by Contagious Edits

This is a work of fiction. Names, characters, businesses, places, events, and incidents are either the products of the author's imagination or used in a fictitious manner. Any resemblance to actual persons, living or dead, or actual events or places is purely coincidental.

❀ Created with Vellum

To Ashley. This one is just for you.

CHAPTER 1

DEAN

THEN...

"Where's Kara?"

I knew the question was coming, yet Mom's words still cut through me, making me pause in my step as I move toward the fridge to get a beer that I desperately need.

"At home. She's exhausted from staying up late working on homework."

I hate that the lie rolls off my tongue so easily. It's not hard to believe my wife is actually at home resting after pulling an all-nighter working on her master's degree in education. In truth, we got into an argument over Sunday night dinner at my parents' house.

But that was only part of the issue.

"Poor dear," Mom says and grabs a Tupperware container from under the cabinet and thrusts it at me. "Don't forget to get her a plate to go."

I smile, forcing the pain away, and thank Mom. Setting the Tupperware on the counter, I open the fridge, get out two beers, and go through the kitchen to the backyard.

"Help me up," my sister says as soon as I step onto the patio. "I have to pee."

Laughing, I set the beers down and extend a hand. Quinn takes it and dramatically groans as she hefts herself to her feet.

"You look like you're about ready to pop," I tell her.

"I feel like it." She rests both hands on her stomach. "I'm three days away from my due date and am dying."

"You're the one who wanted to have another baby."

"Yeah, yeah." She waves a hand in the air. "Save the speech for Archer." She looks across the yard at Archer, her husband and my best friend, who's pushing their two kids on the swing set. "I know how much you like being reminded that he's the one who knocked me up."

"Gross, Quinn."

She laughs. "You make it easy. Now I see why Logan and Owen gave you so much shit when we were kids. I feel like I missed out by trying to be the peacemaker."

I let out a snort of laugher. "You, the peacemaker?"

"Yeah. I was. And still am."

"If you say so." I grab my beer and pop the top. "But that's not how I remember it."

"And how do you remember it?" Quinn rubs her belly and makes a face. "Stop kicking my ribs, baby. That doesn't feel good."

"I was the peacemaker and basically the middle child. I'm between two extremes. There's Weston, who was always a rule follower and incredibly boring, and Logan and Owen, who are, well…Logan and Owen."

Quinn laughs. "What does that make me?"

"You were the *little princess* of the family," I remind her, laughing as well. "You could do no wrong."

She just rolls her eyes. "I really have to pee now."

I grab the other beer as she slowly makes her way into the house and walk across the yard.

"Uncle Dean!" Emma squeals, reaching her arms out. I smile at my niece and feel the rest of my anger start to melt away.

"Hey, Squirt!"

"Will you play chase with me?" she asks, madly kicking her feet to try and get the swing to stop.

"Hey," Archer says to me, grabbing the back of the swing to slow Emma down. "You ready to lose again tonight?"

"Psshh, you wish," I laugh. "You'll be on?" Archer has been my best friend since college, and while it was weird for a bit when he started dating my sister, he's part of the family for real now and things couldn't be better.

Except…they could be.

"Yeah," he says, and sets Emma down. She takes my hand and starts pulling me toward the slide. "But don't let me stay up too late," he laughs. "The baby will be here any day now and we won't get much sleep." He goes back to Arya, who cries as soon as she sees her sister climbing up the steps to go down the slide.

"You ready for another?" I hold out my hand, spotting Emma as she climbs.

"We already have two. What's one more?"

I laugh. "So you're all set?"

"As much as we can be. But the cats have been sleeping in the crib."

"Your kids are all damned to be crazy cat ladies like Quinn."

"Probably." He gets Arya out of the swing and she stops crying right away. "Though my money is on this one being a boy. Quinn had really bad morning sickness with both girls and it hasn't been that bad this time around. And she says the curse was broken after Paige was born." Archer makes a face. "Something about the balance of girls and boys being equal in the Dawson family," he chuckles. "It's crazy but makes sense at the same time."

"What was your boy name again?" I ask causally.

"Hah. Nice try. Quinn would kill me if I told anyone. Even you."

"It's Dean, isn't it?"

Archer laughs. "I can tell you it's not, at least. And I know it was my idea to wait to find out what we're having, but it's driving me crazy now."

"Everyone is going crazy not knowing." I move to the bottom of the slide to catch Emma when she comes down. We hang outside with the kids for a little while longer and then Mom calls us in for dinner.

Wes and Scarlet just arrived, with their kids Jackson and Violet. Logan and Danielle come in right after them, and Logan is holding their six-month-old, who somehow managed to stay asleep through all the chaos of kids talking and dogs barking.

"Can we start eating?" Quinn asks, sitting on a barstool at the large island counter. "I'm starving."

"Owen and Charlie aren't here yet," Dad says. "Not that we're surprised."

Mom gives Dad a pointed look. "They'll be here. Charlie won't let Owen be too late."

"They're a mile away," Logan tells us, sitting next to Quinn.

"Can you sense it?" Quinn asks. "Like a *twin thing?*"

"No," Logan says and cocks an eyebrow. "I never took the tracking app off Owen's phone." He shrugs. "Never know where he'll end up."

"Logan," Mom scolds but we all laugh.

"Why don't you get your plate started?" Mom hands Quinn a plate and Quinn turns, holding the plate out to Archer. He takes it with a smile and gives her a kiss before going around to the stove, getting her plate ready for her.

"How's the progress on the Robocop?" Wes asks Quinn, straight-faced.

"We're still working out a few flaws and trying to find material strong enough to protect the hard drive from fire."

"Ha-ha," I say dryly. "I'm not falling for it this time."

"It's real," Quinn presses.

4

"Just like the Batmobile," I scoff.

"I've seen the prototype," Wes goes on. "It is real. I'll admit the Batmobile wasn't, though even Jackson knew we were making it up."

I finish my beer and just shake my head. A few months ago, Quinn told us she was working on inventing some sort of robot that will help put out fires, going into places too dangerous for firefighters.

I didn't buy it then, and I'm not buying it now.

Though, it is a cool concept.

Quinn goes on and on about it, getting way too excited about the details of how she's coding the software—details that are lost on all of us—until Owen and Charlie show up.

Then its pure chaos again as everyone gets their plates and crams around the dining room table. I look around, feeling a tug on my heart that I've been ignoring for years.

Paige wakes up and starts to fuss. "I'll get her bottle," Logan says and stands. He gives the baby to our mother instead of Danielle and slowly walks into the kitchen.

Mom immediately starts baby-talking to her, and Dad leans over, holding out his hand for Paige to grab.

"Sister?" Dad mumbles, brows furrowing. Logan comes back into the dining room, standing behind Danielle's chair. "What does her shirt say?"

Mom holds the baby out, with her back to the rest of us. "Big sis—oh my gosh! You're pregnant!"

Danielle beams, reaching up to take Logan's hand. "I am!"

The entire table breaks out in happy cheers, and I congratulate them with a smile on my face. My first thought is to call Kara and tell her, and then I get irritated all over again that she refused to come to dinner with me tonight.

"Finally," Charlie laughs. "I wasn't sure how long I'd be able to keep that a secret anymore."

"You knew?" Mom looks from her to Logan with wide eyes, giving him a silent *why didn't you tell me first* look.

Danielle laughs, looking up at Logan again. "I told her before I told him."

"I didn't find out until the next morning," Logan goes on, smiling as he looks down at his wife. "She fell asleep before I came home from work."

"We were both asleep," Charlie laughs. "I went over for dinner and passed out on the couch."

"I came home to an empty house," Owen deadpans, slowly shaking his head.

"There's nothing like pregnancy to suck the life right out of you," Quinn says. Then she gasps and looks at Scarlet. "You only have a few days to get knocked up so we can all be pregnant together."

"Nope," Wes and Scarlet say at the same time, and Wes puts his arm around Scarlet. "Two are plenty for us."

"And I'm older than you all," Scarlet reminds Quinn, who waves her hand in the air.

"Not by much."

"Anyway, Wes is going to get—" Scarlet holds up her fingers and makes a cutting motion. "We just made the appointment."

"Which doctor?" Archer asks, all too interested. Wes just gives him a look and shakes his head. Happy chatter breaks out across the table, and that tug on my heart I've been ignoring reaches out and yanks that fucker right out of my chest.

I turn, looking into the kitchen at my phone which I left on the counter. The angry words Kara and I exchanged before I left still burn on my tongue, and a sour feel starts to bubble in my stomach.

I turn back just in time to see Logan take Paige back from Mom and sit back down next to Danielle, who leans in for a kiss. Reaching for my beer, I lean back and look around the table at my family—my happy family—and I can't deny it anymore.

I want this, and it's what's been the source of why Kara and I have argued so much the last few months.

I want this, and she doesn't.

I can't understand how she doesn't, but maybe she can't understand how I do. Maybe I was too hard on her. Not understanding enough. Didn't explain myself well enough.

Things have been rocky between us, but she's my wife and I love her. We were happy once, can't we be happy again?

I down the rest of my beer, trying not to acknowledge something else I've been ignoring. No one wants to admit they've been falling out of love, and the pain builds slowly. You don't notice it at first, and then one day, you wake up under the crushing weight of a broken heart.

I don't want us to get to that point.

Though part of me thinks we already are.

And now that I want a family and Kara doesn't...it doesn't help.

When we got married, we had plans to travel, to see the world, to live it up as best we could. Having kids wasn't part of that plan. I didn't want kids for a good while. In three years...five years...hell, even seven years, then maybe we'd think about it.

But we've been married for a while now and haven't traveled as we imagined. Haven't lived it up. Though does anything go according to plan?

"Dean," Quinn calls, pulling me out of my thoughts.

"Yeah?"

"Scarlet, Jamie, and I are going to see a movie tomorrow? Can you ask Kara if she wants to join?"

"Yeah," I tell her, though I have a feeling Kara will decline her invitation. She told me it feels weird to hang out with Quinn and Scarlet since they've become so close. When I tell her she could become close to them if she actually accepted their invites every now and then, she gets mad at me.

And I get mad right back.

7

Arya starts to fuss, wiggling around in the highchair. She throws her bowl of mashed potatoes on the floor and all four dogs swarm around her, pushing each other out of the way to lick up the mess. Quinn starts to stand but Archer stops her, telling her to take it easy and he'll handle their toddler.

"Thank you," Quinn says softly, looking at Archer the say way she looked at him on their wedding day.

It hits me then that while I get pissed at Kara, I'm not without my faults. She does stuff that irritates the shit out of me, but I do the same to her. We're dangerously walking the line of falling completely out of love, and I'll be damned if I let that happen.

∿

"You're leaving already?" Dad pulls a cheesecake out of the fridge.

"Yeah. I'm going to bring Kara her dinner and force her to take the night off from studying."

"She's almost done with her class, isn't she?" Dad sets the cheesecake on the counter and gets out another Tupperware to get me a few pieces to take home.

"Yes, thankfully. It's been a hectic last few years."

"It has been. We miss seeing her around here."

I nod, agreeing with him. "I think I'm going to surprise her by booking a vacation over her winter break. Going somewhere warm would be nice."

"Winter is a good time to go on vacation," Dad notes, talking about work and not the weather. Dad worked his way up from a carpenter to starting and owning his own construction and contracting business, and I work with him. I'll take over the family business when he retires. We slow down a bit in the winter, not able to do much exterior work when it's bitterly cold. Though we already have a full lineup of new houses set to go up in the spring.

"Ohhhh, that's so sweet," Quinn says, having overheard me talking to Dad. "We can't wait until we can go on a vacation again."

"Didn't you just go to Disney World?" I ask her.

"It was months ago." She pats her stomach. "And I couldn't go on the good rides."

"And aren't you going again in like six months with Archer's parents?"

"Yes."

I laugh. "That's not that far to wait, sis."

"It feels like forever," she laughs. "Text me later and let me know if Kara wants to come with us. I'm going to buy the tickets online tonight so we can get good seats. Preferably at the end of the aisle since this baby is fifteen pounds and sitting on my bladder."

"That baby weighed six pounds at the last scan," Archer quips, coming into the kitchen to refill Emma's water cup.

Quinn rolls her eyes. "Always such a doctor."

"I can't let you forget," Archer tells her matter-of-factly. "You're leaving?" he asks, seeing the to-go containers in my hands.

"Yeah. Kara's been working hard and is probably hungry."

Quinn, who's annoyingly perceptive, narrows her eyes and opens her mouth to question me, but the baby kicks her hard again and she winces. *Thank you, little guy, for having my back.* I grab the cheesecake and say a quick goodbye to the rest of my family and then head out.

I pick up my phone once I'm in my truck, set on calling Kara to tell her I'm on my way home. I drop it on the passenger seat, thinking it'll be better to surprise her with the food, an apology, and a vow that from this day forward, I'm going to try harder.

Then maybe we can be happy again.

We can stop the fall. Turn it around. Fall back in love instead of out.

We were happy once. We can be again.

I turn up the radio, singing along to Tom Petty, and make the fifteen-minute drive from my parents' farmhouse to our house in the downtown area of Eastwood.

There's a car in our driveway, parked right in the middle, blocking me from pulling into my spot. Kara has had a few friends from her master's class come over lately, but the ones she usually studies with live in Newport, which is a bit of a drive. She didn't mention having any over tonight, but I don't mind. It'll give me time to look up vacation details while she finishes up her schoolwork.

I park on the street and go in through the garage, stepping into the mud room that's attached to the kitchen. Two empty glasses of wine are on the counter…along with a pair of pants.

Men's pants.

I set the food on the counter and swallow hard. Somewhere in the back of my mind, I know what's going on.

But my brain won't let it come to the surface.

Blinking, my feet move on their own accord, following the trail of clothing.

Kara's shirt is on the stairs.

Her bra is hanging off the bannister.

Blue striped boxers are at the stop of the landing.

Everything echoes around me, and I think the meatloaf and potatoes I had for dinner are going to come up. I mentally check out as I keep walking, going down the hall to the master bedroom.

The door is cracked, and the closer I get, the sicker I feel. Kara is talking to someone. And that someone is talking back. I'm not fully aware of what I'm doing as I pause in the doorway and push the door open.

"Dean!" Kara exclaims, pulling the sheets up over her…and *him*. "It's…it's not what you think!"

The shock wears off and I'm pissed as fuck. All I want to do is pound my fists into that guy's face, but I know—even through my anger—that won't solve the issue.

My wife is in bed with another man.

In *our* bed.

Balling my fingers into a fist, I turn, and punch the wall. My hand goes through the drywall and gets sliced open by a nail. The pain doesn't even register.

"Dean!" Kara calls again and starts to get out of the bed. I don't want to hear whatever fucking excuse she's going to give me.

I thought we could fix things.

Be happy again.

But we can't.

CHAPTER 2

RORY

PRESENT DAY...

E verything is fine.
I grip the steering wheel and squeeze my eyes closed, allowing myself a few seconds to feel—to let it actually sink in.

And I know it's not going to be fine.

My stomach flip-flops with worry, and my mind plays out a record-setting game of *worst-case scenario*. The car behind me honks, and I jerk my head up, blinking back the tears as I slowly step on the gas, accelerating through the intersection.

I'll get another job, as an operating room nurse? Not in Silver Ridge. But there are a few other options here, and I have an impressive resume already for only being twenty-eight.

Though some employers might see me as flighty and not able to commit to a job, which isn't the case at all. I love commitment. Commitment and I are best buds.

If the hospital didn't get bought out by a big corporation who's more concerned with making money than actual patient care, I would have stayed at Silver Ridge General until it was time to retire. I had a whole plan: move up to unit manager, then charge nurse, then go for the Director of Nurses position.

I drive another block and flick on my turn signal, slowing to a stop at another intersection. My phone chimes with a text, and since I'm at a complete stop, I pick it up out of the cup holder and read the message. It's from Mike, the guy I've been dating for the last five or six months, and he wants to know if I can come over —and that he just ordered a pizza.

I type out a quick reply, saying I can now since I'm on my way home from work, and he replies with a thumbs-up. He's not the most chatty, and while texting isn't exactly my ideal way of having a riveting conversation, the stupid thumbs-up annoys me.

I go around the block, backtracking a bit to get to Mike's house. He lives downtown, and I'll be there in just a few minutes. I suck in a breath and blink rapidly, trying to pull it together. I want to enjoy a few minutes of normalcy as I eat my feelings, and I don't want pity.

Once I'm parked in front of his house, I pull my name badge over my head and hang it on my rearview mirror like I always do, but it's not like I'm going to need that stupid thing anymore.

Not only did I get let go, I wasn't given any notice. I do believe Marissa, my nursing director, genuinely felt bad, as she was just following orders from her own boss, but come fucking on. Can't you give a girl the proper two weeks? Two days would have been better than this.

I dig through my oversized purse for my lip gloss, try to fluff up my hair, though it's no use. Being in the operating room means pulling all my hair back and tucking it under a surgical cap, and my brunette hair is naturally wavy and totally unruly after a day in the OR, sweating from standing under the bright lights.

It was an eventful day today, with three back-to-back appen-dectomies and one emergency gallbladder removal. Time flew by, every surgery went without a hitch, and my patients were doing

13

well when my shift ended. It's the kind of day that reminds me what I love so much about being a nurse.

My hand gets stuck in a knot in my hair, and I give up and twist my long locks back into a messy bun. Taking another deep breath, I get out of the car and hurry up the snowy sidewalk. It's late February, but we still have another few months of snow here in Michigan.

Mike never locks his door when I'm coming over, and I step inside, getting hit with the smell of pizza right away. I didn't have time to eat lunch today and I'm starving.

"Hey, babe," he says, watching me stomp the snow off my shoes before taking them off. I pull off my coat and hang it on the coatrack behind the front door. "You look hot today."

"I'm in scrubs," I laugh.

He wiggles his eyebrows. "I know."

"Please tell me there's at least half a pizza left."

"Half a pizza?" he laughs.

"I didn't get a lunch break." I stop, clamping my jaw shut and pressing my lips together. I'm acting like everything is fine, which isn't the healthiest thing to do, I know. But all I want is to drown my sorrows in pizza grease and pretend like things are going to be okay. The dread and anxiety will hit me hard tonight, when I'm trying to sleep. So why not deny like a normal person?

Mike motions for me to follow him into the living room. The pizza box is still closed and on the coffee table. "I haven't even opened it yet."

"Did you check to see if they got your order right?" I laugh as I go into the kitchen to wash my hands. "That time they sent us anchovies and pineapple pizza instead of extra cheese scarred me."

"Oh, me too." He grabs two beers from the fridge, forgetting—again—that I don't like beer. I don't drink much in general. I'm not a "look all classy holding a glass of red wine, slowly sipping it throughout the night" kind of girl. I don't like the taste of alcohol, and when I do have some sort of mixed drink or sweet wine, I tend to overdo it.

Trading the beer for a water bottle, I join Mike in the living room. He turns on *Gold Rush* and we dig into the pizza. As soon as I finish my last piece, Mike rests his hand on my thigh, slowly inching it up.

"Oh, I almost forgot," I start, letting my leg fall to the side, against his. "Sam was able to get off work and come home for the weekend for my parents' anniversary dinner. Mason's here too. You haven't met them yet. Have you met Jacob?" I think back, unable to remember a time I've introduced Mike to any of my brothers.

"Yeah. He's the vet. I've taken my mom there with Muffin before."

"Well in that case, everyone with an animal in Silver Ridge has met him. Everyone is going to be there, and my cousins Lachlan and Lennon will be there too. Lachlan plays hockey for some famous team." I make a face. "I don't really follow hockey, though. And Lennon and I grew up together. I used to pretend she was my sister," I laugh. "Growing up with three older brothers made me desperately want a sister. They'll all be happy to finally meet you."

I look at Mike, waiting for him to say something along the lines of "I'll be happy to meet them too" but all I get is radio silence.

"Want to go in the bedroom?" he asks suddenly.

"Uh, sure. That's the only reason you wanted me to come over, wasn't it?" I tease, poking at Mike.

"I wanted to talk to you too," he starts and gets to his feet, pulling me up with him. "But I never turn down sex."

"Well then." I wiggle my eyebrows. "Take me into your bedroom, kind sir."

≈

15

I come out of the bathroom and get back into bed, cold from walking through the room naked. Pulling the comforter up to my chin, I snuggle closer to Mike.

"Can we talk now?" he asks as soon as I'm snugged up and comfy.

"Talk?" I push up on my elbows. *Not again...* "Uh, sure. About what?"

"I've really liked the time we've spent together, Rory."

My throat is suddenly thick and my heart pounds in my chest. He's breaking up with me? Now? After we *just* had sex?

"But I'm not ready for something serious. And I know you... you want more. Meeting your family...I'm just not there yet. I want to travel and devote more time to my music."

His words echo in my head.

Travel?

He considers that plucking he does on his guitar music?

All I asked was for him to come to dinner not give me a promise ring before dessert.

"You couldn't have told me this before I got into bed with you?"

He shrugs. "I wasn't sure if you'd sleep with me after I told you."

The world feels like it's spinning, and while I can't say I was in love with Mike, I enjoyed being with him.

Though now it just feels like a waste of six months. I gave so much to Mike. I watched him play at every shitty bar in the county, staying out late when I had an early shift the next morning. I was supportive. A good girlfriend. Way better than he deserved.

"You're a manipulative jerk," I spit.

"Don't be like that, Rory."

I get out of bed, angrily shoving a pillow out of the way as I search for my clothes. I force my feet into my underwear and yank them up.

"And we can still do this. I know you're not a one-night-stand kind of girl," he adds quickly. "So think of it more as friends with benefits. Nothing has to change, really."

"That would be tempting," I say, and I angrily pull my scrub top over my head, not bothering with my bra. "If I enjoyed having sex with you."

Mike gasps.

"That's right. I faked it almost every time just to get it over with." It's only half true, though I feel like I had to really work for those few times I did come during sex. I can't blame him entirely, though, as much as I want to right now. I'm one of those lucky women who need a bit more stimulation to orgasm. But I'm pissed and my petty side is coming out.

I grab my pants and my bra, balling them up as I stomp out of the room. Mike calls after me, but I'm too busy pushing my feet into my shoes to give him the time of day. I throw my coat on, grab my purse, and storm out of the house, slamming the door behind me.

"Ah, hello, Rory, dear," Mrs. McMillan calls from the sidewalk. She was my high school science teacher, the mother of Amber McMillan who teased me relentlessly in high school, and is now walking down the snow-covered sidewalk; arm linked through Mr. McMillan's, who's my banker.

Their chocolate lab lets out an excited yip, and normally I'd be all over crouching down to pet Godiva, but I'm not wearing any pants.

Can today get any worse?

"Mom, wait up!" Amber jogs to catch up, blonde hair flowing behind her, looking like she just jumped off a *Northface* ad in a magazine.

You have got to be fucking kidding me.

Snow crunches under Amber's boots and comes to a stop next to her parents, taking Godiva's leash from her dad.

"Rory. Wow, it's been a while." She bats her lash extensions and flicks her eyes to my bare legs.

"Hi," I say and try to nonchalantly pull my coat closed. Maybe it looks like I'm wearing a dress.

A short dress.

And Crocs.

Dammit.

"Nice, uh, evening," I say, feeling my cheeks turn the same cherry red as my nail polish.

"It's a little chilly." She flips her hair behind her shoulder, and I hate her for looking so good in a hat. "How have you been? It's been, gosh, years."

"Really good."

Mrs. McMillan looks at my feet. Snow is coming through the little holes in my shoes and my feet are freezing. *Please think I'm wearing a dress...* She blinks a few times and takes a step forward. "Tell your mother I said hello."

"I will." I force the world's most awkward smile, closing my eyes in a long blink. I'll be home soon, and since I don't have to get up to go to work in the morning, I can start—and finish—that bottle of sangria I've been saving *for a special occasion.*

Embarrassment burns on my face, bringing hot tears streaming down my cheeks. I angrily wipe them away and I step in a snow bank. My shoe fills with snow and I clench my jaw. It's the icing on this shitty-ass cake I call my life, that's for sure.

I'm trembling by the time I get to my car, and intend to sit here a minute and let it warm up. But when I see Mike open the front door, I tear out of my spot. I've never been more thankful for my four-wheel drive in my life.

The McMillan's look at me as I speed away and I can already see Mrs. McMillan clucking her tongue and shaking her head as she gossips about me to her neighbors. And God knows what Amber is going to say to her "besties" from high school she still hangs out with.

Who still call me Weird Rory because they never fucking grew up.

Curse of a small town, I know.

I speed the whole way home, crossing all the way through town. I live in a large, old house that was divided into three apartments fifty or so years ago. Everything is terribly dated, but I say its part of the charm.

Parking in front of the big house, I pull my scrub pants on, fighting a bit to get them over my shoes, and then get out.

Missy Davis, who lives in the apartment above me, comes out with her two Yorkies in her arms as I walk toward the house. Each dog is wearing a jacket, a scarf, and boots on all four feet.

"Hey, Rory," she says, fussing over one of the dogs, who keeps flicking the boots off her paws. "Did you hear the news?"

"News? What news?"

She motions to a *For Sale* sign front and center of the yard.

"What is that?" It's perfectly clear what that is. Mr. Thomas, who owns the building, has been talking about selling for years. Maybe I was naive to assume I'd be out before that happened, but obviously I was wrong.

And I...I can't.

My job.

My boyfriend.

They say things come in threes.

Might as well add my apartment to that list.

Nothing is going to be okay.

CHAPTER 3

DEAN

" **M**otherfucker."

"What?" I ask, not taking my eyes off the glowing TV screen in front of us. Archer and I are sitting in the theater room in the finished basement of his house.

Archer trades his PlayStation controller for his phone, holding it up with a frown on his face. I glance away from our game just long enough to see it's the hospital calling.

"Sucks to be you," I say and kill his character. Archer takes his headset off and answers the phone. He's on call tonight, which is the only reason the hospital is calling at half-past eleven. "You gotta go in?" I ask when he hangs up.

"Yeah. I have a stab-wound to fix."

"You sound way too excited about that."

"By the smell, the nurse thinks it might have perforated the bowel."

"Sick," I laugh and start to shut down the game. "Sounds bad."

"Oh, it is. They're prepping the guy for surgery now and I'll be assisting another surgeon on the procedure."

We put our controllers and headsets away and go upstairs and into the kitchen. Archer grabs something to eat on the way to the hospital and goes up to the second level to tell Quinn he's leaving. I rummage through the fridge, finding yesterday's leftovers behind jars of homemade baby food.

I stick it in the microwave and sit at the large island counter, looking at my phone while I wait for the food to heat up. My finger hovers above the little blue Facebook icon. I hesitate and then put my phone done at the last second.

"You wanna stay for a while?" Archer asks, coming down the back stairs that empty right into the kitchen. "I don't like leaving Quinn and the kids alone at night."

"I can." The microwave beeps and I get up to grab the glass container of pot roast.

"Thanks, man. And Quinn will appreciate it. She's convinced the house is haunted."

"Again? Are you sure it's not more cats living on your back porch?"

"I'd rather it be ghosts this time." He rolls his eyes. "And she and Scarlet found a Ouija board at an antique store and Quinn bought it. Now she's convinced she summoned something."

"I don't get how someone can be so smart and logical like she is, yet she's terrified of ghosts."

Archer laughs and grabs a water bottle from the pantry. "I'm sure it has nothing to do with all of her brothers tormenting her about her childhood home being haunted."

"That was Logan and Owen," I counter, though I remember helping those assholes set up a fog machine in the hallway in the middle of the night.

Archer leaves the house in a rush, and I take my food back to the island counter. As soon as I sit, a white cat comes running, jumping up and immediately going right for my bowl. I push her away and get bombarded by two more.

Annoyed, I stand, holding the bowl in my hand, and lean against the counter. The same white cat paws at me, meowing.

"Fine," I say, and give the cats each a little piece of roast. I finish the food and put the bowl in the sink, yawning. I got up at five AM this morning to meet my construction crew on a job site, and spent the day filling in for one of the guys who left with food poisoning. I finished the day with a workout, ran home to shower, and then came over to Quinn and Archer's for dinner.

I'm exhausted and should crash. It'll be another early morning tomorrow, filled with client meetings and approving designs before sending them to our architect. But just the thought of lying down causes anxiety to ripple through me.

Night is the time I remember I'm alone.

That I've been alone, even before the divorce was final.

The time I question if any of my marriage was real, or if it was bullshit all along.

I'm not going to risk feeling. Risk admitting what I've been denying to everyone—and myself.

"You ate it all," I tell the cats, who are still winding around my feet, meowing for more food. I step over them, going back into the basement to watch TV. I make it halfway through an episode of *The Witcher* when my phone vibrates with a text. It's Maria, and if she's texting me around midnight, I know exactly what she wants.

Maria: Hey, handsome. Whatcha doing?

Me: Hanging out at my sister's.

Maria: You gonna be there long?"

Me: Probably. Her husband just got called into work and I said I'd stay. She doesn't like to be home alone at night.

Maria. Awwww that's so sweet of you. You're a good guy.

I wince. I broke my rule of *don't hook up with the same woman twice* with Maria. I was drunk when we hooked up the second time, thinking of my failed marriage and putting the blame on myself. I needed something—some*one*—to distract me, and Maria was more than willing to spend all night being said distraction.

Not wanting to lead her on, I laid it all out from the start. I'm

22

divorced. Not looking for anything serious. I committed once and won't make that mistake again.

Maria starts typing again and then the three little dots go away. Letting out a sigh, I turn off the TV and get up. I'm not above pouring myself some whiskey before passing out, letting the alcohol flood my veins to help me sleep.

Yawning, I flick off the lights and feel my way up the stairs in the dark, tripping over another damn cat. It growls and runs away, sounding like an elephant is running through the house instead of a ten-pound feline who's supposed to be graceful on its feet.

Trying to be as quiet as I can, I head up another flight of stairs, going up the back staircase. It leads me right by the master bedroom, and I stop at the door, looking in at Quinn.

"You awake?" I whisper, but my sister doesn't answer. Two cats are in bed with her, and I stifle a laugh. No wonder Archer complains about them. Silently, I walk down the hall, checking on my nieces. Arya and Emma each have their own rooms—and they're huge fucking rooms at that—but they prefer to sleep together, snuggled up in a twin bed.

Emma kicked the blankets off and Arya is huddled up, probably freezing. I tiptoe in to cover them up. Emma's eyes flutter open when I pull the blanket up over her and Arya.

"Love you, Uncle Dean," she mumbles, not surprised to see me. I stayed here for a few weeks right after the divorce, and the girls still miss me and want me to move back in.

"Love you too," I whisper. "Go back to sleep."

"Okay."

Sneaking back into the hall, my foot hits a toy that's been left in the hallway. It doesn't knock over, but scoots a few inches on the hardwood floor. Wincing, I turn back around and pray I didn't wake up the girls.

They're still fast asleep.

Letting out a breath of relief, I go across the hall to Aiden's room. The door is wide open, but a cat is in the crib instead of my nephew. Assuming he's in bed with Quinn and not eaten by one of Quinn's many cats, I walk into the guest room.

I strip down to my boxers and climb in bed, mind going a million miles an hour now that I have nothing to distract myself with. I toss and turn for what feels like hours, but in truth probably only a few minutes. I never had issues sleeping before.

My life wasn't a fairytale, but I thought I had things figured out. Turns out everything I thought I knew was a big fucking lie.

Giving up on sleep, I get up and go downstairs. One of the guys on the construction crew makes his own moonshine, and that shit is strong. Strong enough to not need much to help me pass out, and I know there's a jar or two stashed in the back of the pantry.

A few cats come running when I open the panty door, thinking I'm going to give them treats. I gently shoo them away, closing the door behind me once I get the jar of moonshine, and go to the counter, grabbing a glass from the cabinet.

I down my first drink too fast and feel the burn right away. Closing my eyes, I try to silence the voices in my head. Soon enough, there will be nothing, and the numb, empty void is almost worse than the pain.

Refilling my glass, I sigh and turn around. I sip this one slower this time, and right as I'm almost done, soft blue light glows from the stairwell. What the hell? I narrow my eyes. I didn't drink *that* much.

Setting the glass down, I push off the counter and walk over to the stairs and see Quinn slowly creeping down holding a lightsaber.

"It's me!" I say when she startles.

"Dean!" she exclaims and comes down the last few steps. "The fuck?"

"Hello to you too, sis." I go to take the lightsaber from her and she jerks it back.

"You scared me! What the hell are you doing here?"

"Archer didn't tell you I was staying?"

"No! I didn't know he left either. Aiden kicked me in the face —that kid sleeps like an octopus—and it woke me up. I assumed you both were still playing games in the basement, but then I saw his text about being at work. I thought you would have left too."

"Wait a minute," I laugh. "You thought someone was in your house and you come downstairs with a fake lightsaber? You do know the sheriff of this town is our brother, right?"

Quinn purses her lips. "I didn't think it was a person. The alarm would have gone off if it was."

"Ohhh, you thought it was a ghost." I'm laughing even harder now. "And that would have saved you? Quinn, it's just plastic."

"Shut up." She whacks me with the lightsaber. "I wanted to make contact with the spirit and thought if I turned the light on it would go away."

I go back to the counter and put the cap back on the Mason jar. "Ghosts aren't real, Quinn."

"They are, and I'm pretty sure one is in the house."

"You have all those high-tech cameras and motion sensors. Wouldn't they have set them off?"

"Eventually they will. I just ordered an infrared camera and a thermal scanner. They'll be here in a few days and I'll prove to everyone I'm not crazy."

I sweep my hand out at the five cats that are now in the kitchen, thinking Quinn is up to feed them. "We already know you are."

"Hah," she quips, and then notices the moonshine in my hand. "Why are you down here, drinking alone in the dark?"

She doesn't have to ask; she already knows and is trying to get me to admit it.

Just like Mom does.

Weston too. He's been through a divorce as well, and out of all my siblings, comes the closest to knowing how it feels to give everything to someone who takes it all and then some…only to have the floor give out beneath your feet.

"You want to talk?" Quinn asks gently, setting the lightsaber on the counter.

"You know I don't like to talk."

"Too bad. You're standing in your boxers drinking moonshine in the dark. We're talking."

She picks up a tabby cat and motions for me to follow her into the two-story living room. Letting out a sigh, and feeling the alcohol start to take effect, I follow her into the living room.

"Why are you drinking alone?"

"I didn't think you or the kids would want to drink with me."

"Dean," she says sternly, looking and sounding so much like Mom it's not funny. "You're starting to remind me of Owen before he and Charlie got back together. Maybe you—"

"I don't want to get back together with Kara," I interrupt. "Owen broke up with Charlie because he was young and dumb. Kara cheated on me…for weeks before I found out."

"Trust me," Quinn starts, bringing her hand up. "No one wants you to get back together with Kara. If you even had the slightest notion, I'd have Archer check you into a psych facility. She's a cunt," she says bluntly. "Even before the…the…*incident* we didn't like her. She never wanted to hang out with me and I'm a really fun person. But what I was going to say is maybe it's time you stop with the one-night stands and look for something more serious. It's been over a year," she adds gently.

"I did the serious thing, Quinn, and you know how that turned out," I say, words coming out harsher than I meant.

"But Wes—"

"Is Wes," I stand, anger filling me. I'm not angry at Quinn. I know she has the best intentions. And I'm not angry at Kara, not anymore.

We wanted different things in life.

I wanted kids and a family.

She didn't.

Even if she hadn't cheated, we wouldn't have worked out in the end. If we'd stayed together, we would have both been miserable.

"I don't want anything serious," I press, though even to me, it feels like a lie.

"Aren't you getting tired of the one-night stands?" She wrinkles her nose in disgust as she talks.

"Not at all. Like you would know."

"I've had a one-night stand," she protests. "Then I got pregnant and married the guy but—"

"What?"

"Ohhh." She winces again. "I forgot no one but Scarlet knows. Well, and Archer. And Jamie. And Marissa."

"I don't want to know. Wait. I do, so I can beat up Archer if I need to."

Quinn dramatically rolls her eyes. "Just don't mess with his hands. He needs them for surgery...and for me."

"Gross."

She laughs. "Now I feel like enlightening you." She wiggles her eyebrows, knowing how much I hate this.

"And now it's time for me to go to bed."

"Just think about what I said?"

I give her a look. "About you and Archer? No fucking way."

"Hah. Not funny, Dean. I'm worried about you. You've always been a relationship person. You're happiest when you're with someone."

"I am with someone. Someone new every night."

She lets out a heavy sigh. "Can I set you up with someone? Please?"

"As long as you make it clear that I want a no-strings night, then sure."

"I love you." She stands and looks upstairs. "Just...be honest with yourself. I miss the old Dean."

"The old Dean was married to a cunt, as you delicately said. I'm happy now, and I see why Owen loved the single life for so long."

"Yeah, because he was trying to make up for the fact that he was desperately in love with Charlie."

"I'm not in love with anyone." I let out a breath, knowing this can turn into an argument in a few seconds flat. Quinn can be dramatic, and I can rival her, if I'm being honest. "I appreciate your concern," I say, hoping to close this out and actually go to bed. Quinn starts to say something else, but then Aiden cries, calling for Mama.

"Oh, he's in my bed," Quinn rushes out, jumping up. "I don't want him to fall."

"Go. Take care of my nephew."

I lean back on the couch and let out a breath, hating that there's no way I can deny it.

Quinn is right.

CHAPTER 4

RORY

I sit up, groaning, and glare at the sun coming through the window.

"What are you so bright and cheery about?" I grumble. Pushing my hair out of my face, I flop back down and stretch out. I'm desperately thirsty but am afraid I'll puke if I move. I squeeze my eyes closed and wait for the wave of nausea to pass. Why did I drink so much again?

Oh right.

I got let go from my job.

Got dumped by my boyfriend.

And have ninety days to find a new place to live, and the only other available apartments in Silver Ridge cost at least twice as much as I'm paying now.

And, again, I don't have a fucking job.

Taking in a deep breath, I slowly sit up again, needing to pee. My feet hit the floor and I stumble, tripping over the pile of clothes I discarded on the floor. I don't even remember stripping down naked and getting into bed, but hey, at least I'm in my bed —alone—and not passed out on the living room floor, right?

"Don't judge me," I tell Figaro, who's standing in the doorway,

29

wondering why it's half-past nine and I haven't fed him yet. "You're lucky you're a cat and don't have a girlfriend or need a job."

I drink straight from the faucet, use the toilet, and groan all over again when I catch a glimpse of my reflection in the bathroom mirror. Somewhere between the first bottle of sangria and episode number four of *The Vampire Diaries* reruns, I cried so hard my eyes hurt. Then, somewhere between episode number five and the second bottle of sangria, I apparently removed all my clothes and dragged my pity-party-for-one ass into bed.

I go right back to bed, stomach gurgling, and pass out for another hour before getting up. This time, I force myself up, put PJs on, and feed Figaro. I down another glass of water and regret it immediately. Grabbing a box of saltine crackers from the pantry, I trudge into the living room and plop heavily on the couch. I turn *The Vampire Diaries* back on, staring at the TV and avoiding real life.

"You know what's the most unrealistic thing about this?" I ask aloud to Figaro, who's now sitting on the back of the couch, grooming himself like he always does after he eats breakfast. "How good everyone looks when they first wake up."

I break a cracker in half, not caring about the crumbs that will inevitably bother me later.

"I know this show is about vampires. But trust me, I'm more likely to meet a sexy vamp than look *that* good after I've cried myself to sleep." I motion to my face. "Case in point."

I let out a heavy sigh and nibble on crackers, telling myself I'm never drinking that much ever again. My phone, which I left on the coffee table last night, chimes with a text. I can see Mom's name, and I'm sure she's reminding me something about tomorrow night's dinner.

I was looking forward to it. I haven't seen Sam or Mason in forever, and now that Lennon is teaching full-time *and* working as the unofficial assistant principal at the high school in Detroit, we hardly have time to see each other either.

They're going to ask me how I'm doing, you know, the obligatory polite question to ask someone when you haven't seen them in a while. But unlike most people, my family cares., especially my brothers.

Tossing my head back, I sigh again, this time even more dramatically than before, and tell that voice of reason to shut the hell up.

I get emotional when I'm tired.

I get dramatic when I'm upset.

"Dra-motional" as Mason put it years ago. I need to get my ass up, shower, and start looking for jobs. It's slim pickings here in Silver Ridge, but I can't just sit here and wallow for the rest of my life.

Though watching Damon and Stefan fighting on TV for the next few hours doesn't seem too bad either.

"What?" I groan when my phone chimes again with another text from Mom. A message from Sam pops up next, then a bunch from Mason, and I grab the phone to read through the group text.

Mom: I can't wait to see all my boys tonight!

Mom: And you, Rory, of course.

Sam: Nice save, Mom. We all know I'm your favorite though.

Mason: Mom had to have two more boys after you to get to the favorite. Obviously it's me.

Mom: Stop it! You know my favorite child changes daily, and Jacob did just bring me lunch...

Sam: pathetic mama's boy

Jacob sends a GIF of someone rolling their eyes and I smile, feeling a little tug on my heart, but dreading having to tell everyone that my life imploded within a matter of three hours yesterday.

31

Sam: My last surgery got rescheduled because the patient stopped at McDonalds on the way in for surgery, so I'll be leaving soon.

Mom: Yay!!!! Will you make it in time for Friday night dinner? I can make chicken pot pie.

Sam: Just for me?! Who's the favorite now? And yes, assuming I don't die in a fiery car crash on the way up north, I should be there around four.

Mom: That's not funny, Samuel James Harris.

Mason: ...so you like me more now, right?

Mom: You boys are exhausting. Drive safe, Sam. Everyone come for dinner if you can. And Mason, aren't you driving right now? STOP TEXTING!!!

Since I didn't charge my phone last night, the screen goes black and I drop it to the couch, grabbing another cracker.

"One more minute and I'm getting up," I tell Figaro. But when that minute goes by, I don't get up. And that little asshole does nothing to hold me accountable.

After this episode I'll get up.

And then when it ends, I still make no move. My eyes start to feel heavy, and I set the box of crackers on the coffee table and lie down, picking the blanket up off the floor. I snuggle up on the couch, wanting to bury myself and get up when things magically sort themselves out.

I have to get up and use the bathroom again, though, and when I throw the blankets back, nothing has changed. It'll be okay in the end...somehow it has to be.

I'm not going to end up homeless on the street. I have time before I need to leave here, and I have money in savings that will tide me over until I can get another job. Once I've showered and cleared my head, I'll fire up a good old-fashioned job search.

On the internet, that is.

"Would it be too much to swaddle you in my baby blanket and bring you to dinner tonight?" I ask Figaro, who's sunbathing on the living room floor. "Might as well accept my fate as childless, crazy cat lady now." He stretches and rolls over, which I take as a yes. "Just remember, you agreed to it."

I grab my phone and take it into my room, plugging it into the charger. Then I pull a pair of black leggings and an oversized grey sweater from my closet and toss them on the bed, preparing my outfit for the day. I'm still dragging as I cross through the apartment and into the bathroom. Brushing my teeth, showering, and then drying my hair perks me up a bit, and I make myself a bowl of yogurt topped with blueberries and granola after that.

A heavy feeling is still sitting on my chest, and it has everything to do with how much I'm not looking forward to telling everyone that I'm a jobless, undatable loser and I guess Mason was right for being embarrassed to be seen with me when we were in high school.

I don't wear mismatching clothes and tell people to call me Luna Lovegood anymore, but the sentiment is still the same.

Yes, I'm being dramotional again.

Deciding to look for apartments now that I have a clear head, I open up my laptop and go back to the new ones I looked at last night. Maybe I got the prices wrong in my sangria-hazed state of mind.

I didn't.

The apartments are gorgeous, but way overpriced for Silver Ridge. We've grown a lot in the last few years, but I just can't see people paying that much to live in our humble downtown, which I'm already biased toward.

"What about houses to rent?" I mumble out load as I type in a new search. There are two nearby and are affordable, but don't allow pets. Well, that's out.

"Oh! This one allows cats!" I click on the picture and flip through the images, almost able to see myself living inside the quaint Craftsman-style house, sitting in that window seat with a book in my hand.

And then realize the listed rent didn't include utilities. Talk about misleading. I close my computer, needing a mental break, and try not to feel too sick about not getting a paycheck next Friday.

I'm going to have to start cutting things out and stick to a strict budget. Dad taught us to live below our means, since he and Mom struggled financially when they were newlyweds. They're well-off now, but it wasn't without years of struggle.

I've been a little lenient on my budget lately, going out to eat, getting Starbucks a few times a week and online shopping. But I had a good job that paid well.

I'll get one again.

I close my eyes, blinking away tears, and repeat it in my head. I will get another job. I have an impressive resume. I'll find something, and it might not be my dream job, working in the OR again, but it will be *something.*

~

Snow crunches under my tires, and my Grand Cherokee rolls to a stop behind Sam's BMW. Mason's Range Rover is next to his, making the snowy driveway look like a photo shoot from a car magazine. But then I see Jacob's truck pulled to the side and laugh. It's covered in mud, blocking out most of the lettering on the driver's side door that reads *Jacob Harris, DVM.*

I put my Jeep in park and run my hand through my hair, hoping that if I look put together, everyone will assume I'm all there mentally as well. I feel better than I did this morning, mostly because I'm not hungover anymore.

A blast of cold air greets me as soon as I step out of the Jeep. I flip my hood up and hurry into the house. I pull open the garage door, stepping aside to let the barn cats sneak in to get warm before they make the run from the back porch to the barn later when Dad goes out to feed the animals.

The house smells amazing as soon as I step inside, and I immediately feel ten times better just to be back in my childhood home. I have a lot of good memories here, and though I was bullied more than I wasn't in my youth, my home life was always safe and comforting.

"Hello?" I call, stomping snow off my boots. I kick them off, grimacing when I step on a ball of snow and my sock gets wet.

"Rory?" Mom calls back, sounding like she's in the living room. "Is that you?"

"Yeah, it's me." I unzip my coat and shake my foot, getting all the snow off as I walk in through the mudroom and into the kitchen.

"I thought you were working until seven."

I glance at the clock. It's a little after five. "I was." I swallow hard, feeling the lump rising in my throat. My family isn't judgmental—at least not toward each other—but I still can't help but feel embarrassed. "But I don't have a job anymore."

There. I said it. Ripped it off like a band-aid.

Mom, who was going around the island counter to pour me a cup of coffee, stops short. "What?"

"The new company that bought out the hospital made a lot of cuts. And I was one of the lucky one."

"Oh, honey!" Mom sets the coffee pot back down and comes over, wrapping me in a hug. "I'm so sorry."

"Thanks," I say, feeling awkward already. "I'll find something new, I'm sure."

"You will. You're a smart girl. And maybe you can get better hours. You always worked so much."

"Most nurses do," I remind her.

"What about a school nurse? They get holidays off."

"It would be nice, but I'd be taking a pay cut and the school already has a nurse." I hold up my hand. "I don't want this to take away from this weekend, okay?"

"Of course, honey," Mom says, knowing that I mean more

than just taking the fun out of the weekend. I don't want to talk about it, and I don't need pity. Mom goes back to getting me coffee and I go into the living room, where my brothers are watching TV.

Sam sees me first and stands with a smile on his face, and crosses the room, wrapping me in a hug.

"It's good to see you, sis."

"You too. It's been too long. You need to come visit more. It's only a four-hour drive."

"Only." Sam laughs and lets me go. "How's life in the OR?"

"You owe me twenty bucks," Mason says to Jacob. "They didn't even make it thirty seconds before brining up *the OR*," he says in a voice meant to mock Sam. I turn, scowling at Mason, but it's hard to be mad at my brother when I haven't seen him in months.

"How's the knee?" I ask, changing the subject. Mason got injured chasing down a criminal and is supposed to be taking it easy until he heals, and he's not dealing with the time away from the action well. As an FBI agent, he's not allowed to tell us details of what happened, only that whoever he tackled was wanted internationally. "It's fine." He rolls his eyes and shakes his head. "I should be out there back on the case—"

"And now you owe me twenty bucks," Jacob tells Sam, and then looks at me. "Wanna guess how many times we've heard this story since he's gotten here?"

"At least three," I say and step over to the coffee table, grabbing a handful of popcorn. "But it's good to hear you're doing well, Mason. We were all worried you'd gotten shot or something."

"Shot at," he says casually. "But they missed. They've all missed…so far."

I sit on the couch, carefully scooping up Cookie, a large gray cat who Jacob nursed back to health his first year as a vet. The poor thing was found nearly frozen to death in the snow, with her long fur matted together in clumps of ice.

"I have to finish up alterations for a client," Mom says, walking through the living room. "Then I'll start dinner before Dad comes home. Nana is napping in the guest room, so try to keep it down. Physical therapy wore her out."

"How's she doing?" Sam asks. Nana had a hip replaced not that long ago, but it hasn't slowed her down.

"Wonderfully, though I think she wears the staff out just as much as they wear her out," Mom laughs. "She has her PT in stitches by the time I pick her up." Mom stops before going into her sewing room, looking around the living room with tears in her eyes. "It's so good to have you all home."

A bit of guilt bubbles up inside of me. This is a happy weekend, celebrating forty-five years of marriage. My parents were high school sweethearts and got married only days after graduation. I don't want to be a damper on anyone's mood with my string of bad luck.

I grab another handful of popcorn and eat it piece by piece, trying to focus on whatever my brothers are watching, which turns out to be a documentary on serial killers.

"How's that guy…Matt? No…Mike? Yeah. Mike," Jacob asks, reaching for the bowl of popcorn. "Is he coming tomorrow?"

"No, he is not." I run my fingers over Cookie's soft fur. "We're not together anymore." As much as I told myself it was okay, that I wasn't emotionally invested, my words sting.

I'm struggling not to take it personally. My throat feels thick and tears pool in my eyes.

"What did that asshole do?" Mason asks, looking like he's ready to jump up, get in his car and drive to Mike's house and start throwing punches. We're only eighteen months apart, and while I couldn't stand him most of my youth, he's always had my back.

"Nothing," I sigh. "Nothing I can get really mad about, well, except that he kind of manipulated me into sleeping with him one last time before breaking up with me." I blink away the tears and refocus my energy on the sense of freedom I have now.

"He what?" Jacob's brows go up. "Where does this fucker live?"

"Guys, chill. He didn't want anything serious, and I can't fault him for that. Though it would have been nice to know before I wasted six fucking months with him."

"I'm sorry," Sam says, and I know he means it. "The guy's an idiot."

"Thanks." I let out a heavy sigh and watch crime scene photos play out on the TV.

"Hey," Sam goes on, playfully nudging me with his elbow. "At least you have the OR to keep you busy, right?"

"Actually…" I bit my lip and look at my brothers. "Anyone want to drink with me?"

～

I PUT MY HEAD IN MY HANDS AND SIGH. "I HAVE NO JOB, NO boyfriend, and pretty soon, I won't have a place to live." I'm sitting at the kitchen table with my brothers, and Sam made us all Jack and Cokes. I haven't touched mine yet, stomach still queasy over the thought of putting any more alcohol in it.

"Don't say that too loud or Mom will try to move you back in here," Jacob says as he breezes through the kitchen, grabbing two banana-nut muffins from the plate on the center of the island counter. "And you'll find another job."

"I'm sure I will eventually," I reply, being the optimist that I try to be. "Though nursing jobs in Silver Ridge are few and far between." I heft back in my chair and let out a sigh. I'm not dramatic or anything, not at all. "Until then, I should start digging up the backyard in hopes of finding a mammoth bone or something I can sell to science."

"I don't think you'll get too much for it," Jacob says, wrapping the muffins in a napkin. "And the ground is still frozen."

"Fine, then I'll be a black widow."

"Like the superhero?" Mason asks, brows going up.

"Yes," I tell my brother, rolling my eyes. "I'm going to find the real-life Avengers and have them hire me as the newest member of their team. I hear their dental insurance is amazing."

"Hilarious," Mason grumbles and goes back to his food.

"Then what do you mean?" Sam asks, eyeing the cookies and muffins on the counter that are meant for dessert. It's been a Harris family rule for, well forever, that we don't eat until everyone is here. Dad is still at work and Mom is in her office, finishing last-minute alterations to a pretty ivory-colored wedding dress.

"I mean, I'll marry rich old men only to kill them and take their money." I nod as I think about it. "It'll probably be less stress than working as a nurse, actually."

"Right." My oldest brother slowly nods. "Avoiding murder charges sounds super relaxing."

"I'll be good enough not to get caught." I cross my arms over my chest. "Ohh, maybe I could be their caretaker and make it look natural. Oh, sorry, Mr. Bennet, but I warned you not to sneak any more cookies. Your blood sugar skyrocketed, and even though I tried to save you, it was too late."

All three of my brothers stare at me incredulously.

"You know I have to take threats of murder seriously," Mason says slowly.

"She's joking," Jacob says. "Right? It's hard to tell sometimes." Jacob shakes his head. "I got a colicky horse I need to go see. Tell Mom I should be back by dinner. Don't kill anyone, sis. Orange is not your color." He pats my head on his way out the door, much like he used to do when we were younger, purposely messing up my hair just to piss me off.

I let out another sigh and try not to worry. I'm a nurse, and I like being a nurse. It's what I've always wanted to be, and when Sam was going through hell in med school, I knew I made the right decision. I get to take care of people, improve both my patients' and their families' lives, and really feel like I'm making a difference. "There's just not a lot of options around here," I lament.

"I might be able to help you out, sis." Sam leans back and the old wooden chair creaks. The sound is familiar, reminding me of family dinners from years past. It's funny how he still sits in the same spot that he did when we were kids. We all do, actually, and there's something comforting in knowing that we'll always have a place around this old, worn table.

"Are they hiring where you are?" I ask hopefully. Sam is an anesthesiologist at an award-winning trauma-center in Chicago. He's only been there for two years now, but he loves it. "You can put in a good word for me and think of how much fun it would be to work together." I give my brother a big smile.

"We just hired two new physicians and five nurses. But I know somewhere that is looking for a new OR nurse. Do you remember my friend Archer Jones? We roomed together during our residency?"

"Ohhhh," I say as his face comes into mind. "The sexy surgeon. Yes, I very much remember him. Is he single and looking to settle down with a hot, slightly neurotic, yet very skilled nurse?"

"Only slightly neurotic?" Mason mumbles, earning a glare from me.

"No," Sam says with a laugh. "He's happily married with a few kids."

"Dammit. All the good ones are taken. Maybe Nana was right to say that any guy worth settling down with would have settled down before he turned thirty."

"Hey!" Mason looks up from the pie he's shoveling in his face. I seriously don't understand how he's so fit when he eats like that. I just look at that pie and gain ten pounds. "I'm single."

"Exactly." I raise my eyebrows. "I said all the good ones. Even Sam has a girlfriend."

"If I wanted to settle down, I would," he counters, and really believes it. And it probably would happen, even with him getting reassigned all over the country for work. That's Mason's luck for you. "But why stop now when I'm on a roll? Women dig men in uniform, and I score more ass than—" He cuts off when Nana Benson whacks him on the back of the head. Ditching the walker she's still supposed to be using, I didn't even hear her come into the kitchen.

"Talk like that and no lady will want to settle down with you." She picks up his Jack and Coke and takes a drink. "You keep those numbers to yourself." She gives him a wink. "If I'd gone on blabbing, your granddaddy wouldn't have asked me to marry him." She chuckles. "He thought I was a virgin on our wedding night. God rest his soul."

"Nana," Sam spits out, face pulled back with horror. "Please don't ruin the sweet old lady image I've had of you in my head all these years."

She finishes the drink. "There's nothing sweet about me." Setting the glass on the counter, she comes over to me. "Don't worry, Rory. You'll find a job and a man. Ideally in that order. Don't forget, anything a man can give you, you can give yourself."

Mason and Sam exchange looks and if Nana was closer, she'd smack them both upside the head. "Get your minds out of the gutter." She turns her gaze back to me. "You're smart and capable. You'll figure it out."

"Thanks, Nana." I smile, nodding to reaffirm it to myself. I will figure it out. "So, Sam, when do you think you'll be able to talk to Archer?"

"You really want me to?" Sam asks. "The hospital is in Eastwood, Indiana. It's probably five hours away."

My stomach tightens. "That's far."

"It's not," Mason counters. "You can do that in a day."

"But I can't come home for dinner."

"You've never left Silver Ridge," he goes on.

"I did too. College," I remind him.

"Listen, sis," he says gently, which is out of the norm for say-how-he-feels Mason. "Just try it. Getting out of here could be good for you," he urges, not having to bring up my lack of friends in town or how being labeled as the "weirdo" in school has stuck with me even today. "You don't have a job or a house right now, so it's the perfect time to branch out. If it's not a good fit, move back. Mom would let you stay here until you figured things out."

I grind my teeth and reach for my Jack and Coke, still not taking a drink but needing to feel the cold glass against my fingers. "I guess you're right."

"I *am* right. If there was a time for you to take a bit of a risk, it's now, when you have nothing to lose."

I look up, pursing my lips. "Thanks."

"You know what I mean. Look, if I didn't take a chance, I never would have gotten where I am today. Silver Ridge will always be my home too, and I'll end up here when I retire, I'm sure, but you got to live a little. You just said you want another nursing job and there aren't any here. So you only have one option: go somewhere else."

"Just agree with him," Sam mumbles as he takes a drink. "It's weird hearing Mason make sense."

"I know, right?" I quip. "It's like hell froze over or something."

"Hah." Mason glares at us both and gets up to make himself another drink. He limps slightly, making me look at Sam.

"Are you supposed to be bearing weight on that leg yet?" Sam asks, going into doctor-mode.

"I'm fine," Mason huffs. "I should be out there, following leads. We were close to a breakthrough on this case before I got hurt," he grumbles to himself as he adds a double-shot of Jack Daniels to his drink.

"I was in Eastwood not long ago," Sam goes on. "They have a

new hospital that's pretty fucking nice with state-of-the-art surgical equipment. You'd be busy all day too. No more sitting around hoping for a tractor accident."

"You two are fucked up in the head, you know that, right?" Mason limps back to the table.

"He's the one who works in trauma," I point out and then shudder. "You know the burnout rate is—"

"Very high, yes," Sam interrupts. "Which is why I'm taking Stacey to Hawaii for Valentine's Day."

"Ohhh, so romantic," I gush. "Are you going to propose?"

Both Mason and Sam stare at me incredulously.

"No," Sam spits out, recoiling from my question. He's been on-and-off dating a woman named Stacey for the last year or so now. We've never met her, and if I judge solely off her social media posts—which I hate doing—I think she's a gold-digging bitch.

I roll my eyes. "You're not getting any younger."

"Neither are you." Sam gets out his phone. "Do you want me to text Archer? At least see if you can get an interview?"

"Do it, sis," Mason encourages. "You've always been the oldest young-person I know."

I sink my teeth into my bottom lip. Have I been playing it too safe? Maybe. But I don't see the harm in that.

And I don't see the harm in interviewing and checking out the hospital. Mason is right. I can come back if I hate it…but there's a chance I might love it.

After the shitshow that is my life, a fresh start sounds amazing.

"Yeah," I say and feel a bit of excitement flood through me. "Text him."

CHAPTER 5

"You look like shit."

I pick up the weights, feeling the fatigue in my muscles already. I was out until three AM, had a client meeting at eight-thirty, and am meeting my brothers at the gym now at noon.

"I wasn't going to bring up your dad-bod, but now I am," I tell Owen, who immediately turns to check himself out in the mirror. Logan snickers.

"You've really let yourself go," he eggs on, making a face in disgust.

"No, I haven't." Owen lifts his shirt and flexes his abs, making Logan and me laugh even more.

"As long as people don't mistake you for me, it's all good."

"Fucker," Owen throws his water bottle at Logan. "Though you do look like shit, Dean. Did you close down the bar again?"

I internally wince. First Quinn now Owen? "Like you're one to judge."

"Oh, I'm not judging. I'm just pointing out that you look like shit."

"I'm tired." I go to the weight bench to start my workout. I had coffee for breakfast, half a leftover donut from yesterday that was left in the conference room at the office, and I haven't had lunch yet.

I *feel* like shit.

"Don't forget, when I lived my life of debauchery, I was younger than you, old man."

"I'm only a few years older than you," I quip and then take in a breath and start lifting. I make it through one set and feel like I'm dying. Okay fine. I probably look like shit. "But it was worth it. Did you know that crab-ass Mr. Farlow has granddaughters? Twin granddaughters."

"Please tell me they're over eighteen," Logan deadpans.

"Fuck you, and yes. They were at the bar last night."

"Ben was the bouncer last night," Owen goes on without missing a beat. "He sucks at checking for fake IDs. You probably boned seventeen-year-olds last night."

"I think I'd know," I shoot back. "They were very…mature."

"Twins, though." Owen checks himself out in the mirror again. "Impressive, though don't go thinking you're special. Twins love twins."

I make a face, pointing from Logan to Owen. "So you… together? I knew the *it's a twin thing* meant more than you were letting on."

"Why do you think we liked sharing a room?" Owen says seriously and a guy nearby on the leg press stares at him.

"Yep," Logan says dryly, rolling his eyes. "And tell me one time you hooked up with twins."

"Just one time?"

"He's full of shit," Logan goes on. "Though he has slept with most of Eastwood. And now you have, so maybe you should compare notes?"

"You guys are disgusting." I look up and see Quinn's reflection in the mirror as she and Archer make their way over. A few months after Aiden was born, she started coming to the gym with Archer, wanting to get back into shape. I don't mind her coming to the gym at the same time as us, and she usually goes and jogs on the treadmill while we lift, but the last few weeks she's been having Archer help her with the weights.

"Hello to you too," Logan tells her.

"Though he has a good point," Quinn goes on. "At the rate you're going, you're gonna run out of women soon. I have this great—"

"No." I look past her at Archer, who does a good job avoiding my gaze. He knows Quinn pestering me about dating someone annoys the shit out of me. And he knows that Quinn won't stop until she's set me up with every one of her single friends. Being put between your best buddy and your wife can't be fun.

"What about a dating app?"

"Those are basically booty calls," Owen tells her.

"Really? But the commercials make marriage seem so promising."

"I don't want to date anyone, and I certainly don't want to marry someone," I huff and go back to lifting.

Logan says something to Quinn, which makes her pout and shake her head, but she goes and gets on the treadmill without another word.

"You know she's just looking out for you," Archer says, adjusting weights on the bar before starting squats. "And there's no harm in going out with someone. If it doesn't work, then it doesn't work."

Owen steps over. "What he's not saying, is just let her fucking set you up so she'll stop."

"It'll buy you some time at least," Archer agrees. "And I'll give the final stamp of approval on who she sets you up with. Though lately, her thing is getting you and Hilary out together."

"Hot Nurse Hilary?" Logan and Owen ask at the same time.

"That would be the one," Archer laughs. "She keeps going

back to an old boyfriend, so I don't think you ha
about her hoping for a second date."

"I'll consider it," I huff, gritting my teeth as I push through
final rep. My nutrition sucked ass yesterday and then again
today, and I vow to get back on track. I was in decent shape
before but threw myself hardcore into working out and eating
right after Kara and I split up. It kept me busy, gave me something to focus on, and proved that *revenge bodies* aren't just for
women.

Though I've moved on from wanting revenge to just feeling
sorry for Kara. I had a hard time after, as expected, of course. We
were together for years before we got married, and the split sent
me into an existential crisis questioning if anything I felt was
actually real.

I thought it was.

Even when I knew we were spiraling out of love at a dizzying
rate, I still believed we could fix things.

Maybe I'll let Quinn set me up on a date just to appease her…
or to prove that it doesn't matter who she sets me up with. It's
not going to work. My heart's been ripped in two and smashed to
a bloody pulp.

It's beyond revival. Hell, it's not even beating anymore.

Why put it back together only so it can get broken again?

Along with feeling betrayed, it made me feel really fucking
stupid. Yeah, I'd been busy with work. We had a record number
of projects going on, including the renovation of the historic
courthouse in downtown Eastwood. Dad's been slowly stepping
back, giving me more free rein over the company as he prepares
to officially retire.

But I was still there. Bringing her dinner. Asking how her day
went. I knew most of her students' names. I listened to her vent
about difficult parents, about the lack of state funding for the
school. No, I wasn't perfect, but I cared.

I tried.

...ε TIGHT ON THIS BUDGET." I SLIDE THE HOUSE ...me and tap the curved staircase. "This alone is goi... ...nore than you'd think."

I quickly scan over the "must-have" list and see a lot of expensive items as well, including the Wolf oven range. "But I think we can get something really similar and work with what you're able to afford."

"Really?" Katie, the client I'm meeting with this morning, squeals.

"Yes. We'll have to go over this list in more detail once I get a plan from our architect." I tap at the floor plan she printed from an out-of-state builder's website. "This is a copyrighted plan, so we'll have to change it enough to make it legal."

"Oh. I didn't even think about that. I don't want to get in trouble."

I nod. "We do everything right here at Dawson Construction. We have clients bring in floor plans like this all the time and we're able to make it work."

She claps her hands together. "Devon will be so happy to hear this! I went to your niece's birthday party last year and fell in love with your sister's house. I knew you guys built nice houses, but wow."

I smile. "Her house was fun to design and build." Quinn and Archer's house is a fucking mansion, but it's been good for business. The photos of their double curved staircase in their two-story foyer we posted on our Facebook page went viral, which got us a spot in a popular home-and-garden magazine.

Business has been booming ever since.

"My daughter and Emma are in the same preschool class," she explains. "You were at the party. I think."

I was there—physically—but not so much mentally. Quinn went into labor at my wedding. She started having contractions before the ceremony even started and toughed it out until the end.

And Kara was bitching about it the whole time, saying Quinn was stealing all the attention from her. She kicked her out of the bridal party just for being pregnant and got pissed when I hung out with Archer—like he and Quinn planned to get pregnant just to fuck with us. Though really, Quinn was pregnant before we picked our wedding date. Archer brought that up to her once and she wouldn't talk to me for the rest of the night.

What the fuck was I thinking, marrying her? My baby sister was smiling through labor pains so she could be in our wedding photos and Kara acted like she went into labor on purpose just to ruin our day.

Emma was born a few minutes after midnight, so her birthday is the day after my would-be anniversary, but it brings up too many emotions. I love my niece. I'm Emma's godfather, and I don't want anything negative associated with her.

That was honestly the driving force that caused me to get my ass in gear. To go to the therapist that Scarlet recommended and to find a way to move on, to finally let go of my anger.

Kara fucked me over once, and once is enough. I'm going to live my life, and I'm living it the way I want to right now.

"It was a busy party," I say, keeping my professional air.

"It was. Super cute too. My daughter still wants a Rapunzel-themed party because of it." Katie smiles and now her five-thousand-square-foot dream house on a three-thousand-square-foot budget makes sense. It's something I've seen before, and something Dad has taught me how to handle well.

It's the *Keeping up with the Joneses* syndrome, and this time it's literal. Quinn and Archer Jones have the biggest, fanciest house in all of Eastwood. It's easy to want to try to keep up with them, to feel insecure that you don't have what they do. It can get people into a lot of trouble, taking out a loan for something they can't afford.

In the end, clients will do what they want, but Dad and I always try our best to convince them not to take on something that won't really fill the void. They'll find someone else to compare themselves to and feel shitty all over again.

"I'm going to email you a few forms," I go on, wanting to wrap up this meeting so I can go get something to eat. "It'll help narrow down your "must-haves" and will give us a better idea of your design style. Everything is still completely custom, but we've found giving you examples or showing you different options available helps move the process along."

Katie claps her hands together again, and it takes another ten minutes to get her out of the office. I walk her out and then go back to my desk, answering emails and scheduling painters to come in and do touchups to one of our newest projects.

Nearly an hour later, I'm finally heading out for lunch. I'm meeting Quinn, Scarlet, and their kids for lunch today. It's a ploy to try and set me up on another date, I know, but Quinn offered to pay, and I never turn down free food. Plus, I love my nieces and nephews, though Jackson is at school and won't be joining us.

Its freezing rain out today—gotta love January in the Midwest —and the drive into town takes twice as long. Quinn and Scarlet are already at the café, and it looks like they ordered food already.

"Hey!" Quinn slides a plate in front of me. "Just in time. They just set the food down. I got you your regular, is that okay?"

"Heck yes, thank you." I take one bite before Arya and Violet pounce on me, wanting a hug.

"Give Uncle Dean some space," Scarlet says, shaking her head and causing her golden hair to dance around her face. Two guys seated at the diner counter lean closer, whispering something about her.

"You're totally being checked out," Quinn says, breaking apart food for Aiden.

"Those hilljacks at the bar?" Scarlet flips her hair. "They've been checking me out since the moment we walked in. You too," she adds. "You're a babe."

"Please." Quinn rolls her eyes. "I've had three kids."

Scarlet just shakes her head. "Well, I'd do you."

"Aw, thanks. I'd do you too."

I roll my eyes and take a big bite of my burger. "Want me to tell them to fu—I mean, eff off?" No swearing around the kids… gotta remember that.

"Nah." She looks up again, and this time purposely catches their eye. "I could con them so hard."

Quinn laughs. "Should I be concerned?"

"No," Scarlet sighs. "I've happily traded my life of crime for a law-abiding husband."

"Weren't you afraid you'd get caught?" I ask.

"That was part of the fun," she admits. "I'm still waiting for the day Wes needs me to go undercover and get top-secret information for a police matter. Though, the Robocop Quinn is making will be able to handle pretty much everything."

"Laying it on a little thick there, aren't you?" I ask flatly and take another bite of food.

Both Quinn and Scarlet laugh, as Quinn pulls out her phone. "Come over tonight and I'll show you." She swipes through photos that are probably Photoshopped. "It's real, and it's not a Robocop like the movie. Wasn't that one half-human or something?"

"Or something?" I lean back, shocked. "Have you not seen Robocop? It's one of the greatest movies of all time."

"Sure it is."

"And I am coming over. Archer already invited me."

"You two should just get married at this point."

I bring my hand to my chest. "I've always wanted to be a

doctor's wife. But really." I hike up my eyebrows. "Why do you want me to come over? Who else is going to be there?"

Quinn shrugs and is suddenly really interested in the applesauce she's opening for Aiden. "Just some of my friends. We're playing D&D."

"Just when I think you couldn't be more of a nerd."

"Oh shut up. Owen and Charlie played it with us last time and had fun."

"Owen is losing his touch. Being a dad has made him lame."

Scarlet looks at Quinn, nonverbally saying something. Quinn nods. "Wes and Scar are coming."

"Wes is even lamer than Owen. No offense, Scarlet."

"None taken. His lameness is part of what I love about him."

"I'm playing video games with Archer tonight. And I'm not interested in any of your nerd friends."

"Not even her?" Quinn flips to another photo of a woman. "She's pretty, isn't she?"

I lean in and look at the photo. "Yeah. She is."

"Can I set you two up?"

I think back to what Owen said yesterday, about how I should just let Quinn set up a blind date so she can be done with it. "Fine."

"Really?" Quinn's green eyes widen.

"Yeah. Actually, let's make a deal."

Quinn gives Aiden the applesauce. "I'm listening."

"You can set me up on three dates. But after the third one is a bust, you have to promise to stop with this. It's annoying."

"Three dates?" She brings her hands together and smirks. "I know the perfect people."

"They have to be spaced out too. One a month."

"One a week?" Her eyebrows go up.

"Every two weeks."

"I can agree to those terms."

"Last part of the deal," I go on. "Archer gets final approval over who you set me up with." I smile smugly. He's been my best friend since college. He'll have my back.

Quinn laughs. "Please. I'm the one who's sleeping with him. He'll do what I say, and trust me, you won't be sorry."

Oh, but I will be. Because there's no way in hell I'll want to go on a second date with anyone ever again.

CHAPTER 6

RORY

"I got the job!" I'm smiling as I say it, holding the phone out in front of me. I just got back into my Jeep after the interview, and have Mom and Sam on speaker phone.

"Oh, honey, that's great!" Mom cries.

"I knew Archer would like you," Sam says.

"I didn't even talk to Archer," I tell him. "Just the nursing director and the unit manager, but they did say Dr. Jones put in a good word."

"Pays to know people," Sam laughs.

"When do you start?" Mom asks, and I can tell her excitement is waning.

"They said I can start as soon as I can get here, but I told them I'll need a few days to move." I start the Jeep, shivering from the cold already, and wait a few seconds for the call to switch from my phone to the speaker in the car. "I'm not familiar with the town at all."

"I might be exhausting my favors, but I can see if Archer has time to show you around," Sam says. "Or maybe his wife, though I think she's still working and they have three kids."

"I'll gladly just email her so I can get an idea of a good part of town to move into."

A page for Dr. Harris echoes in the background. "I have to go give an epidural," Sam rushes out. "I'll text Archer and will let you know what he says."

"Thanks, love you!"

"Are you excited?" Mom asks, after Sam leaves the call.

"I am," I tell her, and actually mean it. It was weird how the moment I drove into town, I felt like this is exactly where I need to be. I'm away from everything that went wrong before, and an added bonus, not having to run into the McMillans and explain why I wasn't wearing pants the other night. "But I'll miss you."

"I'll come visit every weekend."

"Every other weekend is fine," I laugh. "I'm going to drive around town and find somewhere to eat."

"All right, honey. I'm proud of you! Love you!"

"Love you too, Mom." I end the call and slowly back out of the parking space and head into town. It's too cold to walk around, so I park in front of a used bookstore and pull out my phone again, looking for nearby restaurants. There's a diner not far from here, and I drive around the block looking for a closer spot.

I'm halfway through my chicken tenders and fries when Sam texts me, saying Archer's wife, Quinn is going to call me so I can ask any questions I have about Eastwood.

Ugh. Why didn't he tell her to text me? I hate talking on the phone with people I know. I hate talking on the phone with people I don't know even more.

I go back to my book, reading about sexy vampires and badass witches, thinking I have time before Quinn calls. But only two sentences later, my phone rings. I have a mouthful of chicken, and I swallow quickly and end up coughing. I down water, hack up the chicken I almost choked on, and answer the phone on the last ring.

"Hello?"

55

"Hi, is this Rory?"

"Yes, it is. You must be Quinn." I smile politely, forgetting she can't see me.

"Yep. So, your brother said you just got a job here. Congrats!"

"Thanks. The new hospital is great."

"Yeah. It is." A beat of silence passes between us, and I start to feel super awkward. "So, um, what do you want to know about Eastwood?"

"Oh, geez," I laugh. "Is there a bad part of town I should avoid living in?"

"Not really. Are you looking to buy or rent?"

"Rent for now."

"There's one apartment complex in Eastwood. It's dated but nice. We lived there while our house was being built."

"Do they allow cats?"

"Yes, they do. You have cats?"

"Just one for now. Maybe I'll get another to keep me company since I'll be alone in a new town," I say and then regret sounding like a crazy cat lady.

"I have seven cats."

"Lucky! Oh my goodness, that is goals, for sure."

"Right? Thank you for agreeing," Quinn laughs. "And if you do want another cat, I volunteer with the county's cat rescue and can help you find a good fit."

"Oh, I might have to call you back later then, once we're all settled."

"For sure," she says, and we spend the next few minutes talking about our cats. "I'll text you the info for the apartment complex, along with a few houses that are for rent. Two have been updated recently and I think are pretty nice."

"Thank you so much."

"You're welcome! And welcome to Eastwood."

I end the call smiling.

~

"Morning," I say cheerily, breezing into the locker room at the hospital. I've been at my new job for a few weeks now and am loving it. I set two coffees down and take my coat off and stuff it in the locker.

"Hey, Rory," Hilary, one of the nurses I work with, says with a yawn.

I hand her one of the two coffees I brought in with me.

"Oh my God, thank you." She pops off the lid and inhales the sweet scent of flavored coffee.

"Late night?" I ask, shivering as I take off my zip-up hoodie I had on under my jacket. We have an early surgery this morning and need to change for the OR right away.

"Yes." She takes a careful sip of coffee and smirks. "Jeremy called and I answered."

"No! You were doing so good avoiding him!"

"I know," she says with a wince. "But it's been like two weeks since I've had sex and he's so good when he's trying to win me back." She wiggles her eyebrows. "He'll go down on me for hours."

"I'd be sore if someone had their head between my legs for hours," I laugh. "And you think two weeks is a long time? Try a month for me." I mentally count back. I've been in Eastwood for a month, and I officially started a week after losing my old job. "Or longer."

"You need to get laid."

"Tell me about it." I rake my hair up into a tight bun. "You got any hot single friends you can set me up with?"

Hilary takes another drink of coffee and then pulls her name badge from her purse before shutting her locker. "Actually, I do. Well, I don't know if he's hot, but I do know he's single."

I give her a look. "Sounds promising."

"You'd actually be helping me out a lot if you did go out with this guy."

"How so?"

"I agreed like a week ago to go out with one of Dr. Jones's friends. But now that Jeremy and I are back together…" She puts on a dramatic pout and bats her lashes. "Please, Rory."

"Tell me about him."

"Well, I don't know much, only that he got a divorce last year. I think he moved in with his parents and might still be there."

"Well, maybe he can take me back home and we can play a rousing game of Uno with his parents."

"See! It'll be fun."

I roll my eyes. "The best time. What about work? What does he do?"

"I remember Dr. Jones saying something about his friend taking a break after the divorce, but that was a few months ago. So who knows."

"Ugh, this guy sounds like a loser. No wonder you don't want to go out with him."

"Well, if Dr. Jones is friends with him, he can't be *that* bad, can he?"

Doctor Archer Jones is quite popular at the hospital, not only because he's a young, hot surgeon, but because all the nurses love working with him— again not just because he's a hottie. He's easy to work with and respects his nurses. He treats us as equals and makes sure we know how much he values having a good team to work with.

It's refreshing, really, to be told thank you by someone who technically outranks me. But it's so fucking true. I don't know how many times I've corrected doctors' errors, or noticed that the new meds they just prescribed cause a severe allergic reaction and the allergy is clearly listed in the patient's chart they obviously didn't bother to even open.

"When and where are you supposed to be going?"

with a guy I have no interest in. I don't owe him anything. Just when I'm about to cave and ask if we can go out another night, he replies with "okay".

Well, at least he doesn't seem too torn up about it. I sit back on the couch and open up Pinterest, looking for ideas on how to decorate my tiny living room. The apartment is nice. Not amazing or great, but nice. It's in desperate need of updating, but the carpet is new, the paint is a neutral gray, and it didn't have any sort of smell when I moved in. If I decide to stay in Eastwood for good, I'll look into renting a house or even buying one in the future.

But for now…it'll do.

I waste a good amount of time pinning decor ideas that are way too expensive to ever follow through with. Yawning, I get up to go into my bedroom and change, but right as I'm about to reach behind me and pull the zipper down on my dress, I catch my reflection in the mirror.

I put way too much effort into my appearance to just strip down, throw my hair up in a messy bun, and call it a night. I've heard the nurses talk about a bar called Getaway more than once, and it seems to be the hangout place in Eastwood. According to Jane, who frequents the joint, the drinks are good and the food is even better. And the best part is the bar being owned by hot identical twins.

They're both married, of course, furthering my theory that all the good ones are taken and I'm destined to be alone. Maybe I'll make a detour to the cat rescue on the way to the bar, though I'm sure by now they're closed.

"Figaro," I call, grabbing a pair of heeled booties from my closet. "Dinner time." He follows me into the little kitchen and meows at my feet as I open up a can of food. I plop it down on his plate, refill his bowl of dry food that he hardly touches anymore since he likes the wet food much better, and make sure his water bowl is clean and full. I run my hand over his sleek fur.

"Don't wait up for me," I say, turning on the lamp in the living room. I hate walking into a dark house, and while this place is small and it would be hard to hide in without being seen, my imagination gets away from me at night. If I were home more, I'd get a dog who would bark when murderers snuck in while I was sleeping.

Putting on my coat, I give myself a final look-over in the mirror, and then head out.

CHAPTER 7

"That's a fucking relief," I say a little too loud, getting a nasty look from the lady behind me.

"What is?" Danielle asks, putting a pie in a to-go box for me.

"That blind date Quinn tried to set me up on canceled."

"You didn't want to go?" She adds an extra cookie, probably feeling sorry for me. But as far as I'm concerned, I dodged a fucking bullet.

"On a blind date? Hell no. I don't want to go on any date."

"I can see that." She closes the box and slides it across the counter. "Does Quinn know yet? She just—"

"Wants me to be happy, I know," I sigh. "And going out with random people she sets me up with isn't doing the trick."

Danielle goes to ring me up, giving me the family discount of course. "I don't have any advice, but I wish I did. I can't stand people who cheat, and I can't even image how you feel," she says quietly so no one around us hears. "And I'll say something to Quinn if you want. We're all going over tomorrow so the kids can have a play date."

"I would really appreciate it."

"I can't promise it will do anything, but I'll drop some subtle

63

hints. Make her think it's her idea and not mine to leave you alone."

I laugh. "I like the way you think." I tap my phone against the screen on the register, paying for my cheat-day treats.

"Are you going to be at dinner Friday?"

"Yep. I'll see you then."

"Great. Bye, Dean."

"See ya," I say with a wave and pick up the pie, feeling a weight lifted as I walk out into the cold air. I've been mentally preparing myself for this date all night, wishing I could cancel without breaking the terms I agreed to with this blind-date shit.

This was date number three, and part of me just wanted to get it over with. Since I wasn't the one who canceled, I'm saying this counts. I've held up my end of the bargain and I'm not going out on any more stupid fucking dates.

There's no point. It doesn't matter how long you know a person. How much you tried to "do things right." They'll still screw you over in the end, and it's only a matter of time before it happens again.

Fool me once…

I'm not getting fooled twice.

I SINK MY FORK INTO THE PIE AND SLICE OFF ONE LAST PIECE. If the blind date hadn't canceled, I'd be at the restaurant right now. I'm still relieved I'm not there, putting up a fake-ass front that I'm enjoying myself.

But…if I were there…I would be distracted.

I wouldn't be sitting here, trying to shake off the emptiness before it settles into my chest, sinking deeper and deeper until it consumes me.

I'm not lonely.

I don't want anything more.

Why would I?

I have a house to myself. Get more action now than I did when I was married. I have no one to answer to but myself. No one to nag at me. Annoy me.

Keep me company. Make me laugh. Wrap my arms around in the middle of the night, when the house is cold and—dammit.

I set my fork down and lean back, sighing. I might be able to keep the emptiness away for now, but I can't shake this restless mood or deny how much I *don't* want to sleep alone tonight. I look around the living room, and the fact that I'm the only one here presses against me like a heavy, wet blanket, slowly suffocating me.

I've only been here for a few months, and my plan was just to stay until I found something else, something smaller and easier to manage. Yet here I am, all alone in this big house, with rooms to fill and a large dining room begging to be used for family meals.

It was a model home for one of the neighborhoods our company developed and has been professionally decorated. We put a lot into this house, with tons of upgrades in the kitchen, a huge tiled shower in the master bathroom, and crown molding throughout the downstairs.

It's been on the county *Spring Home Tour* for three years in a row now, and every year it gets high ratings from everyone who passes through. But houses aren't meant to sit empty, and I know Dad was throwing me a bone by suggesting I buy it. I got a hell of a deal on this place, of course, and we still bring clients in to show them examples of our work.

And I agreed to have it on the home tour again this spring, which I'll probably regret.

This house was built for a family, with an open-concept floor plan and a large bonus room over the garage which would a perfect playroom. Don't get me wrong, I'm not complaining that I got really nice house for dirt cheap. This place is fucking sweet, and the women I bring home are always impressed by it.

But it reminds me just how alone I am.

I slide the pie to the back of the counter, a habit I got into years ago. We always had dogs growing up and most were terrible food hounds, stealing anything they could off the counter. I get something to drink and then go back into the living room with the intention of playing video games and keeping myself occupied that way, but I know that won't be enough, because I don't want to be alone tonight.

"Fuck it," I say, not caring that I have a ten AM meeting in the morning. These clients are perpetually late, and we're meeting here at the house so they can look at the wainscoting in the guest room upstairs. I'm a generally neat person, and I vacuumed the entire house yesterday, so it's not like I have to rush around cleaning before the meeting.

It's plenty of time to get home…or to kick someone out.

Either way, I'll have a warm body next to me tonight. It'll be enough…for now.

CHAPTER 8

RORY

"Why are you calling me?" I slow and pull into the gravel parking lot of Getaway. "Are you dying?"

"Not tonight," Lennon laughs. "And I'm driving. So you get to listen to my beautiful voice. I know you miss it."

"I do," I say and drive through rows of pickup trucks as I look for a spot. "So if you're not dying, then why are you calling me?" We text occasionally, not as much as we have in the past, but we've both been busy with work.

Which isn't a good excuse, I know.

"You're never going to guess where I have an interview next week."

"Orlando."

"Ewe, no, my hair and all that humidity do not mix," she laughs. "Guess again."

"Um, Vegas? I know you love the dry heat."

"I do, but I'm not that lucky. You're never going to guess so I'll just tell you. Newport."

"Yay! Wait…Newport? That's by me!"

"I know! I wasn't sure about taking this job, but they're

desperate for an assistant principal at one of their middle schools, so I agreed to come and talk face to face."

"Ahhh, that's awesome!" My lips pull up in a smile. I lost contact with the few close friends I had in college, and most of the nurses at my previous job were older than me. We got along just fine and went out to lunch together a few times, but they were busy with their teenage children so hanging out as friends never really happened.

Lennon and I were always close, and even though we don't see each other that often since she took a job in Detroit, things are never awkward between us. We're only seven months apart, and she really is just like my sister.

"When is your interview?"

"Next Tuesday. I'll be coming in late Monday night and my interview is Tuesday morning. My flight doesn't leave until the evening, so please tell me you're not working."

"I'm off Tuesday!" I say

"I knew this was meant to be."

"It totally is! How cool would it be if you moved here?"

"That would be awesome. How are you liking it, for real?" she says.

"I'm settling in. I actually just got to a bar. By myself."

"What? Elory Harris is going out alone?"

"Hah. I do things alone. Just not very often in social settings."

"Well, have fun. You deserve it. I know you haven't gone out since you've moved."

"I haven't, but—"

"No excuses, but really, Rory, have fun. Meet a cute guy. Flirt a little and have him buy you a drink."

"Remember when we used to pretend to be British?" I laugh.

"Our accents were terrible."

"But it worked. We always got guys to buy us drinks."

"Nix the accent, but don a fake name," she suggests. "No harm in having a little fun, right?"

"You are right," I say, letting her words sink in. "A little fun never hurt anyone."

"Well…" she starts and then laughs. "Be safe."

"You too. Love you, Len."

"You too, Ror. Night!"

I end the call, check out my reflection one more time since I have a terrible habit of smearing my lipstick without realizing it, and get out of the Jeep. Cold air hits me in the face, and I hurry in, regretting my choice to not wear my coat into the bar. It's freaking freezing, but I don't want to have to worry about my coat once I'm inside.

Nerves flutter through me as I step into the bar. I don't go out on my own like this very often, and I've never set foot inside a bar without a boyfriend or several girlfriends on my arm. I take a second to look around and then feel a sense of empowerment flood over me, washing the nerves out to sea.

This place is crowded, and country music plays above the sounds of dishes clanking and people talking and laughing. It's exactly how I pictured a small-town bar to be, yet more at the same time.

It's big.

Full of all sorts of people.

Modern in some ways and country in others.

I immediately love it.

Smiling, I weave my way through the crowd, spotting a seat at the bar.

"Rory!" someone shouts, and I turn to see Jane, another nurse from the hospital waving at me. She usually comes in as I'm leaving, but we've chatted a few times and she's nice enough. She's young, only a year or two out of nursing school, and always cheery.

"Hey, Jane!"

She waves me over, holding a beer in her other hand. "You finally came!" Turning to the guy next to her, she motions at me.

"We work together, and I keep telling her to come out here some night when we're both off." She takes a drink of her beer only to realize it's empty. I'm guessing that's not her first of the night. "This is Damon, my boyfriend. This is Rory. We work together."

"You already said that," Damon laughs and wraps his arm around her waist. "You're so fucking cute." They kiss and I'm left standing there awkwardly. Isn't love so fucking grand?

"I need to introduce you to someone," Jane blurts, breaking away from her boyfriend. She takes my arm and pulls me over to her table. "Guys, this is Rory. We work together."

"Hi," I say, lifting my hand up in a little wave.

"This is Nick. He's single," she adds quietly, wiggling her eyebrows. "Ohhhh! Perfect timing!"

A cocktail waitress brings over a tray of tequila shots. Jane downs one and trades it for another, handing me one as well.

"Do a shot with me!"

I wrinkle my nose. "I had way too many tequila shots in college. I can't do it anymore."

"What do you want?" Nick asks, giving me a smirk. "You look like the kind of girl who prefers a glass of expensive wine."

Is that a compliment or a backhanded insult? I'm not sure. But I smirk right back and straighten my shoulders. "Actually, I like whiskey."

"Damn," he says. "A woman after my own heart." He flags down the cocktail waitress and orders two shots of whiskey. Do people take whiskey as a shot? I don't drink enough to know. And when I do drink it has to be something sweet where I can barely taste the alcohol at all.

"Thank you," I say, trying to be coy, and take the whiskey from the tray. The smell of tequila coming from Jane is strong and makes me shudder, reminding me all at once of that one night I spent on the floor of a Taco Bell bathroom after a little too much partying.

"You okay?" Nick asks, smirking again.

"Yeah, I'm just remembering a night years ago when I had way too much tequila. I was on my way home from this crazy costume party—I was dressed as Hermione and—"

Nick's phone rings, and he turns away from me to answer without a word. What is happening? The call must be urgent... maybe? His body language is making me think he's trying to score a booty call or is a total mama's boy and is checking in with his mother. Jane and her boyfriend are locking lips again, and I'm just standing here feeling awkward. I wait a beat, and Nick is still on the phone, and Jane is practically in her boyfriend's lap now.

"I'm, uh, gonna find a seat by the bar," I say, lowering the shot glass. A few seconds pass and no one looks my way. "Thanks for this." I raise the glass and turn, walking toward the bar, feeling more and more awkward. I don't want to have a pity party, but maybe there was something to Mike not wanting to commit. Nick answered a call mid-conversation.

Am I that boring?

I'm no supermodel but I think I'm decent enough to look at.

And I showered so I know I don't stink.

I make it a few more paces before someone bumps into me, jerking my arm.

Whiskey sloshes out of the glass and spills down my chest. *Dammit.* Thank goodness it was only a shot and not a full drink at least. Holding my arms out, I look around for a napkin, stepping back to avoid the rowdy crowd in front of me.

But right as I move back, I bump into someone else. Tonight, obviously, is not my night. Teetering on tall heels, I start to lose my balance as I turn to apologize to the person I bumped. Strong hands grasp my shoulders, keeping me upright. I turn to see who saved me, and I open my mouth to tell him thank you, but the words die before they can leave my lips.

The man before me might possibly be the most gorgeous man

71

I've ever seen. Even in this dim light, his eyes are striking: sky blue with a rim of dark navy. His dark hair is effortlessly pushed away from his face, and the perfect amount of stubble covers his sharp jaw.

I need to step away. Break his magnetic gaze. Because a man this good-looking means nothing but trouble.

"Th…thanks," I finally say, clutching the shot glass, still a little stunned. "I uh…I need a napkin."

His full lips pull up into a smirk and he looks at my chest, watching a bead of whiskey roll between my breasts. "That's a waste of perfectly good whiskey."

He meets my eyes again, and that smirk turns into a cocky half-smile, one he knows looks beyond sexy. He's aware of exactly what he's doing, furthering the voice in the back of my head telling me to run far, far away. I'm new in town and don't need his brand of trouble.

Though there's no harm in having a little fun, right?

I swipe a finger across my chest and stick it in my mouth, tasting the whiskey. "It is. I should find the jerk who bumped into me and tell him that."

"No need," Blue Eyes says, reaching past me to grab a napkin off the bar top. "I'll buy you another shot." He hands me the napkin, eyes back on me as I blot up the spilled alcohol on my chest. "I'm Dean," he says.

"And I'm…I'm…" Cursed. Damned to have another string of bad luck. *Not looking to start anything new, especially with Mr. GQ who has "heartbreaker" written all over him.* "I'm very glad I ditched my date and came here."

What? Who said that? Rory Harris isn't a flirt. It's not for lack of trying, it's for lack of skill, I'm willing to admit.

"Ohh, ouch. The poor guy." Dean signals to the bartender and pulls out a stool for me.

"Yeah, it was set up by a friend, actually, and the guy seemed like a total loser. I dodged a bullet." I smooth out my dress and take a seat on the stool. "I'm talking in his thirties, still lives with his parents, no career ambition or anything, and an overall boring, whiny man-child from what I was told."

Dean laughs. "Why would you agree to go out with him?"

Laughing as well, I shake my head. "I guess I felt a little sorry for him and was trying to help out the friend who set the date up."

"His loss is my gain," Dean says as the bartender comes over. "Do you want anything else?"

"A glass of Moscato would be great, actually."

"Pink?"

"Red, if they have it."

"They do."

A pretty blonde bartender comes over and takes our order. She seems very familiar with Dean, which doesn't matter. He could come here every day, drink himself silly, and take home a different woman every night and it wouldn't matter.

It's his business.

And I'm not going to let him be mine.

Though...dammit...I really want to.

"Thanks," I say after he puts in our order. I look around; glad I got here when I did. The place is filling up fast. "It's busy for a Tuesday night."

"Getaway is always busy," Dean notes, taking the stool next to me when the guy sitting there gets up, beer in hand as he stumbles to a pool table. "Which is good."

"It is?"

He nods. "Very. My brothers own it."

"Oh. Well, then, yes, business is good." And that could be why the bartender knew his usual drink. He's not a—it doesn't matter.

"If you're surprised by Getaway being busy on a Tuesday, I'm guessing you've never been here before."

73

"You guessed right." The waitress comes back with our drinks. "Thanks," I tell her, taking my Moscato. "I just got a job at the new hospital and moved here."

"It's brought a lot of newbies into town."

I take a sip of wine, which is much better than any whiskey would have been. "Unwelcome newbies? This isn't a town that hates outsiders, is it?"

Dean chuckles. "If they look like you, we'd all be okay with it."

I blush and take another sip of my wine. And then another. "Well, I'm from a smallish town up north, so if you were to say you don't welcome outsiders, I'd oddly be okay with it."

"Up north?"

"In Mich—" I start but quickly cut off. Tonight is all about having fun. "Canada. I'm from Canada."

"Ah, I see. So this is tropical weather for you then."

I laugh, take another sip of wine, and nod. "It hit forty-three today. It felt like a heat wave."

"It's weird even for us locals." He brings his glass to his mouth and takes a drink. I have no idea what he's drinking—an Old Fashioned maybe—but I really want to taste it off his lips right now. "How long have you been here?"

"About a month."

"And you're just now getting out?" He raises his eyebrows and I nudge him with my foot.

"Hey, now. Are you judging me?" I swallow another mouthful of wine. Is it too soon to feel it hit me? Since I ditched my date, I also ditched dinner. I'm starving and this wine tastes too good right now.

"I judged you the moment I saw you," he admits candidly.

"Oh yeah?" I cock one eyebrow and rest my elbow on the bar; still not knowing who this woman is, being all flirty and not too awkward. Not yet, at least. "Tell me…what did you think when you first saw me?"

That cocky grin is back on his face. "The first thing I thought was how much I wanted to lick that whiskey off your chest."

Cue more blushing—and oh shit. The big sip of wine I just took went down the wrong pipe. I turn my head, coughing. Still want to lick me, buddy?

"But before that I saw something…something different in your eyes." The cocky grin fades and for a moment, the confident air he's putting on disappears. The moment is fugacious, over before it's really even there.

"Different?"

"You look like you have a story."

"Don't we all?" I raise my glass a bit and then take another drink, mentally telling myself to slow down since the glass if halfway gone now.

"Oh, we do. But not all are worth telling. Even fewer are worth listening to."

"Tell me, Dean," I say and lean in. "Do you have a story?"

He laughs, casually plowing his hand through his thick brown hair, messing it up perfectly. It should be illegal to be that good-looking.

It's a distraction and causes severe lack of judgment.

"I have several, and trust me, they are more than worth hearing." He takes another drink. "But you didn't come here tonight to listen to me tell you my story, did you?"

"No," I say and bring the wine to my lips. "I didn't, and I get the feeling you didn't come here to talk either."

I didn't mean it the way it sounds, but there's no taking my words back now. And more importantly…I don't want to take them back. This is fun, and the way Dean is looking at me like he wants to devour me makes my whole body come alive.

"I did not." His eyes wander over me, not hiding that he's checking me out yet not being overly obvious about it. It's like he's not afraid for me to know he likes what he's seeing…or more so, he *wants* me to know he likes what he's seeing.

Holy shit.

I'm squirming in my seat, and suddenly words have left me. The sexy Rory has checked out and now awkward, foot-in-mouth Rory is threatening to stand in for her.

Racking my brain for something to say, I buy myself time by taking another drink of wine. The double doors open as a large group comes in, and a gust of cold air rushes through the bar, making me shiver.

"Cold?" Dean asks, reaching out and running his hand slowly up my forearm, feeling the goosebumps that break out along my flesh. Oh my goodness, his touch is warm and his palms are rough, and it's been so long since I've been touched like this.

Actually, I don't think I've ever been touched like this.

Gentle yet deliberate. Friendly, yet promising what's to come.

"If I had a jacket, I'd give it to you, but I left mine in the car."

"Me too," I say, voice all breathy. I suck down the rest of my wine and set the empty glass on the bar top and adjust the wrap of my Coach wristlet on my arm. The bartender comes over to get my empty glass, and I unzip the wristlet to get out cash to pay for my drink.

"I got it," Dean says and tells the bartender to put it on his tab.

"Well, thank you."

"You're welcome. Do you want another?" he asks.

"I'd rather have a side of cheese fries," I admit. "I didn't have dinner."

"I didn't either. Well, I just had pie."

"Ohhh, now pie sounds good. Do they have pie here?"

Dean shakes his head. "No, and if you want to get pie, you need to go to the bakery on Main Street. My sister-in-law owns it."

"Must be nice to have family members who own a bar and a bakery." I inch a little closer. "My brother owns his own vet clinic. I get a family discount on wormer."

Dean laughs, and it rumbles right through me. I don't think

I've ever heard a laugh I can describe as sexy before, but everything about this man is turning me on.

"It is nice getting free food and drinks."

"I bet. Though I'd probably weigh five hundred pounds after a month of all that free food."

Dean grabs a menu and hands it to me. "The house pretzel with cheese is better than the fries."

"That does sound good. It's not too late to order food?"

He shakes his head. "The kitchen is open until ten."

"Good. I feel bad when it's way too close to closing time."

"That's very considerate of you."

"I worked in retail in college." I give the menu one more glance and decide on the soft pretzel and cheese. "It was irritating when people came in right before closing."

"I try not to go anywhere if it's within fifteen minutes of closing, unless it's my sister-in-law's bakery. Then I'll go in a minute before and order whatever takes the longest to make."

I laugh and meet his eyes, feeling another rush of heat go through me.

"I'm kidding," he says. "And she'd probably tell me to get the fuck out anyway."

"Oh, I would too."

"So…where did you go to college?"

Shit. I have no idea of the names of any Canadian colleges. "The, uh, Central University of…of…" Canada is divided into territories, right? "…of the Northern Territory."

"Never heard of it," he says right as I realize my so-called college would be abbreviated to CUNT.

Oh my fucking gosh. If I were to drop dead right now, the universe would probably be doing me a favor.

"It's a small school. Private too. And girls only." Just pick up the shovel, Rory, you're doing a good job digging yourself a hole to crawl in. "Do you come here often?" I blurt, needing to change the subject.

"If I say yes it makes me sound pathetic, but since my brothers own the place, we all come here to hang out."

I smile. "It's nice you like being with your brothers."

"They can be assholes, but for the most part, they're good guys," he laughs. "And the free food and drinks don't hurt."

I feel my phone vibrating with a text. "Excuse me," I say as I dig it out of my little purse. It's Lennon, reminding me not to leave my drink on the bar when I turn away.

"That wouldn't be your boyfriend, would it?" Dean asks, doing a good job of looking not too interested as he makes sure I'm single.

"No, it's my cousin." I quickly reply that I'm always careful and put my phone back done. "And I'm guessing you don't have one either?"

"A boyfriend?" Dean gives me a smartass smirk. "Not at the moment." He finishes his drink and moves his stool a little closer when a new song comes on, base loudly thumping around us.

The pretzel and cheese comes already, making me think the bartender pulled a favor for Dean to get the food here so quickly. It's huge, practically spilling off the plate.

"Want some?" I ask, sliding the plate in between us. "There's no way I'll be able to eat this all."

"I suppose I can help you out."

"And they say chivalry is dead," I laugh and break off a piece of the pretzel. We eat a few bites in silence, and when the bartender walks back, Dean orders a refill of both our drinks, along with waters.

"I didn't catch your name." He dips a piece of the pretzel in the cheese sauce and looks at me. Our eyes meet and heat rushes through me again, settling between my legs. We're talking, having a nice time, but I know Dean's intentions weren't to come here to make a friend.

He's here to take someone home, and right now, that someone is me.

I already told him I graduated from Cunt University, and chances are I won't see this handsome man again after tonight. There's no harm in having a little fun, right?

I push my hair behind my ear, aware that Dean just checked out my breasts for the second time. "I'm Blaire."

CHAPTER 9

RORY

"**B**laire from Canada," Dean say, and the fake name is sultry on his lips. He smiles at me, and for a split second, I think my cover is blown, that he knows there is no way I'm actually from Canada and that CUNT is a bullshit lie. "I'm very glad you ditched your date tonight."

I laugh, high-pitched and nervous. "Poor guy is probably heartbroken over it."

"You said he lives with his parents?"

"Yep," I laugh, shaking my head. "I mean, there's nothing wrong with that. I lived with mine for the first year after I graduated college so I could save up my first year having an adult job, but bringing a date back to meet your parents..." I make a face and shake the head.

"Doesn't really set the mood," Dean laughs. I tear off another piece of the pretzel and push the plate to Dean. "Have the rest. I can't eat anymore. And you were right. That was really good."

"Do you want another drink?" He picks up the remainder of the pretzel and dips it in the cheese sauce.

"Yeah, I do."

"Another glass of wine?"

I think for a second. "No. I haven't had a Long Island in a while."

"I haven't either," he chuckles, and orders me one when the bartender comes back.

"Are your brothers here tonight?" I ask, trying to surreptitiously wipe around my mouth, making sure I don't have lipstick smeared on my face after eating.

"Not anymore. They had to go home to their wives and children."

"Lame," I laugh.

"Right?" Dean's face breaks out in a smile, but his eyes don't mirror the same sentiment.

"But also, not," I go on, letting out a breath. "It would be nice to have a family. I mean, someday. In the far-off future."

"The idea of it is nice," Dean says, and the cocky confidence is gone for half a second. Then he inhales and angles his body toward mine, putting that sexy smirk back on his face like armor. "But for now, I enjoy my freedom."

"Me too. Because as a single adult, I can go out and buy a cake whenever I want to, and no one can stop me."

Dean doesn't say anything for a good three seconds and then he laughs. "I have not taken full advantage of that. Though I did buy a pie today. And ate nearly half of it."

"Good. I can have some when I go home with you and see what the hype is all about."

"When you come home with me?" He actually looks shocked. Happily shocked, but shocked nonetheless.

Though he's probably not as shocked as I am. I don't feel like I'm living a lie, though, and it's weird. I'm saying exactly what I want without the fear of repercussions. I've always been a people pleaser, trying to think one step ahead of what I say or do, overanalyzing how my behavior will affect someone.

I don't want to upset anyone.

Or offend anyone.

Or act too weird, which is easy for me to do.

Being one hundred percent honest is liberating. Am I actually turning myself on? I think I am.

"I mean, if you want me to, that is."

The smile is back on Dean's face. "Let's see where the night leads."

I'm confident if I suggested we leave right now, he'd throw down money on the bar and whisk me away.

Another text comes through, vibrating my phone that's face down on the bar. I flip it over and see it's from Mason.

"Still not a boyfriend," I joke and open my phone to read the text. "It's my brother...warning me about a serial killer." I roll my eyes and laugh. "It's kind of his thing."

"Serial killers?" Dean cocks an eyebrow.

"He prefers them, actually," I go on, watching Dean's reaction.

"Because of all the new documentaries or something?"

I laugh. "No, because he's a..." I trail off, realizing I almost got myself caught. FBI agents are US citizens. I'm pretending to be Canadian. Dammit.

"A detective with a background in criminal psychology."

"That's intense." The bartender brings our drinks, and Dean closes out his tab and leaves a generous tip. "Wait, there's a serial killer we need to worry about?"

I wave my hand in the air. "According to him. He's been forced to take time off from running after criminals after an injury and is obviously way too bored."

"So there's not a serial killer on the loose?"

"Oh, I'm sure there are tons." I give a one-shoulder shrug. "Anyone in here could be one. I could be one." I lean back. "You could be one."

Dean holds up his hands. "Busted. It's not until I've bound and gagged my victims until they figure it out."

"I'm a fast learner."

"I can tell." He laughs and I pick up my drink. "You have two brothers then?"

"Three older brothers. Made growing up fun."

Dean's eyes light up, and that cocky air is gone again, and it's like the real guy is showing through. "I have three brothers too. And one younger sister."

"She's the youngest?"

"Yep."

"I thought having three brothers was awful." I recoil and make Dean laugh.

"We gave her hell growing up, but we get along well now."

"Same with me. Mason—the detective—is only like a year older than me, and we did not get along when we were kids. But we're all close now, though we all moved away from Silv—Silver Mapletown."

I internally wince. My poker face isn't what it used to be, and when Lennon and I would go out pretending to be British sisters, we had a hashed-out backstory.

Why the fuck did I have to go with Canada? I've only been there once, and it was ten years ago. I need to be better prepared next time.

"I miss them," I go on, unable to shut my damn mouth. "But I'm not *that* far and I'm sure we'll all get together for holidays, which is nice and all, but it's not Friday-night dinner. At my parents' house, I mean. We all go to dinner. On Friday night."

I bring my drink to my mouth, making myself stop talking.

"My parents still do Sunday-night dinner," Dean says softly, almost as if it's to himself. He looks away, lets out a slow breath, and turns back. Smug Dean is back, and damn, that smirk is doing bad things to me.

I suck down another mouthful of the Long Island, forgetting how strong these things are, and make a face. I set it down and trade it for my water.

There's a lull in our conversation now, and these things can easily turn into sand traps for me. Yet I feel comfortable around Dean, which is silly since I just met him.

"Have you lived in Eastwood long?" I ask, stirring my drink with the straw.

"My whole life."

"And you never wanted to leave?"

"Oh, I did," he tells me. "When I was younger all I could think about was getting out of this town."

"What changed?"

"I went away for college and realized how much I looked forward to coming home. And it wasn't just a house that was home, but the people in the house. It's lame, I know."

I smile, knowing exactly what he means. People can be home. "I don't think it's lame. You could have the best house in the world but if you came home alone, what's the point, right?"

"Yeah. My friends and family are all here." He shrugs. "It's home."

"I'm really liking it so far."

"That's good to hear. You'll like it better in a month or two when the weather finally turns."

"Yes, I am very much looking forward to being able to wear sundresses again." I motion to my short hemline. "And not freeze."

"You look good, if that helps."

"It does. Though I'd be lying if I said I wasn't looking forward to getting under my heated blanket in the near future."

"That does sound nice on a night like tonight."

"Yeah," I agree, not realizing that I've been messing with my necklace with my other hand, running my fingers over the little moon charm that hangs right above my breasts. I let it fall to my chest, and the metal, warm from my hand, feels good on my skin. Dean is looking me over again, and acting like I don't notice, I lean back, stretching my long legs out.

And then I let myself look Dean over.

He's tall, taller than me in these heels and is probably several inches over six feet. His hair is effortlessly pushed back, messy yet sexy, and his eyes are intense and hypnotizing at the same time. He's simply dressed in dark jeans with a leather belt, and a gray Henley shirt. He looks firm and muscular through his clothes, and my body begs me to reach out and see if he feels as good as he looks.

I look up and see Jane, who I'd honestly forgotten about. Sitting here talking with Dean made the rest of the world stop turning, and it shocks me how much he sucked me in.

"Want to play darts?" I blurt when I think Jane has spotted me.

"Sure. You any good?"

"You'll have to find out." I wiggle my eyebrows and hop off the stool, feeling the alcohol hit me as soon as I stand up. I take a small sip of the Long Island and bring it with me.

The bar is getting really crowded now, thanks to the big group of over a dozen people here to celebrate someone's birthday. Dean reaches for my hand and I take it, feeling a thrill go right through as soon as our hands touch.

Someone from the birthday crew shouts something about a "twenty-one-shot challenge" and everyone in the group erupts in cheers.

"Good luck," Dean chuckles.

"He's going to need it." I shake my head. "Do people actually follow through with it?"

"Not here," Dean tells me. We wind our way through another group of people standing around the pool tables. "I might be spilling a Getaway secret, but when people do attempt that twenty-one-shot challenge, they get cut off after just a few and are given club soda instead."

"That's pretty funny," I say. "And a good idea. I had one glass of red wine on my birthday and fell asleep during the joust at Medieval Times."

"You went to Medieval Times for your twenty-first birthday?" he asks with a glint of amusement in his voice.

"Yes," I answer, putting my hand on my hip. "You say that like it's a bad thing?"

He's still holding my other hand and gives it a squeeze. "It's not. I didn't expect it. You look like you'd be one of those girls renting a limo and going to a club or something."

"And is that a bad thing?" I laugh, and remember when Amber McMillan did exactly that. She invited everyone from our graduation class who was still in Silver Ridge that summer. Well, everyone except for me.

"I don't know." His eyes meet mine; searching for something I'm not sure he's ever found. "I came here for my twenty-first birthday. It's a rite of passage in Eastwood. This place was around for ages before my brothers bought it."

"It's a neat place." I look at the exposed brick on the exterior wall by the bar. "Is the building original?"

"Parts are. It's been expanded a lot."

"It looks like it could be expanded more." We go around another couple who are heavily making out, and snag a place in front of one of the dart boards. I set my drink down on the table next to us, sliding it against the wall. I pull a napkin from the dispenser and stick it over my drink, punching my straw through it. It's not foolproof, but makes it just a little harder for someone to slip something in unnoticed.

Dean hands me a dart and I line myself up, swaying a little on my feet. I close my eyes, find my footing, and let out a breath. Then I open my eyes and throw the dart, just missing the bullseye by a hair.

"Dammit," I mutter and hold out my hand. "Let me try again." Dean gives me another dart, and this time I hit the bullseye dead on.

"Well, you've officially busted my *let me show you how it's done* trick," he laughs. "And I don't think I want to follow that."

"I'm kind of competitive when it comes to throwing sharp things."

"And that's not something you hear every day."

I step back and take another small sip of the drink, not really wanting it but not wanting to waste it.

"Archery has been a hobby since I was a kid. And the same range that taught archery had spears and throwing axes and that sort of stuff." I wave my hand in the air, mentally telling myself to stop now before I go on to say how I used to be part of a LARP group who dressed up like elves and fought battles against targets we tied to bales of straw.

I was one of the few who could ride a horse *and* use my bow and arrow. It made me a badass in that group. But a nerd at school, though I didn't let it stop me.

"Your turn."

"Don't judge me," Dean chuckles. "I grew up being told *not* to throw sharp things. You know, like most normal kids."

I laugh and dramatically toss my hair over my shoulder. "Being normal is boring." I take a seat at the tall stool at the table and watch Dean throw the darts. He's not bad, but I'm better.

We take turns throwing the darts, talking and laughing the whole time. I have no idea how much time passes, but the bar seems to be thinning out a bit.

Is it getting close to closing already?

"You ready to head out of here?" Dean asks, putting the darts back.

"Yeah. I am."

He takes my arm and leads me outside and into the parking lot. Snow and gravel crunch under my feet, and it feels like the temp dropped ten degrees in the hour or so I was in the bar. I clasp my hands on my elbows and my breath clouds around my face. I fall in step next to Dean, inhaling the intoxicating scent of his cologne mixed with the cold, fresh air.

The wind blows my hair into my face, and when I shake my head to get it out of my eyes, sparkling stars catch my eye.

"Look!" I call, pointing to the sky. "A shooting star!"

Dean stops next to me, tipping his head up as well. "I think I missed it."

"Just wait. Sometimes there's—oh, another!"

"Wow," he breathes as two more tiny golden lines streak across the sky. "There's a meteor shower tonight. I'd forgotten about it."

"I didn't even know we were supposed to have one."

He closes the distance between us and puts his arm around me. "You're freezing."

"This helps." I lean in as he envelopes me in his arms. I bring one hand up, resting it on his firm chest. We stand there, watching the sky, and it's as if the whole world stands still. Dean slowly runs his hands up and down my arms, doing his best to keep me warm.

"It's so beautiful," I whisper as another gust of wind blasts us. Dean tucks my hair behind my shoulder.

"Yeah, it is."

"It's crazy, isn't it?" I start, looking from the sky to Dean for a second before watching for another shooting star. "How far away space is? I mean, obviously it's far, but when you think about it... it's just crazy."

"And we're on some big floating ball."

"Yes! It's almost like a mind fuck," I laugh.

"It is. Do you believe in aliens?" His lips curve into a half smile.

"I wish I didn't because it kind of freaks me out, but I can't deny that there *isn't* life out there." I sweep my hand out at the sky and shiver. I bring it back against my body, and Dean holds me closer. "And I don't think they're *Independence Day* aliens who are going to come and invade earth. Humans have kind of ruined this planet. Why come here, right?"

"I actually think the same exact thing. It's…it's almost narcissistic in some ways to think we're the only intelligent race in the whole universe."

"Yes! And you know something really trippy? If they are out there, do you think they're looking at the same stars we are? Maybe there are two aliens doing the same thing we are, right now."

"That is trippy."

I'm shivering, and by now Dean has to be cold as well. The wind blows again, hitting us with a dusting of snow.

"Your skin feels like ice." Dean runs his hand up my arm before slipping it over my shoulder. His fingers sweep along the line of my spine, and he presses his palm into the small of my back.

"It is cold," I comment, turning my head to look at him, and the moment his blue eyes lock with mine, something passes through me. It's not the pure lust-fueled heat that I felt before.

No, this time it's…different, and I cannot explain it to myself even if I wanted to.

I left with the intentions of hooking up with a stranger, of having primal feel-good-while-it-lasts sex. Yet here I am, delicately pressed against Dean's chest, watching stars fall around us. My heart skips a beat and my lips part, realizing that if we were in a romantic movie, this would be the part where Dean kisses me. Where we go back to his place and have said primal sex, but when the morning comes, we both know it's something more.

Only, it can't be, because I started this with a lie, and it has to end that way. I could come clean, tell him that I didn't graduate top of my class from Cunt University and that my name is actually Rory. That I moved here after my life went to shit back in my home town and it's actually been really nice being somewhere new where people don't know me as the weird girl who got in trouble for bringing a wooden stake to school in the sixth grade because I thought the new janitor was really a vampire.

Even if he didn't run away screaming, it would ruin the mood, wouldn't it? He wouldn't be holding me like this, standing here in the bitter cold so I can look at the stars.

"You're trembling," he says softly. "Do you want me to get my coat?"

Not leave, but get his coat so I can keep watching the fucking sky. Stop being so irresistible, Dean.

"No, I…I…I'm ready to get out of the cold."

"Are you sure?" He tucks my hair behind my ear again. "You didn't have too much to drink, did you? I can drop you off at your place if that's what you want."

Mother. Fucking. Hell.

Leave it to me to find the perfect guy and completely screw it up.

CHAPTER 10

"No," she says, full lips parting. "I didn't drink too much." She's shivering in my arms, and the cold is starting to get to me too. I have jeans and long sleeves on. That dress looks amazing on her, but she had to be cold the moment we stepped outside.

I look into her green eyes and feel something I haven't felt in years. Blinking, I look away and think about how hard her nipples must be right now since she's cold. Even that visual isn't doing it for me, and I can't shake the feeling that this is the ending of a really good first date.

What the fuck?

"My car is right over here." I dig my keys out of my pocket to hit the autostart and warm it up as we walk the rest of the way, which is what I should have done as soon as we stepped outside. But Blaire is a bit distracting.

She watches the headlights come on and smiles. "You drove a Mustang in the snow?"

"The roads are mostly clear."

"Mostly," she laughs.

"I have a truck, but it's full of tile samples at the moment."

"Tile samples?"

"I'm a contractor."

"Oh, cool."

I keep a hold on her as we walk, and when we get to the car, it's hard to take my arm from her. There's something about her that's different.

Refreshing.

She's not trying to impress me, and her confidence is sexy as hell. I open the car door for her, feeling something inside me tell me this is a bad idea, that I should just take her home, or go back inside, buy her a burger, and make sure she's good enough to drive before I leave and go home alone.

I don't want to feel more than physical longings to push my cock inside of her, feeling more than thinking. That's the whole point of this no-strings thing I have going on.

And I do want to fuck Blaire.

But I wouldn't mind hanging out and talking a bit more either.

Dammit.

"Do you live nearby?" she asks when I get into the car and turn down the music enough for us to talk over.

"Not too far." I pull my seatbelt over my lap and click it in place. "Two corn and one soybean fields away."

She laughs and tosses her head back. Her hair cascades in a wave over her slender shoulder, and her breasts rise and fall. The black dress she has on hugs her curves in the best way, and the deep V-neck leaves little to the imagination.

"Right. That's how you measure distance in a small town."

"Eastwood is actually big in terms of space," I say as I pull out of the parking spot. "Since we have a lot of farmland."

"Do you have more cows than people or am I stereotyping?"

"You are, but we do. The Langers have a large cattle farm. You might smell it as we drive by."

"I look forward to it." She settles back in the seat and I turn on the seat warmers for her. "Thanks," she says and reaches forward, turning the music back up. *Free Falling* is playing, and it's one of my favorites. "I like this song."

"Me too."

"Obviously." She turns, smiling at me, and I'm hit right in the middle of my chest by her beauty. "It's your playlist."

"Hah. Valid point. You're a Petty fan?"

"I'm a fan of a lot of things, and it changes depending on my mood. Or what genre book I'm reading."

I laugh, not sure if she's being serious. She is. "What's on the current playlist then?"

"Right now, lots of Billie Eilish, Ruelle, and Hidden Citizens."

We chat about music the rest of the way to my house, and this night is turning out very different than how I thought it would go.

I rarely enjoy talking to the women I bring home. I think the same can be said for them, as it's apparent we're leaving together solely to hookup. And that's all this is.

A hookup.

No strings.

No feelings.

No attachments.

If I'm lucky, I'll never see Blaire again. Though the chances of us running into each other in passing is likely in a small town.

Dammit.

I hit the garage door button and slow when I get to my driveway. "Should have taken the truck," she says when the Mustang's tires spin going up the slight incline of the driveway.

"Shhh, Betty can handle it." I pat the dash.

"Betty? You named your sports car *Betty*?" She bursts out laughing. "I thought you'd give it a sexy name like Francesca or something."

"It's a white car." I put the Mustang in park.

"Oh my God. Your car is named after—or in honor of—Betty White?"

We both laugh. "It started as a joke," I tell her and close the garage door, not wanting her to get hit with another blast of wind when she gets out of the car. "But it stuck."

"That is awesome. I always thought people naming their cars was kind of silly, but Betty White has swayed me in the other direction." She makes a face. "And that is something I never thought I would say."

I go around the car to the door leading into the house and enter the password to unlock the motorized deadbolt. Running my hand up the wall, I flick the light on and step inside, going through the mud room and into the kitchen. I kick off my shoes, and Blaire follows.

"Your house is really clean." She slowly looks around the kitchen. "It's impressive."

"Thanks. We have clients come here to look at some of the upgrades and custom options we're able to build. It's a pain, but I try to keep it clean in case they want to come over at a moment's notice."

"How responsible of you."

"Not really. I just like things to be easy."

That coy little smile is back on her face, making my dick jump. "Do you now?" She takes her purse off her wrist and sets it on the island counter. "I would have taken you for the kind of man who's always up for a challenge."

Goddamn this woman.

She leans back against the counter and brings one hand up, playing with her necklace. My heart pounds in my chest and blood rushes to my cock. Slowly looking her over, I step forward, wanting nothing more than to unzip her dress, stripping her naked right here in the kitchen.

And she's looking at me like she wants the same.

More than what I want, it's what I need. I need to lay her

down and fuck her hard; losing myself in how good it feels to have my cock buried inside her. I want to make her come, hear her scream my name, and leave her begging for more.

Everything else will fade away, and for that time, everything is all right. For a short while, I won't be alone.

She shivers and drops the silver moon charm against her chest. It bounces off her skin before settling right above her breasts. Her eyes meet mine and she smiles, and I don't know how it's possible for someone to look so fucking adorable and sexy as sin at the same time.

Her hair is messy from the wind, and I long to run my hands through it, moving it to the side so I can unzip that dress and watch it fall to a fabric puddle on the floor.

Stepping forward, I suck in a breath and go to her, stopping just inches away. My hands settle on her waist and she hooks hers around my neck. It's strange, how standing here with her like this feels almost…almost normal.

Like we've done it before.

Yet the thrill of not knowing what she tastes like, not knowing how her lips feel against mine sends a jolt through me, causing my cock to harden. She leans in, hips pressing into mine. She smiles again when she feels my hardening cock through my pants, tipping her head up.

Her tongue darts out, wetting her lips, and suddenly, I'm aware of everything.

The way her breasts rise and fall as she breathes, the warmth of her skin against my hands, coming through the thin material of her dress. She's several inches shorter than me, even in her heels, and my cock is pressed up against her stomach. I lean closer, breathing in the subtle sweet smell of her perfume.

The clock on the wall ticks, and my heart pounds right along with it. The wind blows again, blasting against the side of the house. Everything is moving in slow motion, yet time is passing too fast.

I slide one hand to her back, trailing my fingers up the line of her spine. Her eyes flutter closed, and she tips her head back a bit, lips parting. I can't help it anymore.

I need to feel more of her.

I want to get lost, not just in sex, but in *her*.

My hand goes to the back of her head, balling her hair into my fist. She drags one hand down, resting it against my chest.

And then I kiss her.

It's just a one kiss, yet it makes everything inside me come alive, fueling me with desperation. I bring my other hand to her ass, giving it a squeeze as I press her against me. I kiss her hard and then break away, moving my mouth to her neck.

She moans softly as I nip and suck at her skin, and she runs her hands down my chest, letting them hover right over my belt. Just the thought of her slender fingers wrapping around my shaft is enough to do me in. I put my lips to hers again, kissing her harder than before.

She kisses me back just as hard, and I put both hands on the curve of her hips as I slip my tongue into her mouth. She's melting into me, breasts crushed up against my chest.

Her heels click on the hardwood floor as she widens her legs, welcoming me in between. I bunch up her dress and step in, sweeping a hand down to her thigh. She sucks in a breath and wraps her arms around me, just as desperate as I am for more.

Without warning, I pick her up and put her on the counter. Her legs fasten around my waist, dress riding up around her middle. I look down, admiring her in the dim light. She balls up the hem of my shirt, and I raise my arms up over my head, letting her strip me.

Her teeth sink into her bottom lip, and she lets the shirt drop to the floor. I take her in my arms again, and my fingers dance over the zipper on the back of her dress.

Blaire sucks in a breath, arching her back slightly as the zipper is pulled down half an inch. Then another. And another.

But then I stop. I'm in no way prepared for this to be over anytime soon. It's been a long fucking time since a woman got under my skin the way Blaire has, and the harder I try to ignore what's in front of me, the more blatant it is.

There's something different about her, and it's going to take effort to remind myself that this is a hookup, that I won't see her again after tonight.

One and done.

It's fun.

It's safe.

Your heart can't break if it's not in someone else's hands.

We only have tonight, and I'm going to make it a night she's never going to forget.

I jerk away from Blaire and push her back. She rests on her elbows and I drop to my knees, parting her legs and moving in between. Her lips part and a small gasp leaves them as I slowly trace the tips of my fingers up her thighs.

Hooking my fingers around the back of her knees, I slide her forward, aligning her pussy with my mouth. Parting my lips, I turn my head and kiss the inside of her thigh, soft at first, teasing her with my touch.

She's propped up on her elbows, and I can feel her eyes on me. Moving slow on purpose, I kiss my way up her thigh, turning my head and letting my breath warm her pussy. Then I suck at the flesh on her other thigh. Her muscles tense, body anticipating what's to come.

Not taking my mouth off her thigh, I reach up and slip my fingers under the waist of her panties and start inching them off. She rocks back, letting me pull them off her. I stand and pull them off one leg at a time and watch them drop to the floor.

Blaire looks at me, eyes wide and a slight flush covering her cheeks. She bites her lip and gives me a wicked smile. Unable to resist any longer, I dive back down, hard cock pressing against my jeans.

As Blaire's hand lands on the top of my head, her fingers tangling through my hair right as I put my mouth to her, kissing my way up her thigh. I gently urge her back and hook one of her legs over my shoulder. And then I move in, tongue lashing against her clit without warning.

She lets out a cry of pleasure and angles her hips up toward my face. I work my tongue, licking and sucking, and then move my head to the side, doing the same to the tender flesh inside her thigh.

"Dean," she moans, pushing herself up again. Her fingers grace my hair, but she falls back once I circle my tongue around her entrance. I work withfever, reading her body and taking notes on what she likes. I slip a finger inside of her, and my cock aches to replace my damn finger.

She wraps her other leg around my shoulders, moaning in pleasure and sounding so fucking hot. I flick my tongue over her clit in rhythm to rubbing her inner walls.

"Holy…shit…" she pants and tightens her legs. She's right there, so close to coming. She sucks in a sharp breath and then her body shudders with pleasure as the orgasm ripples through. Her pussy spasms around my finger, but I don't stop. I add another finger, filling her more, and go right to her G-spot, lightly pressing against it as I continue to lick her pussy.

She's squirming, pushing me away only to bring my head back between her legs. Her body is on overdrive, and my cock begs to be touched, to have her wrap her lips around it and suck hard, moaning as I come, swallowing everything I give her.

Blaire plants her hand on the counter and tosses her head back. She hits the large vase on the center of the island. It had to hurt, but it's like she didn't even notice, too distracted by the second orgasm I'm about to give her.

I push my fingers deeper inside of her, groaning as I lick and suck at her sweet pussy, thinking about how good it's going to feel to push my cock inside of her.

She tightens her legs around me as she comes again, and the heels of her shoes dig into my shoulders. I slowly pull my fingers out of her and kiss her thigh once more before moving back up. She's lying on her back on the counter, chest rapidly rising and falling.

I straighten up, realizing just then how much my knees hurt from kneeling on the hardwood floor. Though the discomfort hardly registers in my mind as I look at Blaire, panting with her dress up around her waist. She's fucking gorgeous, and if I don't get inside her I'm going to explode.

"I'm going to pick you up," I tell her, knowing she can't walk.

She nods and makes a feeble attempt to sit up. I scoop her up, holding her against my chest, and go into the family room that's directly off the kitchen. I lay her down on the couch, grabbing a blanket, and move on top of her. Covering us both up, I move between her legs.

Her eyes flutter shut, and I gently sweep the hair that's in her face back behind her ear. A few seconds pass before she inhales, opens her eyes, and flashes that same devilish smile.

"It's your turn."

CHAPTER 11

RORY

H oly.
       Fucking.
Shit.

My entire body is humming. Alive. Feeling pulses of pleasure I never thought were possible. I've never had a man make me come that hard. And Dean made me come harder than I ever have before twice.

I blink my eyes open and bring a hand up, still feeling the aftereffect of the orgasm flooding my veins, and run my fingers down Dean's back. His skin is smooth and warm, and even though I'm still recovering, still panting and my heart still racing, I want more.

Dean is making me greedy.

And I want to please him as much as he's pleased me.

I bend my knees and drag my fingers up and down his back, my nerves prickling through my entire body once again. Dean smooths my hair back and kisses me. I can taste myself on his lips and it turns me on even more. I buck my hips, feeling his erection through his pants.

Fumbling in my movements, I bring my hands down, putting

them between us as I try to undo Dean's pants. He lifts himself up, giving me more room, and I get the button on his jeans undone only to remember he's wearing a belt.

Getting impatient, he sits up and undoes the buckle. Then I push his hands out of the way and pull the belt from the loops. The force of his erection pushes against his pants, forcing the zipper down. I lick my lips, eyes going to the gleaming tip that's sticking out of the top of his boxers.

I could feel that he was large when he was pressed up against me. My breath hitches as I shove his pants down to his thighs. That thing is huge and I'm not sure if it's going to fit inside of me. Nerves flutter through me as Dean dives back down, kissing me harder than before.

Widening my legs, I welcome him in between, groaning when his cock rubs against my already-tender clit. I arch my back, rubbing myself against him.

I'm still wearing my shoes, and one of my heels gets stuck in Dean's pants as he pulls them down his legs.

"My shoes," I start, voice coming out all breathy. "Should I take them off?"

"No," Dean says gruffly and lets his jeans fall to the ground. He wraps his arms around me and sits up, changing our position. I'm in his lap now, straddling him, and there's only the thin layer of his dark blue boxers between us. "But you will take your dress off."

His voice is deep and demanding, sending a jolt through me, and he looks at me, hunger on his face, and waits for me to obey. On shaky legs, I move off his lap and take a step back. Heart racing, I reach behind me and slowly pull down the zipper of my dress. The sound cuts through the night, drowned out only by my pounding heart.

With anyone I'd be shy. Embarrassed. I'd regret my late nights of eating too much pasta and sleeping in instead of going to the gym. But Dean is looking at me like I'm the only thing he wants.

The only thing he'll ever need.

And suddenly I realize the power is in my hands. I flick my eyes to his massive cock. I'm the one turning him on like this.

Me.

I sweep my hand up my chest, slowly moving it to my shoulder and push one of the straps down. Dean leans forward, eyes widening of their own accord. I do the same to the other side, and let the dress slip off my arms, falling in a whoosh to the floor, leaving me standing before him in only red high heels and a black pushup bra.

"You are so fucking hot," he groans, looking me up and down before reaching out and taking my hands. He tugs me forward, and I sink back down onto his lap, rocking my hips so my clit rubs against his cock.

Holy shit, I could come again right now. But then Dean picks me up again, and in a swift movement, has me pinned down between his muscular body and the couch. His lips go to mine and his tongue slips into my mouth. He kisses me hard and desperate, and I rake my fingers down his back, stopping at the elastic on his boxers.

Dean moves his mouth to my neck, having discovered already that's a sensation that drives me crazy, and I plunge my hand into his boxers, giving his butt a squeeze before bringing my hand around to his front.

Suddenly Dean stops kissing me and pulls away, looking into my eyes. The desperation is still there, but I see something…something else.

Something I can't quite define, yet it's familiar.

Because I've felt it too.

He's looking for something he doesn't think he'll find. There's loneliness behind the cocky grin, a longing for more behind the lust. It's the heart-wrenching need to be part of something, to feel a love so strong you know you can get through anything.

He turns his head, looking almost startled by his own

emotions. His eyes close in a long blink, and he puts his mouth to mine again, kissing me hard as he slides his arms under me, lifting me off the couch just enough to unhook my bra. I twist one arm up, pulling it out of the bra strap, and Dean pushes the other strap down, pulling my bra off and tossing it over the back of the couch. I'm naked underneath him, and his body on mine feels so good.

He's warm and firm, and the tip of his cock rubs against me, making tingles of pleasure run rampant through my entire body. Dean kisses his way down my neck, flicking his tongue over my nipple. I've never been one to find particular pleasure in having my nipples touched, but Dean knows what he's doing.

He's done this before, many times.

I'm new to the one-night stand, but he's not, and right now, I've never been so thankful to be with a well-experienced man. My mouth falls open as Dean reaches down, stroking me, spreading my wetness around my core. He circles my nipple with his tongue once more, and grazes me with his teeth as he moves back up, putting his lips to mine.

My body aches to have him inside me, and I've never felt such desperation in my life. If that monster cock doesn't push in me, doesn't fill every single last fucking inch of me, I might not make it.

"I need you," I groan as his fingers dip inside my entrance, teasing me.

"You're not very patient, are you?" he growls, somehow able to keep his composure. "What if I'm not ready for you yet?"

"Then...then tell me what to do," I pant. "To...to..." He plunges his fingers deeper inside of me, rubbing right against that sweet spot. My eyes roll back as I feel another orgasm start to build. I've never come from vaginal penetration before.

I think I'm in for a world of firsts tonight.

Pulling his hand up, I put his fingers in my mouth and rock my hips, rubbing myself against him again.

"Fuck," he grunts and aligns himself with my core. I slowly pull my fingers out of my mouth, feeling his hungry gaze on me. Dean puts his lips to mine again, kissing me hard as he slowly enters me.

"Ohhhh," I moan, feeling him fill every single inch of me. He groans as he slowly pulls back and thrusts into me again.

And again, a little faster that time. I angle my hips up, and his cock rubs against my G-spot as he rocks his hips. Hooking my legs over his, I bring my hands up to his shoulder, pressing my nails into his flesh.

He takes his mouth from mine and buries his face in my neck, kissing my skin as he fucks me, rocking me so hard my head hits the arm of the couch.

"I'm...I'm...almost..." I pant but am unable to get the words out. I go nonverbal as I come for the third time, and the orgasm starts deep within me, rocketing my body into a state of pleasure I never thought was possible. My ears ring and my toes tingle. I lie there, clutching Dean's impossibly fit body as my own trembles with pleasure.

He slows his movements, giving me a few seconds to recover, and then pushes in balls deep, groaning as he comes. He rests his head against my forehead, cock pulsing inside of me.

Holy. Shit.

My body is humming, pussy spasming. I didn't know I was capable of feeling so much in such a short amount of time, especially at the hands—or in my case, mouth and cock—of someone else. I open my mouth to tell Dean just that, but can't catch my breath.

He slowly pulls out and lies next to me, keeping us both covered with the blanket, and spoons his body around mine, holding me tight as our hearts stop racing.

Then he grabs his boxers from the floor, offering them to me to clean myself up enough to hurry into the bathroom. I'm still naked, and he's still lying on the couch when I return.

"Fuck, you're gorgeous," he says quietly, tipping his head when I walk back into the room, dropping my heels next to the couch. He stands and grabs me around the waist, pulling me back onto the couch with him.

This is the part of a one-night stand where I have no idea what to do. I came home with Dean for one thing and for one thing only, and we just did said thing.

Should I leave? Ask him to take me to my car? Stick around and go for round two?

I sink onto the couch, next to Dean, bending my legs up and covering up with the blanket. Now that I'm not under him, I'm cold, and goosebumps break out on my arms.

Dean turns to me, running his hand through my hair as he pushes it behind my shoulder. He opens his mouth to say something, but the lights flicker and then everything goes black.

We wait a beat, expecting the power to come back on. When it doesn't, Dean stands, tucking the blanket around me.

"The whole neighborhood is out," he says, voice cutting through the dark. "Hang on."

"Okay," I say, looking around. I can't see a damn thing, but hear Dean moving about. He's in the kitchen, which is right off the living room. The glowing screen of his phone comes from several yards away, and he gets something from a drawer in the island before coming back into the living room.

I watch as he starts a fire, and only a minute later, the room fills with soft yellow light.

"That comes in handy," I say as he comes back onto the couch, slipping under the blanket. His arms go around me and he pulls me to his chest, laying me down with him.

"It does, and I don't use it that often."

"You're really good at starting fires. I'm impressed."

"I wish I could take all the credit, but it has a gas start," he chuckles. "Makes it easy to start."

"Cheater."

"Hey, now. You didn't lay out any rules."

"I think I should put out the fire and give you two logs to rub together."

He laughs. "We'd freeze to death before I get a fire started that way."

"I'll save the survival challenge for the summer then."

"That doesn't sound much better." He runs his hand up and down my arm. "I've grown quite used to my cushy first-world lifestyle."

"Me too. Though I did go through a phase like ten years ago where I was convinced we'd have some sort of apocalypse—most likely zombie—and I took this crazy intense week-long class about surviving in the wild. I might have cried the entire time."

"You're not joking, are you?"

I shake my head. "It was being offered not far from where I lived, and while sleeping on the ground wasn't fun, I think it built character. We started the class with over a dozen people and by the end, only me and three others finished. And at least I wasn't naked, right? Though I was afraid most of the time."

"Everyone would have stayed if you were naked."

"Hah. No one wants to see me naked after a week of living in the woods."

"I think I still would."

"Hopefully we'll never have to put that to the test. But if it ever comes to it, I could keep you and two others alive for a week on the run."

"I will keep that in mind." He kisses the side of my head and continues to run his fingers up and down my arm.

We lie there together, watching the logs pop and burn. Not a word is said, but the silence is anything but awkward.

Dean's phone buzzes, and he reaches out to grab it off the coffee table.

"Someone slid off the road and hit a pole," he says, reading the text message. "That's why the power is out."

"Ouch. Hopefully they're okay."

"Yeah. The roads can be slick this time of year. I wish people would just slow down."

"Right? Like, I get accidents can happen no matter what, but I wish people would use more care when driving in ice and snow."

"This time of year makes me want to move to Florida."

"Hah. Same. As long as I'm close to Disney, I'd be happy."

"You're a Disney fan?" he asks, but there's no judgment in his voice. Not everyone finds it cool or even normal for an adult woman to be so obsessed with fairytales and happy endings.

"A big one. I haven't actually been there in years. But I love anything that has magic and a happily ever after."

"My whole family loves Disney. We all went a few years ago for my sister's wedding and everyone keeps going back now."

"Your sister got married at Disney? Lucky!"

"It was…nice." He looks away as he talks, swallowing hard as if the event brings up too much emotion. It's a millisecond of an expression, and makes my heart hurt for him.

Stop it.

You're Blaire from Canada. This is a one-night stand.

Though sitting here, cuddled up in front of a fire next to Dean…it feels like the start of something more.

CHAPTER 12

RORY

"Are you hungry?" Dean tightens his arm around me.
"A little. Are you?"
"The answer to that will always be yes."

I twist around, turning to face him. We're still cuddled up together on the couch, keeping warm by the fire. "I believe you mentioned pie."

His full lips pull up in a smile. "I did. There's half of it left."

"Well then, I think we should finish it."

"I think we should too." He runs his hand over my hair and starts to sit up. "I'll get something for you to put on, though I'd prefer you to remain naked." He wiggles his eyebrows and I laugh. He kisses my forehead before getting up, and I admire his tight ass as he disappears up the stairs. I sit up, brush my messy hair back, and run my fingers under my eyes in case I have any smeared mascara.

Then I lean back, sticking one leg out from under the blanket. The fire cracks and one of the logs split, tumbling down the little pile. Embers fly out, sizzling on the marble hearth. The soft light illuminates the room, and I take a minute to look around.

This whole house is impressive, and I remember Dean saying

he brings clients here to show off what his contracting company is able to do, which makes sense to have everything be top-of-the-line. It's well-decorated and very tidy.

But it almost feels temporary. Like he's just staying here and not really living here. Not that I think he's lying about this being his house or anything. No, it's his house. But it's not his home.

I hear him walking around upstairs and I smile, letting my eyes fall shut again. Though this time, a weird feeling starts to grow in the pit of my stomach.

I don't know why. This night is going way better than I ever expected a one-night stand to go. We had mind-blowing sex. I enjoy talking to him. And now he's getting me clothes so he can feed me pie.

So why do I feel this knot forming.

I think it's because of all that: the great sex. The way we get along. The pie helps, but it doesn't really matter. But I do know one thing for sure. I don't want this to be our only night.

Stop it, Rory.

This is why I've never had a one-night stand before. I have a hard time separating sex from emotion, so until tonight, I've only slept with guys I was already emotionally invested in. My track record isn't the best, with ten out of ten relationships failing, but I'm a romantic.

It's how I roll.

And it's how I have to roll out of here in the morning. It's getting late, and with the roads being icy, I don't think Dean will want to take me back to get my car tonight. I'm sure I'll stay, and once the sun comes up in the morning, I'll have some new perspective and won't feel the same about Dean then.

I hope.

"Is this okay?" Dean comes back into the room and holds out a pair of black sweatpants and a white t-shirt. He's wearing light gray sweatpants and I want to fuck him all over again.

"Yeah. Thank you." I take the clothes and pull the t-shirt over my head and step into the pants.

"We can eat in here," Dean says, sweeping his hand to the living room. "Stay by the fire. I'll be right back."

I settle back into the couch, looking at the flames again as Dean gets the pie. He returns with the box of pie, two forks, two wine glasses, and a bottle of something dark red. He pours us each a glass and hands me one. I bring it to my lips, taking a small sip.

I'm no wine connoisseur, but all I know is this wine isn't sweet. I try not to make a face.

I fail.

"Don't like it?" Dean laughs, opening the pie box.

"I'm not really a fan of anything that tastes like alcohol," I admit, wrinkling my nose.

"Ah, the red Moscato makes sense now. This Shiraz isn't going to be for you then."

I hike an eyebrow. "You know your wine."

"Not really. My...my...someone I used to know liked wine. I went on wine tours with them." He gets that distant look in his eyes again, like the thought is hurting him from the inside out. "I have a few other bottles in the fridge. I'm not sure what they are." He shrugs. "I don't drink wine, but I get it as gifts from clients a lot."

"You must build some nice houses."

"I like to think so." He opens the box of pie and hands me a fork. We make small talk that's anything but awkward as we eat, and Dean trades the red wine for something white and much sweeter.

Before I know it, half the bottle is gone, along with most of the pie. I drank more than I ate and am feeling a little tipsy. I get up to use the bathroom and come back to the couch to find two glasses of water. I gladly down most of my water as Dean pokes at the fire, rearranging the logs.

The wind picks up, howling against the windows. I set the glass back down on the coffee table and get up, moving to the other side of the room. Two lounge chairs and an accent table are along the window, and I peer out, looking into the back yard.

The dusting of snow we previously got blows along the frozen grass, and dark clouds are starting to cover the sky. If we wake up to more snow in the morning, I wouldn't be surprised.

Dean comes up behind me, hands landing on my waist. I twist in his arms and hook my hands behind his neck. Now that I'm barefoot, I get a better sense of just how tall he is, making my five-foot, six-inch frame seem small next to him.

I inch closer, soaking up the heat coming from him. Men aren't supposed to be this good-looking in real life. They aren't this muscular and aren't that good in bed. They don't rummage through their freakishly organized walk-in pantry looking for sweet wine and serve you the best apple pie you've ever had while stealing glances at you in front of a fire.

Is Dean a unicorn?

There has to be something wrong with him, and I know if I go looking for it, I'll either find more than I bargained for or will push him away.

"Blaire," he says, and the name is like a shock to my system. Shit. I almost forgot. This is a hookup. A one-night deal.

Dammit.

"Dean."

He smiles and goes in for a kiss, and that one kiss is all it takes to spark up the fire between us again, and we can't strip each other fast enough. Dean picks me up, strong arms not faltering, and carries me up the stairs, kissing me the whole time.

We pause in the landing and he smashes me against the wall, kissing me until I'm breathless. My legs are tight around his waist, and I want nothing more than to sink down on his cock. We're on the way to his bedroom, I know, but fucking right here in the hall seems like a fan-fucking-tastic idea too, because I don't think either of us have the willpower to make it a few more yards down the hall, then into his room, *and* onto the bed.

Way too much work.

Dean sets me down, and right when I think he's going to take my hand and lead me down the dark hall, he spins me around and presses me against the wall. He enters me from behind, and I plant both hands on the wall, leaning forward a bit as he fucks me. He grips my waist with one hand and reaches around with the other, playing with my clit until I come, legs shaking as I hold myself up.

He slowly pulls out and turns me toward him. I wrap one arm around his shoulders, needing to hold onto him for support. I let out a ragged breath, body trembling yet still wanting more.

We tangle together again, kissing and groping as we clumsily go down the hall, falling onto the bed together. Dean moves between my legs again, but before he can push that big, beautiful cock into me, I shove him away and move back, getting to my knees.

Hardly able to see him in the dark, I blindly reach out and push him down onto the mattress, climbing on top. I slowly sink down on his cock, crying out from how fucking amazing this feels.

He slaps my ass and I ride him hard, and we both come almost at the exact same time, collapsing to the mattress.

"That...that..." I pant. "That was amazing."

"Yeah," he agrees, rolling onto his side. "It was."

We lie there, catching our breath, for a minute. Then I get up to use the bathroom, and Dean goes downstairs to take care of the fire for the night. I'm already in bed by the time he comes back, moving like a shadow in the dark.

"Are you cold?" Dean asks as he gets into bed, pulling the comforter over us both.

"A little. I usually sleep with a heated blanket in the winter."

"I don't have one, though it's not like we couldn't use it right now. I can bring you another blanket, though. We might need it if the heat doesn't come back on."

"I would very much like that. I'm going to risk sounding like a diva by asking if you have a soft blanket too." A smile pulls up my lips as goosebumps break out over my arms again. Without Dean against me I'm cold.

"Like a fleece blanket?"

"Yeah."

"I do. I'll be right back."

Still naked, he gets up, and Lord have mercy, that man has one fine ass. I silently curse the lack of power, wishing I could watch that fine ass walk all the way down the hall to the linen closet. Less than a minute later, he comes back with a soft fleece blanket that feels super snuggly. He hands it to me, and I wrap it around my shoulders, needing to have the softness against my skin and then the top sheet.

"I promise I'm very laid back," I say as I adjust the covers. "But when it comes to sleeping, I'm a bit of a princess."

"I hope this lives up to your expectations then, your majesty." He gets back under the covers and wraps his arm around me.

"Oh, it does. Though I don't have my sleep mask or white noise," I laugh, though I really do need those two things to have a good night's sleep. "And if I remember, I take melatonin before getting into bed too. Working nights and then switching to the day shift can mess up my sleep schedule. I'm a little high-maintenance, I know."

"Yeah, it would make it hard to sleep switching your schedule around. And if you think that is high-maintenance…" He trails off and chuckles.

"What?" I ask, settling in his arms.

"Then you're not high-maintenance at all. I like to have white noise at night too."

"Really?"

"Yeah. I usually listen to thunderstorm sounds."

113

"I alternate between that, crickets, and new-age music."

"The wind will have to do tonight," he says, sounding like he's on the verge of falling asleep. I'm exhausted. I don't think I'll have trouble sleeping either. My eyes close and Dean tightens his hold on me.

I don't like the quiet at night because it freaks me out. I over-analyze every little noise, thinking there are ghosts in my apartment or someone is trying to break in. And my mind wanders too easily at night, winning at the *what's the worst thing that could happen, no matter how unlikely* game. Having the soft background noise helps to quiet my thoughts.

"Goodnight," I whisper, slipping my arm out of the blankets so I can intertwine my fingers with Dean's.

"Night, Blaire," he mumbles, half asleep already.

His words are like a slap to the face all over again, and my eyes fly open.

Right.

I lied, and I can't tell myself it doesn't matter, because it does. The sex, the conversation, the pie, and the sex again. It's not just me confusing sex with emotions. Dean is a guy I want to see again.

Letting out a breath, I try to settle back down, but this time I can't quiet the voices in my mind. I lie in bed, physically as comfortable as ever, but can't fall asleep.

Careful not to wake Dean, I climb out of bed, keeping the blue blanket around my shoulders. I pad down the hall and downstairs, getting my phone out of my wristlet.

I tap the screen and squint, the light too bright for my eyes. I pull up my texts as I hurry to the bathroom, typing out a message to Lennon as I walk. I sit on the closed toilet seat, shivering already, and let out a breath, shaking my head at myself.

Mason texts me, making me think something terrible happened. But then I see that I accidentally texted him the message of *I royally fucked up* instead of Len, since he was the last person to text me.

Mason: What did you do now?

Me: Sorry. Meant to send that to Len

Mason: Are you in trouble?

Me: Not the kind of trouble you're thinking of.

Mason: But you're okay?

I send a rolling eyes emoji and let out a breath.

Mason: What's going on, Rory? It's the middle of the night.

Me: I'm fine.

Mason: You're fine but you royally fucked something up and are texting Lennon about it in the middle of the night?

Me: Fine. I did mess up, but trust me; you don't want to know about it.

Mason: Now I have to know about it.

I let out a heavy sigh, knowing Mason isn't going to leave me alone until I give him enough of an answer to convince him that I'm not tied up in some psycho's basement.

Me: It's about a guy. I'll talk to Len about it in the morning. It's fine, really, I'm just me being me.

Mason: Did he hurt you?

Me: No. Really, I'm fine.

Mason: When girls say they're fine, it's always bullshit. You're a girl.

Me: Great observation there.

Mason: Shut up. But if you need anything, I'm here, Rory.

I smile and go to type a simple *thank you* but stop. It's no secret that Mason is a fan of no-strings romance. He's my brother and discussing anything romance related was always a no-go, but my stomach is in knots and I don't know what to do.

Me: In that case...(just remember you offered)

Mason: On second thought, I'm not here.

Me: Hah. I'm calling you. Hang on.

I crack the door, looking up the stairs. Wrapping the blanket around myself, I tip toe out of the bathroom and into the kitchen, going into the little hall that leads to the laundry room. I don't think Dean could hear me, even if he was awake.

I call Mason and bring the phone to my ear.

"How's the weather?" he asks as soon as he answers.

"What? It's cold."

"Are you sure?" he presses.

"Yes, it's winter in northwest Indiana."

"Right. It's not *peachy*."

"I'm not being held hostage," I rush out in a whisper, forgetting that "peachy" was the word I was told to use in case I was actually being forced to call home and act like everything was fine. "But I did go home with a guy from a bar tonight."

"Do you need someone to come get you? I can call the local police and—"

"Stop," I whisper. "No. I really like this guy."

"That's why you called?"

"Shut up and let me talk. I met this guy at the bar and told him I was Blaire from Canada. I didn't think we'd hit it off. But we did, and I kept up the whole Canadian act. But he's actually pretty awesome and a total hottie and I don't know what to do."

Mason is silent for several seconds. And then he bursts out laughing. I scramble to turn the volume down on my phone.

"It's not funny."

"It's fucking hilarious. Please tell me you didn't try to have a French-Canadian accent."

"Not this time. But he's going to hate me if I tell the truth, right?"

"Well," Mason says, and I can tell he's getting a little uncomfortable. "I take women home from bars, and I usually don't care what their names are...if you know what I'm getting at."

"I do. I know guys don't bring chicks home from bars because they're hoping to find marriage material, but it wasn't like that. I think it started out that way, but then it turned into…into something more."

"Don't read into it too much, sis," he says gently. "The guy took you home for what sounds like some no-strings sex. Gross. I can't believe I'm talking to you about this."

"Should I call Sam instead?" I ask dryly, knowing Sam is the biggest man-whore I've ever met.

"Hah. He'd tell you to sneak out and find another guy to take you home instead. But really, Ror, this guy isn't looking for anything more, even if you think you felt something. You've never had a one-night stand before, right?"

"Right."

"Then this should be your last. You had your fun, now go back to being the youngest old person I know, okay?"

I let out another breath, getting what he's saying, I don't want to be one of those women who clings to any shred of hope that some guy will fall for me, using sex as a way to try and earn said love.

I'm smart, independent, capable, and a terrible liar.

"Okay."

"Do you need a ride home or anything?"

"No. I'm going to go back upstairs and try to sleep. I'm exhausted."

"Gross," he says with a shudder. "I'm going to call you in the morning and make sure you're okay. Can you text me the address of where you are and the guy's name?"

"Want me to go through his wallet and send you a photo of his ID?"

"Yeah, that would be great, actually. I can run him through the database and—"

"Mason, I'm joking. I'm not going through his wallet. His name is Dean, he's a contractor, and his brothers own a bar called Getaway here in Eastwood."

"That's enough. I'll be able to find him."

I roll my eyes. "I hope you never have a daughter."

"Kids aren't in my future."

"Keep having one-night stands and you never know."

"Not funny. Be careful, Rory."

"I will be. Night, Mason. Love you."

We end the call and I inch forward, certain I'm going to find Dean standing in the kitchen, ready to kick me out after hearing everything I said. Though I'm sure Mason is right.

Dean didn't go to the bar tonight looking for a girlfriend. He was looking to hook up, and that's exactly what we did.

Twice.

Quietly, I creep up the stairs and get back into bed. Dean's breathing is slow and rhythmic. It's comforting and could easily lull me to sleep.

Trying to remember Mason's warning, I slip back under the covers, moving closer to Dean, for the warmth, not because being next to him feels so damn good.

I close my eyes, exhaustion pulling me down. In his sleep, Dean wriggles closer and puts his arm around me.

This is meaningless sex. He won't even remember my name in the morning.

But I'll remember his.

CHAPTER 13

DEAN

I wake up with hair in my face and half the covers pulled off of me. Gray clouds cover the sky, and muted light comes in through the bedroom window.

Without thinking, I roll over, gently pulling the covers from Blaire, and wrap my arm around her. I don't know what time it is, but my alarm is set to go off at eight this morning and it hasn't gone off yet.

My phone could very well be dead, but right now, I don't fucking care. Blaire lets out a sigh in her sleep and pulls the blankets again. Smiling, I move closer to her, pulling the blue fleece blanket up and covering my shoulders. She's on her side, body slightly bent so her supple ass is pressing against me.

We're both naked, and my bed has never felt more comfortable. I should be thinking of ways to get her out of here, but instead, I'm lying here calculating how much longer we can stay in bed together before I have to get up for the client meeting. There are a few dishes I need to stick in the dishwasher, and other than gathering the clothes we stripped off each other, the house is clean.

It'll take me five minutes to get things straightened up, and about fifteen to get to Getaway if I speed. That's thirty-five minutes I need before my clients arrive, and that's assuming they're not early.

Blaire moves in her sleep, turning toward me, and brings the covers up around her shoulders. Worried that she's cold, I carefully adjust the blankets, keeping the soft blanket against her skin, and then cover her with the sheet and then the comforter. I take her in my arms and close my eyes.

I'm asleep in minutes.

~

"Morning." I look away from my phone and smile at Blaire, who's finally waking up. She stretches her arms out and smiles.

"Morning."

"You don't have to work, do you?" I ask, realizing that I never asked her that last night.

"Not today." She lazily sits up, holding the fleece blanket over her breasts. "Is that your subtle way of telling me to leave?" She hikes up an eyebrow, looking so ridiculously cute. "You can just say it."

"No," I laugh. "My client meeting at ten got pushed to noon and I wanted to see if you'd like to go out for breakfast."

"Oh. Well, yes. I would like that. But I probably look like hell."

"You look like I fucked you good and proper last night." I drop the phone to the bed and move to her, pinning her down on the mattress.

"No," she laughs when I try to kiss her. "I know my breath stinks!"

I go in for another kiss, making her push me away, laughing.

"Seriously! I fell asleep before I could even think about brushing my teeth."

"I have an extra toothbrush if you want to brush your teeth," I say without thinking. Then it's like my words hit us both at the same time. I don't offer my one-night conquests toothbrushes. I don't invite them to breakfast. And I don't kiss them like this in the morning.

I roll off of her and look out the window, trying to act interested in the light flurries that are floating down to the frozen ground.

"I'd very much like that."

"It's in the top drawer on the right," I start and motion to the bathroom, remembering that there are two separate sinks. "On the vanity next to the shower."

"Thank you."

She wraps the blue blanket around herself and gets up to use the bathroom. I shake my head, trying to rid the thoughts and feelings about that woman.

She was fun, a lot of fun. Nothing more. Nothing less.

Getting up, I grab boxers and a pair of athletic pants from my dresser. I need to get into the closet to finish getting dressed, and you access the closet through the bathroom. I sit on the bed and answer another email inquiring about meeting to discuss building a house in the near future, trying to be productive and keep Blaire off my mind.

She comes out a few minutes later, still wrapped in the blanket. "I'll, uh, go find my clothes," she says, offering a tight smile. It's the first time since I uttered a word to her that things are a little awkward.

After brushing my teeth and getting a long-sleeved shirt from my closet, I go downstairs and find Blaire sitting on the couch. She's wearing her dress again, but has her bra draped over her arm.

"It's really uncomfortable," she admits when she sees me looking. "It makes my boobs look nice, I know, but you've already seen them in their natural glory."

Her blunt honesty is refreshing, and a smile pulls up my lips. "I thought they were pretty fucking nice in their natural glory." I tip my head, staring at her breasts. "And they still look good in that dress."

"Well, thank you, sir." She looks down and her cheeks redden a bit. "It's cold out there."

"Even better." My mind goes to pert nipples and being able to see the outline through her dress, and then I remember it is actually fucking freezing and she's wearing a short dress and didn't bring her coat. "You're going to freeze in that. Hang on." I jog back upstairs and find a pair of black sweatpants that Grandma got me for Christmas they were a size too small. I set them aside and have been meaning to go through the rest of my closet for items of clothing to donate but haven't gotten to it yet.

My laziness is paying off today. I grab them and a Dallas Cowboys sweatshirt and go back downstairs.

"Here, this will help."

"Thank you." She takes the clothes. "This will go great with my heels."

"Oh, right." I laugh. "Sorry, I can't help you out there. Unless you want socks."

"I'm tempted to say yes." Her smile lights up the whole fucking room. "But I don't think I'd be able to fit my foot in my shoes if I did. Though if anyone questions my fashion choices, I'm blaming you."

"Fair enough."

She steps into the pants and pulls the hoodie over her head. It's just about as long as her dress. "These are comfy. You might not get them back."

"The pants don't fit, but I might have slight emotional attachment to that sweatshirt."

"To this old thing?"

"That's my lucky sweatshirt."

She rolls her eyes again, and I take her in my arms, wanting to feel her body against mine one last time.

"Where are we going?" She eyes the clock. "There aren't a lot of places open for breakfast around town, right?"

"Right. The café is our only option. Have you been there yet?"

She nods. "A few times. I've gone in on my way to the hospital for coffee."

"They have decent coffee. Though there is a rumor we're going to get a Starbucks soon."

"No way!"

I nod. "A new shopping center just got approved. We've been watching it closely so we can put bids in and have our company head up the construction."

"Wow. That's a big project!"

"Yeah, it is. I hope we get it." I grab my coat and my wallet. "Do you want a coat?"

"Nah. I'm fine in this. I already look like a homeless hooker." She sits on a barstool and puts her heels back on. "How do I look?" she asks, standing up.

"You pretty much nailed it with homeless hooker," I chuckle.

She wiggles her eyebrows. "Try to resist me now."

"I'll do my best. You don't mind going out like that?" I ask carefully, surprised at her attitude toward, well, everything.

"I've worn weirder clothes in public. Don't ask. And I wasted a lot of my life worrying about what other people thought of me. They're going to judge you no matter what, right?"

"Right." I shove my feet into my shoes and open the garage door. "Hang on a second, actually. With the snow, I think I should take the truck."

"Good idea. We don't want to be responsible for knocking out the power as soon as it came back on."

I tell Blaire to stay in the house where it's warm and quickly take the tile samples from the passenger seat of the truck, stacking them on my workbench in the garage. I brush off the seat and go back inside to get Blaire.

"You weren't joking when you said your truck was full of stuff," she comments when she gets in, looking at the backseat.

"Yeah, it's all shit I need to take to the office, which I will this afternoon."

"Let's just hope you don't have to slam on the brakes or all this stuff is going to kill us *Final Destination* style."

"No pressure or anything."

She holds up her hands. "I'm not the one driving."

I fire up the truck and back out of the driveway, going slow through the neighborhood since it hasn't been salted or plowed yet. We get a lot of drifting snow in Eastwood, thanks to the flat land and all the cleared fields during the winter.

A few miles pass and Blaire is looking uncomfortable.

"I, um, I need to tell you something," she says, twisting in her seat.

"You're not married, are you?" I blurt. It's one of my biggest fears and something I'd never forgive myself for, though I'd never do it on purpose.

Bringing home a married woman, being the asshole who broke up a marriage, a family, a home.

It wouldn't be done knowingly, and it's not like my women of choice are going to come out and tell me they're married right off the bat.

"No," she says quickly. "I've never even been engaged."

"Good."

"It's good I haven't had anyone want to marry me?"

"Oh, I, uh, didn't mean it that way."

"I'm just giving you shit," she says with a pretty smile. "Are you married?" she asks slowly.

"Not anymore."

"Um, sorry?"

I shake my head. "Don't be. I'm better off now." She's still looking at me like she's trying to figure me out. I've already said

124

too much. She pulls her arms in close to her body and bites her lip, brows furrowed.

"So," she starts, taking a breath. Then my phone rings, and I see it's one of the vendors we work with.

"Sorry, it's work. Do you mind if I take this?"

"Of course not," she rushes out. I answer, and end up talking to three different people before I resolve the problem. And now we're at the diner and I've been on the phone the whole time.

"Sorry about that."

"It's fine," she presses. "Sounds like you got things figured out, though."

"Yeah. We're good now." The parking lot hasn't been cleared yet, and there's about an inch and a half of snow on the ground. Blaire is wearing open-toe high heels. "Stay there," I tell her and kill the engine. I get out and rush around to her side. "I'm going to carry you in."

"Like a baby?"

"If that's what you like."

"Baby-play? Gross."

"Huh?" I push my brows together.

Blaire starts laughing. "You've never heard of baby-play?"

"Something tells me I don't want to." I turn around and have her get on my back.

"You don't, but I'm going to tell you anyway. And when we get inside, I'll look up pictures."

I hurry through the snow, careful not to slip and take us both down. Blaire laughs as I run, holding onto me tightly. I don't set her down until we're in the café. We are able to get a table for two right away, and are seated in a booth in the back.

"This place is so cute," she notes, looking around. "It's like what you'd picture a small-town diner to look like."

"It's looked like this for years. I think a lot of us would be sad if it got a major update, though it's due for one." I motion to the slightly warped table.

"It's part of its charm." Blaire smiles and looks at the menu. We both order coffee, and she surprises me by ordering a big plate of pancakes, bacon, and eggs. "We have a diner like this at home," she says, looking around as she chews a piece of bacon. "The food isn't as good, but I'm probably biased. My dad owns a restaurant."

"Are you a good cook then?" I ask, stabbing a piece of a pancake with my fork.

"That's debatable," she laughs. "I know how to cook, but I don't cook often. Seems a little silly to make a fancy meal when I live on my own."

"Yeah, that makes sense. I don't like to cook." I reach for my coffee. "My mom's the kind of mom who still makes food for me several times a week."

"Must be nice." She nudges my foot under the table. "Mama's boy."

"Like you'd turn down free food."

"Oh, I wouldn't. But I'm still going to call you a mama's boy."

"You can call me whatever you like," I laugh.

"Dean!" someone calls, and I look up to see Quinn, Archer, and all their children bustling through the door. Blaire follows my gaze, and her fork falls out of her hand, clattering to the plate and splattering syrup over the table.

Archer picks up Aiden and the five of them come over on the way to an empty table. Blaire's eyes are wide as she watches, and her cheeks turn bright red.

Right. She looks like a homeless hooker, as she puts it. She's probably embarrassed to be seen by anyone other than me. I'll get rid of Quinn as quickly as I can.

"Hey, Rory," Archer says, struggling to hold Aiden, who's flopping around and trying to get out of his arms. Rory? Who the hell is Rory?

"Well, it seems like I finally found a good match. Though technically I did set you up with Hilary, but I'm still taking credit for her getting her friends to go out instead." Quinn beams at me, flicking her eyes from me to Blaire. "I knew I should have made you take a bet or something. A week of free babysitting would have been nice."

"What are you talking about?"

Quinn cocks an eyebrow. "Obviously your date went well."

"My date?"

"The one I set you up on last night," she sighs.

"I didn't go on a date last night." I look at Blaire, who's looking horrified right now. I lean back, eyes going from Blaire to my sister and back again. "You're not Blaire from Canada, are you?"

CHAPTER 14

I f I could slither under the table and stay there until everyone leaves, I would. But even if the floor wasn't sticky from a morning full of customers dripping syrup and dropping food on the ground, it wouldn't solve my issue.

Because my boss is standing just a foot from the table, looking confused as hell. It's the first time I've seen that look on his face, which is probably a good thing considering he's slicing people open and removing organs.

My mouth opens, but no sound comes out. I can feel Dr. Jones staring at me, along with all three of his kids and his wife, who I remember to be Quinn. Oh my gosh, we talked on the phone, she helped me find a place to live, and she likes cats.

"No," I finally say. "I'm not."

"But why do you…" Dean starts, looking at Quinn. "Why do you think you set us up? The blind date bailed last night."

No. No. No.

Dean was the loser I blew off. Of all the guys in all the world…

"Because she was." Quinn looks at Archer, and everyone realizes what's going on at the same time.

"Why did you tell me your name was Blaire?" Dean slowly turns his gaze back to me.

"Because I'd just met you in a bar," I say, feeling like everything is happening in slow motion.

"I was the loser you were supposed to go out with. The jobless, man-child." He turns back to Quinn. "You suck at setting people up."

"I didn't say that." Quinn picks up a cute little girl, looking as uncomfortable as I feel.

"I...I...I should go." My fingers shake and my cheeks burn as I open my wristlet and pull out enough cash to cover my portion of the bill. I slide out of the booth and stand. "Never mind, I didn't drive." I start to dig my phone out of my little purse. "I'll call an Uber." I look at Dean and am taken back by the anger reflected in his blue eyes.

"I didn't know you were my blind date," I say. "If I did, I wouldn't have canceled."

His jaw tenses, and his brow furrows even more. "Just go."

"Dean," Quinn scolds. "Don't be rude."

"Rude?" He sweeps his hand out at me. "I didn't blow off a date with a *loser* and then lie about who I am."

"Oh please," I blurt, surprising myself. "You took me home for one reason and one reason only, and I think I checked off that box for you. Twice." I take a step and falter, heel catching on the hem of the long pants. "I'll drop off your clothes...later," I add pointedly.

"Wait," Quinn says, setting the little girl down. "I'll drive you. There's like one Uber in Eastwood."

"I can wait."

"You could be waiting for hours."

I let out a breath and steal one last look at Dean, heart hurting more than I expected it to. He was supposed to be one night of unbridled fun.

And he was.

Yet I want more.

Dammit.

"At least eat first."

Quinn waves her hand in the air. "Archer knows my order. It's not that far to the apartments from here. You did move in there, didn't you?"

"I did."

"Then we're going." She gives Archer a kiss and motions for me to follow her. "Come on."

I give Dean one last look and if there was a contest for avoiding my eye, he'd win.

"I'm sorry about him," Quinn says once we're outside. "He's a drama queen."

"So you know him?"

She stops in her tracks. "Right. You have no idea. He's my brother."

"Oh my gosh. That makes this even worse. I swear I didn't know. Hilary didn't even tell me his name, just that she was letting Dr. Jones know I was taking her place. I'm so sorry."

"Look, I get it. You meet a guy at a bar and you give him a fake name. I've done it before."

"At least I didn't pretend to be British this time," I mutter. "I didn't think he'd be so mad. I mean…the first thing he told me was how he wanted to lick whiskey off my breasts."

"Eww, well no. Not because of you, but because he's my brother and he…he's been through a lot the last year. He came home to find his wife in bed with another man. Hence his issue with being lied to."

"Oh," I say, stepping in a snow drift. My poor toes are freezing. "I had no idea."

"I doubt he leads with that. But I'll give you inside information." Quinn unlocks a black Escalade and motions for me to go to the passenger side.

"Thanks, but I don't think he wants to see me again."

"You're the first woman he's taken out to breakfast," Quinn says and pulls her seatbelt on. "So you must have made an impression on him."

"Yeah, a bad one."

Quinn shakes her head and fires up the engine. *Rotten to the Core* comes on and she quickly turns it down. "Sorry. My kids love Descendants. And I do too."

"So do I. I was Evie for Halloween last year."

"No way." She twists in her seat, looking at me with a smile on her face. "Every year, my brothers do this anti-love party at their bar and people are supposed to dress up as bad guys or villains. I'm going as Mal and my friend—and sister-in-law—is going as Audrey during her Queen of Mean phase."

"That sounds fun."

"You should go with us!" Quinn puts the SUV in reverse and slowly backs out of the parking space.

"Maybe," I say, feeling weird all over again. I liked Quinn from the short bit we talked on the phone, and knowing that she's a fellow adult who loves made-for-TV Disney movies gives her bonus points.

"Don't feel bad about the whole Dean thing," she says, as if she can read my thoughts. "He's always been dramatic like that, and after the divorce…it was ugly. He's not a player either, not really. He's…he's regressed or something."

"I can't even imagine walking in on that."

"I can't either. I probably shouldn't tell you this, but I lack boundaries and overshare, so I am, but I never liked his ex-wife. I'm not happy with how things ended, but I think he's better off without her because I never thought they were meant to be. Archer agrees, though he'll never admit that to Dean."

"So Dr. Jones—Archer—is Dean's friend?" I ask trying to piece the little info I have together.

Quinn nods. "Yes. They were college roommates, and I had a huge crush on Archer throughout all my teen years. Blah, blah,

blah, we finally hooked up, I got pregnant, and we've been happily married since."

"You do overshare," I laugh.

"I like to think it's one of my better qualities."

The SUV bumps along the road, and Quinn slows as we drive over another snow drift.

"Your brother, Sam, is nice," Quinn says after a minute of silence. "I've met him a few times."

"He went to your wedding," I say, remembering Sam's relentless teasing about going to Disney World to be a groomsman in his friend's wedding.

And Dean mentioned his sister got married at Disney World.

I don't know how I didn't put the two together, though it's not exactly like I was looking to follow the trail of breadcrumbs even if it was laid out in front of me.

Though now that it is, I'm thinking I should look for a new job in another new state, on the other side of the country. Because I keep messing things up, getting tangled in webs of drama I desperately want to avoid.

"Archer was excited when he took that job in Chicago." We slow to a stop and both grimace, watching a teen driver slide through the intersection in a minivan. "I still go to Chicago a few times a month for work."

"What do you do?"

"Simply put, I develop software."

"Oh, that's cool."

"I love it. I left a big company a few years ago to start up something with friends. Right now, we're working on creating robots."

"Like robots that could potentially take over the world?"

Quinn laughs. "If they do, I'll be able to control them. I'll give you the cheat codes too."

"Thanks," I laugh. "I went through a phase where I was sure the world was going to end and made it my mission to learn all the survival skills I could, but controlling world-dominating robots wasn't something they taught us in prepper-camp."

"That's a real thing?"

"It is," I laugh. "I still feel like completing a week of it is one of my proudest accomplishments. Not graduating nursing school with honors or the lives I've saved using CPR, but surviving a week in the woods shooting zombie-targets with a bow and arrow."

"Okay, but that is pretty badass." She takes her eyes off the road for a second to look at me. "I had a panic room put in our house in case something like that happened. Though now I'm realizing I didn't think it through since I'm pretty sure my house is haunted."

"Ohhhh, I love haunted stuff! What's going on in your house?"

"Just weird noises and creepy feelings. I set up thermal cameras and am just waiting for evidence now. You believe in ghosts?"

"I do. I was a junior ghost hunter with a local ghost-hunting group in my youth." Amber McMillan called me *Spooky Rory* that year, which was stupid. If you're going to give me a mean name, at least make it rhyme or have some cool alliteration.

"That's awesome! Maybe I should start one here in Eastwood. You'd have to join, of course."

"I'd love that." I twist my hands in my lap, almost hating how much I like Dean's sister. She shouldn't be this awkward and cool at the same time.

I shouldn't want to hang out with her after Dean made it clear he didn't have any interest in seeing me again, which is fine. Fair. I didn't expect to see him again either.

And by tomorrow those feelings I thought were real will fade away, I'm sure. Or at least I hope.

CHAPTER 15

DEAN

"I think you're blowing this way out of proportion," Quinn says, picking Aiden out of the highchair. All three kids had a meltdown after she left, crying for Mommy, and I couldn't leave Archer alone to deal with that.

They were meeting Weston and Scarlet here for a late breakfast, and they showed up before I had a chance to run out of here. And now that Quinn is back, everyone knows how last night unfolded.

"She gave you a fake name at a bar." She sits back down, and Aiden snuggles up with her. "Do you want to know how many times I gave fake names to guys at bars?"

"No," Weston and I say at the same time.

Archer turns to her. "I do."

"Like once," she says. "I didn't go out much."

Scarlet leans forward. "I couldn't tell you how many times I used a fake name even if I wanted to. I agree with Quinn here. You're being dramatic."

"She blew me off and then lied," I counter, but I know they're right. If it was anyone else, I wouldn't care. But Rory wasn't just anyone.

Fuck.

"Fine," Scarlet goes on. "Did she steal your wallet?"

"No."

"Take cash from your nightstand drawer?"

"I don't keep cash in there."

"That's smart." Scarlet adds sugar to her tea. "Did she try on your expensive Rolex and 'forget' to take it off? Write down your credit card numbers? Leave with an expensive Gucci purse?"

Weston looks at his wife. "You're speaking from experience, aren't you?"

"If I was, would you arrest me?" Scarlet bites her lip and wiggles her eyebrows.

"As soon as Violet goes down for her nap."

"Eww," Quinn quips but then turns to me. "See? She didn't con you or anything. She just gave you a fake name. Not a big deal. So you should call her and see her again."

"Stop," I say harshly. Letting out a breath, I rub my forehead. I enjoyed last night. The sex was fucking great, but it was more than that, and I don't want to go down that path. Not now, not ever.

Things were ugly after the divorce, as they always are, I suppose. I had to pick up the broken pieces of my heart and rebuild everything I'd worked so hard for, our home and our shared friends.

Eastwood is a small town. It took effort to avoid Kara at first. She was a teacher at the school Jackson attends, but then she took a transfer and works in Newport, still close enough to run into, but the daily risk of seeing her was gone.

I blink and it's like I'm right back there, standing in the hallway looking into our bedroom. I'd never been more pissed in my whole life, and it was a kind of anger I'd never experienced before. It took over my whole body, twisting my mind and darkening my heart.

I couldn't think straight. Hell, I don't even remember exactly what transpired that night.

There was lots of yelling.

Swearing.

Punches were thrown.

Kara ran after me, crying.

And then I ended up at Quinn and Archer's house, sitting on their porch until they came home from dinner. Things passed in a blur the next few days, and I've never been happier to have a lawyer in the family. Charlie handled everything, and while I wanted to make Kara hurt at first, I just wanted everything to be over.

The betrayal hurt like a hot knife to my heart, and my entire life had to be rebuilt. We might not have been the happiest couple, but we had a routine.

A house.

A life.

I've rebuilt it all and am pretty damn happy with what I have.

"I got her number," Quinn says, trying to be casual as she spreads butter on her pancake. "I can text it to you if you want."

"I already have it," I grumble.

Quinn's eyes light up. "So you must like her! You asked for her number."

"No, she texted me an hour before we were supposed to go out to say she wasn't going to make it."

Quinn takes a bite of her pancake and makes a face.

"Something wrong?" I ask.

"It tastes funny. But anyway, if you like her, call her. Go out again. And she didn't think *you* were a loser. She said it was the way Hilary described you."

"That doesn't make it any better. And it's not her fault, it's yours." I point to her and Archer.

"Hey," Archer says, catching Emma's cup of milk a second before it spills. "Sit still," he says through gritted teeth. Emma has

136

been up and down ten times already and knocked Arya's water over twice. Thankfully the cup had a lid on it. "I wouldn't describe you as a loser and then ask if someone who works with me wants to go out with you."

"Then you weren't being honest," Weston deadpans. "Because I don't know how else you'd describe him."

"Hah," I say dryly. "Quinn, I know you mean well, but stop, okay? I don't want to date anyone."

"But you seemed to like her," Quinn goes on, furthering my annoyance.

"We had fun." My mind flashes back to her perfect tits. To how good it felt to be inside her. To have a meaningful conversation with her as well as talk about the most random things and have it feel completely normal...to hear her laugh. *Fuck.* "Several times."

"But you took her out to breakfast because you wanted to spend more time with her, right?"

Quinn is right. Waking up next to Blaire—I mean, Rory—felt good. We didn't just hook up, but we got along.

We clicked.

And I don't remember the last time I felt like I clicked with someone like that.

"Help me out," I say to Weston. "Tell her to shove off."

Weston's eyes meet mine and he nods before turning to Quinn. "I think it's time to slow your roll."

"Fine," Quinn huffs. "You guys are no fun. I like Rory. She believes in ghosts and has a cat."

"You're trying to convince him to go out with her again," Archer reminds her. "I wouldn't bring up ghosts or cats."

"He has a point," Weston whispers to Quinn, loud enough for us all to hear.

I reach for my coffee, which is cold by now, and try to remind myself that all Quinn wants is for me to be happy.

But she doesn't get it.

"Fine, I'll admit she's nice," I say, knowing I'm walking a dangerous line. "Nice to talk to, nice to look at, nice to…" I trail off and raise my eyebrows. "But it doesn't matter. I don't want a relationship," I press. "I've already been down that road and you saw how it turned out."

"Yeah, but—"

"No," I interrupt, pulse rising. "We weren't perfect, but I did everything right. I showed up. I cared. I tried. Maybe I wasn't the best husband, but I did what I was supposed to do and look what that got me."

Quinn frowns. "I'm sorry."

"It's fine." I let out a breath and an awkward silence falls over the table, filled only with whatever Emma is making her Barbie say to a pink unicorn.

"I need to use the bathroom," Quinn says, handing Aiden to Archer. Her brow is furrowed and her cheeks are suddenly flushed. Shit. I upset her.

"You okay?" Archer asks.

"I don't feel well." She puts her hand over her stomach. "I think I had too much coffee this morning." Quinn makes it two feet away before both girls need to use the bathroom too. Violet suddenly has to go too, and Scarlet gets up to take her and help Quinn with the other girls.

Aiden starts to cry the second his mother and sisters leave, and we spend the next five minutes trying to get him to calm down.

"Doesn't this make you want another?" Archer asks over Aiden's cries.

"Nope," Weston shoots right back. "We're very happy with two. Though Scarlet was hot as fuck when she was pregnant. She disagreed." He shrugs. "Jackson's years older than his sister. Having two close together…I don't know how you do it with three."

Archer laughs. "I couldn't without Quinn."

That ache in my heart is back. It's dulled over the last year, but it's a missing part of me, sending waves of phantom pain through me when I least expect it.

The want to have my own family, to be wrestling with my own toddler, annoyed and irritated as all hell but going to bed thankful every night because we have each other.

"So about Rory," Archer says, words cutting through my thoughts. Dammit. I should have known this was coming as soon as my sisters left the table. "You liked her enough to take her to breakfast."

I look at him, trying to ignore the question in his statement. "Yeah. She was fun."

"In your last year of newfound bachelorhood," Weston starts, "when has fun turned into breakfast?"

I ignore his gaze on me as well.

"She's been great to work with." Giving up, Archer gives Aiden his phone, and the kid finally settles down. "Nice. Personable. She fit right in with my surgical team, and I'm doing just as bad of a job trying to convince you to date her as Quinn."

I let out a heavy sigh. "I'm not dating anyone."

"What would going out with her one more time hurt?" Weston asks, looking me dead in the eye.

A million reasons rush through my mind, with the biggest being *what if I fall for her?*

Before I'm forced to give an answer, the girls come running back.

"Daddy!" Arya yells from across the diner, holding Violet's hand as they hurry over, followed by Scarlet. Quinn and Emma rejoin us a minute later. Aiden goes right to Quinn, snuggling up in her lap. The tension has left our little group, and I intend to keep it that way...and not talk about Rory again. Thinking about her makes a knot form in the pit of my stomach, giving me a feeling I can't quite place. It's like knowing you forgot something

139

but you're unable to remember what it is you forgot. It's just that feeling of unknown dread.

"Are you ready to be a single mom in a few weeks?" I ask Quinn.

"Yes," she glares at Archer. "It's not fair you get to go spend a week in Miami and leave us all here in the cold."

"I'm going to a medical conference, not a party." He puts his arm around her. "I'd say I won't enjoy it just to make you feel better, but I love biology as much as you love software."

"I know," Quinn grumbles, then she wrinkles her nose and leans down, smelling Aiden. "Your son pooped, and I just took the girls to the bathroom."

"You want to change a diaper?" Archer asks. "It's been a while."

"And I intend to keep it that way." I look down at my watch. "I need to get going. I have a client meeting."

"I'm glad we ran into you," Quinn says, standing and giving me a hug. "See you Sunday?"

"Yeah. I'll be at Mom and Dad's."

"Great. See ya then."

I say bye to my nieces and nephew, leave money to cover my food at the table, and hurry out the door. I have a few hours before the client meeting, and if Quinn and Archer hadn't busted Rory's cover, I wonder what we'd be doing right now.

Fucking back at her place? Maybe she'd make us lunch and we'd sit on the couch together, watching TV and talking about random things again. Whatever it would have been, it doesn't matter, because it's not going to happen, even though I know I want it to.

CHAPTER 16

"You didn't answer." Mason's voice comes through the speaker of my Jeep. I just left the bar and should have let the engine heat up longer before taking off. I'm shivering, gripping my heated steering wheel tight to warm up my frozen hands.

"Arrest me."

"I could arrange that, you know."

"I do," I sigh. "And sorry if I made you worry. I'm heading home now and am fine."

"Good. Everything work out?" he asks.

"Well, not exactly." I slow to a stop at a red light and let my head flop back against the headrest. "I'm never lying about who I am ever again, though. Rest assured."

"I don't know if asking for details is a good idea, but I'm too damn curious."

"Let me start from the beginning," I grumble. "Hilary, a nurse I work with, was set up on a blind date by our boss, Dr. Jones. The guy was Dr. Jones's friend. Long story short, Hilary got back together with her ex and convinced me to go out on said date instead. She made the guy sound like a total loser, so I canceled at the last minute and then went out."

"That's going to be relevant later, isn't it?"

"Unfortunately." I feel the heat of my embarrassment burn on my cheeks all over again. "Well, the guy I went home with last night was the guy I was supposed to go on a date with."

"No fucking way," Mason laughs, and I can imagine the smug smile on his face.

"Way," I say through gritted teeth. "And I found that out when Dr. Jones and his wife ran into us at breakfast. Like I said, I'm never pretending to be someone else again unless I'm on vacation, far, far away."

"Sorry, sis, but that's fucking hilarious."

"To you. It's not to me."

Though, if it were anyone else, I'd be laughing too. It's not funny because of the regret I'm feeling for fucking this up, because I really liked Dean.

"Give it time and you'll be laughing."

"Yeah," I agree, though I don't believe it. "I'm sure I will. Thanks for checking on me."

"Take care."

"I always do. Love you, Mason!"

"You too."

I end the call and turn on my music, singing along to the *Frozen 2* soundtrack until I get to my apartment. Figaro is sitting in the small entryway, swishing his tail back and forth.

"We've talked about this," I say, leaning against the door as I take my shoes off. "No judging." Leaving my heels in the middle of the floor, I cross through the little living room into the kitchen, getting out a can of food for Figaro. "You didn't even touch your kibble." I motion to the full bowl. "So don't act like you're starving. We both know you'd eat that if you were hungry enough."

I give him his food and then go to shower. I turn on the water and pull Dean's sweatshirt over my head, trying to push the sour feeling in the bottom of my stomach away.

Did I ruin things forever with Dean? Does it even matter if I did? I'm fairly certain I need to take Mason's advice for once and let this one go. Last night was a hookup, and someone with an *out with the old and in with the new* mentality about love isn't someone I want to get involved with.

"This is why I don't do one-night stands," I tell my reflection, raking my hair through my messy curls. I roll my eyes at myself and then finish undressing, getting annoyed that I'm one of those girls who can't separate emotion from sex, unless I'm right, and maybe Dean felt it too.

"Get over yourself, Rory," I huff and get into the shower. Things are going to be awkward at work, but it'll fade fast. I wanted a fresh start in a new town, and that's exactly what I got. I'm not against dating, but I'm not going to fawn over the first guy in Eastwood who made me feel pretty.

Whatever I'm feeling…it will fade too. I'll wake up in the morning with a clear head and these lingering feelings for Dean will be gone, and I'll realize last night was just about the sex and nothing more.

Guys like Dean are good for one thing and one thing only: breaking hearts. I won't let myself make that mistake.

"How was the date?" Hilary pulls her sweatshirt over her head. "With Dr. Jones's friend, I mean."

My back is turned as I shove my clothes into the locker, buying myself some time. Do I tell her the whole truth? Or just say that Dean was great but a total playboy and I won't be seeing him again? I did go out with Dean, just not the way she thinks I did.

"It was okay," I reply, pulling my tank top down and shivering.

143

We're going right into the OR and have to change into our surgical scrubs. "Dean wasn't as bad as you made him seem."

"Yes, Dean, that's his name." She smacks her forehead and laughs. "I'm so forgetful. But just okay?"

"I had a great time, actually, and the sex was amazing."

She wiggles her eyebrows. "Ohhhh, get it girl."

I laugh. "It was a one-time thing, though. He's, uh, not looking to date anyone."

"Huh. I wonder why Dr. Jones would set him up with someone."

"I get the feeling it was his wife's idea. Dean is her brother."

"Oh, wow. That's a tangled mess I'm glad I avoided."

I shut my locker and walk over to grab clean scrubs. "It's interesting, that's for sure. It might be a little weird looking Dr. Jones in the eye," I say, not needing to go into detail. "I mean, he knows I hooked up with his friend."

Hilary shrugs. "We got two gall bladder removals back to back. We'll be too busy for you to feel weird."

"I always feel weird."

Hilary laughs. "But that's part of your appeal, you know that, right?"

"I do." I pull a scrub top over my head and finish getting dressed. We walk into the hall right outside the OR, waiting for our morning meeting. It's Thursday, and nearly a full day has come and gone since I've seen Dean.

I wish I could say the same about thinking of him.

It's stupid, and I keep reminding myself that. I wasn't drunk but was rather tipsy from the time he took me home to the time I woke up. That can make any situation seem better than it really is. "Beer Goggles" is a thing for a reason.

"Good morning," Dr. Jones says, breezing down the hall. *Act normal.* I smile and bring my hand up to give a small wave but end up hitting myself in the face with my own fingers.

Dr. Jones catches my eye and smiles back, and I want to

slink back into a corner. It would one thing if he knew Dean and I went home together, but knowing that I lied about who I was…

It's not embarrassing, I tell myself. I'm a grown-ass woman and can do what I want, including pretending to be Blaire from Canada and sleeping with some hot guy from the bar.

We quickly go over what we have on the schedule for the day, and things are back to normal. We're busy already today, and then get two emergencies come in, with the patients being rushed back into the OR. It's hard to explain to others what being in the OR is like at times.

With a good surgeon—like Dr. Jones—usually the mood is light. We know what we're doing and have years and years of experience between everyone on the team. One of the anesthesiologists we frequently work with is hilarious, and we're often laughing and listening to music.

But the last emergency surgery is tense, with the victim being brought in after a car accident. Another surgeon is on her way in to assist, but we all know right away the chance of our patient making it is slim to none.

Hours later, the whole team is exhausted, and our patient is in recovery. Dr. Jones tells all of the nurses and surgery technicians to go take a break while he assesses the patient, trying to decide if she's stable enough to be transferred to a trauma center in Chicago.

It's a bit quiet in the break room, as we all sit around the table thinking about how easily life can be taken. The woman—a mother I'm guessing—was wearing an Eastwood High School spirit jersey. The basketball team is playing tonight. We pieced together that she must have been on her way to her son's game.

"I am going to need a drink after this shift." Hilary pulls her blonde hair out of a bun and rubs her scalp. "Anyone want to go to Getaway with me?"

"I'm in," Thomas, one of the surg techs says. "I was going to watch my cousin play in the game, but I don't want to see the kid who might lose his mother tonight, well, if he's even there."

"Fuck, it's so sad." Hilary lets out a breath. "What about you, Rory? You want to go out with us?"

Dean told me he goes to Getaway a lot, since his brothers own it, I might run into him there, and—no, I'm not letting one person dictate my life, new town, new beginnings, remember? I'm not avoiding my favorite ice cream place just because Amber bitch-face McMillan goes there.

I have nothing against Dean...only that I want him against me again. *Resist the dark side, Rory...*

"Yeah, why not?" I lift one shoulder in a shrug. "As long as we don't stay out late. I'm on the schedule for tomorrow."

"Me too." Hilary wrinkles her nose. "Meet there at eight-thirty and be home by ten?"

I smile. "Yeah. I can handle that."

"DAMN GIRL," HILARY SAYS WHEN I SLIDE INTO THE BOOTH NEXT TO her at Getaway. "Look at you."

I wave my hand in the air. "I bought this dress like three years ago and have only worn it once.

"Well, it looks great on you. I see you change into scrubs almost every day and didn't know you had such fantastic boobs."

"I have my second-favorite pushup bra to thank for that."

Hilary laughs and takes a drink. "Not your first-favorite?"

That one is still in Dean's truck. "It's in the laundry."

"Babe, you gonna introduce me?" the guy across the table asks, reaching over and taking Hilary's hand.

"Jeremy, I presume?" I ask.

He smiles. "So you talk about me."

"I do," Hilary sets her drink down and takes Jeremy's other hand. I mentally roll my eyes. Here we go again...

"I hope you say good things."

"I only have good things to say."

And now I need a bag to barf in. Turning, I look out at the bar, *not* looking for Dean, that is. Then I spot one of the bartenders and know right away it's one of Dean's brothers. They look alike, and I can tell, even from all the way back here, they have the same pretty blue eyes.

"Are you gonna order any food?" Hilary asks, pulling her hands out of Jeremy's. Thank goodness. "I'm starving."

"I ate before I came, but those big soft pretzels they serve here are good."

"That does sound good. The waitress was just here, and we told her we needed a few minutes to figure out what we wanted to eat. I'll flag her down."

"It's okay, I'll go up to the bar." Several barstools have just opened up and I'll get my drink faster if I go up anyway. "So, two pretzels? Anything else?"

"I'll take a basket of wings," Jeremy says.

"Okay. I'll be right back."

I hike the purse strap up over my shoulder and walk through the small crowd. It's a weeknight, still a bit early, but I know enough now to expect this place to fill up fast in the next hour or so.

Taking a seat at the bar, I put in our food order and then get a glass of red Moscato for myself. I take a sip, not wanting to walk with a full glass, and then get up to go back to the table. But as soon as my feet hit the floor, and I turn my body to walk away, I come face to face with someone else.

Dean.

147

CHAPTER 17

DEAN

Fuck. Me.

Rory stands up, and before I realize it's her, I'm admiring her ass. She's wearing a dark gray sweater dress today, and it hugs her curves perfectly. Unlike the last time I saw her standing by the bar, she's wearing leggings and boots with her dress, much more weather-appropriate. Her hair is pulled back in a braid over her shoulder, and I want to wrap it around my hand as I fuck her from behind.

She turns, sea-green eyes widening when she looks at me. She has some sort of fruity drink in her hand, and I know her lips will taste so fucking good right now.

"Fancy seeing you here," I say with a smirk, looking Rory up and down. Her dress is low-cut again, showing off those big, beautiful tits. The same little half-moon pendant hangs around her neck like a focal point, forcing my eyes to go to her chest.

I blink and get a flash of her tight little body under mine. Fuck, I want her.

"Stalking me?" she quips, cocking one eyebrow.

"I told you I come here often, so I think you'd be the one stalking me."

"Fair enough." She takes another drink, and I watch with envy as she presses that glass against her lips.

"Who are you tonight? Natalia from Russia?"

She narrows her eyes, and the instant annoyance on her face makes me want her even more. "No. If I was going to be anyone, I'd be Arwen from Rivendell tonight, stopping at an inn for a rest and some ale before I head back out on my quest."

"What?"

She lets out a breath. "Never mind. I'm just Rory tonight."

"And *just Rory* wasn't good enough for the other night?"

"Look, I said I was sorry, okay? I didn't mean to pull some mastermind trick on you. We both were clearly looking for a one-night kinda deal and we both got what we were looking for, didn't we? You seemed to very much enjoy *Blaire from Canada* or am I mistaken?"

"Oh, I very much enjoyed Blaire." My lips pull up in a half smile and Rory pushes her shoulders back as a flush comes over her chest. "Enough to do it again."

"No," she rushes out, and then looks surprised with herself.

"Why not?" I go on, unable to stop the words from coming out of my mouth. Taking her home would be fun—very fun—but also a bad idea. I'd be breaking my cardinal rule. "You didn't enjoy being Blaire? You could try being yourself this time."

She presses her lips together, staring at me for a good few seconds before taking a big sip of her drink. "That sounds fun, but I...I..." She sinks her teeth into her bottom lip and tips her head, looking me over. Her thoughts are written all over her face, and her inability to hide what she's thinking is so fucking cute.

At least the feeling is mutual.

"I'm here with friends." She snaps her attention back to my face, shaking her head. "I should get back to them. They're probably wondering where I am."

"I'm sure they can see you standing here, right by the bar."

"Maybe they're near-sighted."

149

I let out a snort of laughter. "You better get back to them. Though if you get bored...you know we'll have a good time. Which reminds me, your bra is still in my truck and you have my clothes. We could go back to your place so I can get them."

"Nice try." She takes another drink, and if she turns and walks away, she'll be doing us both a favor. Sleeping with the same woman twice is a mistake.

Sleeping with the same woman twice within the same week... it's an even bigger mistake.

Yet I can't seem to control myself around her, and the more she pulls, the more I want to push.

"I'm sorry if I gave you the wrong impression the other night, but I'm really not a no-strings kind of person. That was actually my first one-night stand."

The cocky smirk is back on my face. "Why stop at one night?" I step forward and tuck a loose lock of hair behind her ear. Her eyes flutter shut and her lips part, body reacting to my touch. I let my fingers trail down her neck, down her shoulder, and across her collarbone.

"And this one night would just consist of sex, breakfast, and then parting ways?"

"You say that like it's a bad thing."

Someone pushes past her to get to the bar, and she shuffles forward out of their way, moving right up again me. My hand lands on the curve of her hip, and Rory sucks in a breath.

"It's...it's not a bad thing...if...if that's what you want." She pushes her shoulders back and tips her head up to mine. I could kiss her right now. Taste her drink on her lips. Remind her how good we were the other night.

And then do it all over again.

"But it's not my thing," she says, finding her resolve. "I'm not a no-strings kind of person. I like substance with my sex, and I don't think you do. Which is fine. You do you, right?"

"I'd rather do you, but I get what you're saying." I take my hand off her hip. "And I respect that. Though if you change your mind, you know where to find me."

Grumbling something indiscernible, she brings her glass to her lips and walks away, hurrying over to her friends.

"It finally happened." Logan puts a Jack and Coke down on the bar in front of me. "Someone turned you down."

"Technically, no. We already hooked up."

He lets out a snort of laughter. "Must not have impressed her. I knew you were full of shit all this time."

"Trust me, she enjoyed herself multiple times. I'm not breaking rule number one."

"It's sad I know what rule number one is," Logan grumbles as he wipes up a spill on the bar top. "I finally get Owen married off and now I have to take care of your dumb ass."

"I get to be a dumbass for a while." I run my finger down the glass, wiping away a bead of condensation.

"And it's been a while." Logan fills a couple of drink orders for customers and then comes back to me. "Look, man, I won't even pretend to know how it feels. I don't want to think about coming home and seeing Danielle in…in…you know." He can't even say it. "But it's been over a year. If you don't slow down, you're going to run out of women to take home. Unless you go to Newport, and I know the bar there won't give you the family discount like we do."

I pick up my glass, knowing there's truth in his words, and look out at Rory again. She's leaning in toward her friend, twisting her braid around her fingers as she talks.

"I don't see the point in another relationship," I say for what feels like the millionth time.

"I'm going to say something we've all been thinking but no one has actually told you."

I take another drink and stare at my brother. "Spit it out."

"Remember when Daisy left Wes?"

"That's kinda hard to forget." I was the first one he told, actually. He had me come over and watch Jackson, not wanting to upset Mom and Dad before he knew what was going on.

"And remember how we never really liked her?"

"Yes, I do," I say, knowing where this is going.

"And now that Wes is remarried and happy, we can all say we're glad Daisy up and left and it was better for everyone in the end."

"So you're saying you never liked Kara and are happy she cheated on me?"

Logan lets out a breath. "Not exactly. I'm saying maybe this is the same situation in a sense. You two weren't meant to be together and now that you're not…you can find someone else."

"Did Danielle tell you to say that?"

Logan narrows his eyes. "I can think for myself, you know. I'm not going to badger you like someone else in the family does. Just…just don't drive away my customers."

"I'll do my best." I roll my eyes and take another drink. Logan gets busy filling drink orders, and a few guys from the construction crew come in waving when they see me. I could go over, hang out with them for a while and then work my magic and take someone home with me, but I feel off my game tonight, and it's starting to unnerve me.

Because I don't want to take just anyone home. I want Rory.

Dammit.

CHAPTER 18

RORY

Yawning, I shuffle into the locker room and suck down the rest of my coffee. We're going right into surgery and will probably regret drinking so much, but it's either this or I fall asleep on my feet.

"Late night?" Jane asks. She's getting ready to leave as the next shift takes over.

"Kind of. And then by the time I remembered to take melatonin, it was too late."

"Ugh. I hate those."

"Yeah. Me too." I put my empty travel mug in the locker and let my eyes fall shut, giving myself a quick mental break before getting changed. I ended up leaving the bar only half an hour after I got there, drinking only half my Moscato so I wouldn't have to worry about not being able to drive.

But I couldn't get Dean and that stupid smirk off my mind. He knows I'm attracted to him and was using it to his advantage. I sat on the couch, trying to distract myself with cheesy made-for-TV romances, but my mind kept going back to Dean.

It didn't help, and I finally got my butt in bed, regretting not taking Dean up on his offer to go back to his place. I would have enjoyed it, that's for sure. But I would have left wanting more, because as much as I wish I could do the no-strings thing, I can't.

I'd end up getting attached and would get my heart broken when I saw Dean out with someone else. I couldn't be mad at him either, since he told me from the beginning he wasn't looking for anything more than casual sex.

I'm done with noncommittal men. After wasting six months of my life with Mike, I've been there, done that, and I'm not doing it again.

"How was the night?" I ask, forcing myself to get changed.

"Slow, which was kinda nice after the day you all had." Jane takes off her name badge and pulls a sweatshirt over her head. "The PACU is freezing today, though. Something about a busted boiler." She shrugs. "Do new buildings still have boilers? I feel like that was a thing on the Titanic."

I laugh. "I think it was, and I'm not sure. Maybe big buildings do. Are we well-stocked with blankets?" Patients are cold already after waking up from surgery.

"Yes, and Dr. Keller was *pissed* about the weak heat. Someone is bringing in those little desk heaters to put in the recovery rooms if the heater doesn't come back full-force."

"That'll help. And I thought it felt cold in here too."

"I've been freezing all shift. I cannot wait to go home and get in bed."

"Bed," I say wistfully. "I would do anything to be back in bed right now."

Hilary breezes in, looking way too perky for an early, cold morning. "Did you cave and bring Dean home with you—again?"

"Hah. I wish. Well, not really. I'm all for finding a nice guy to date, but he's not that."

"Not nice?" Jane asks.

"Oh, he's nice." I grab scrubs to put on. "Just not into dating. My last boyfriend strung me along for months only to say he didn't want anything serious. I don't want to waste my time like that." I shrug and try to brush everything off. "But for now, I really want to focus on myself and finally get my shit together. I've been thinking about going back to school to get my master's, and I'd love to get in better shape. Maybe I'll join a gym. Then I'll worry about dating after I've been here for more than a month."

"Good plan there."

We change and walk out of the locker room, getting report and then starting our shift. Today goes smoother than yesterday, and I'm so looking forward to having the next three days off. I'm sleeping in tomorrow and then driving to Chicago to have dinner with Mom, Dad, and Sam.

Wanting to stay true to my word, I go home, change, and then drive to the only gym in Eastwood after work. I get nervous working out in front of people, and my heart is racing as I walk up to the counter.

But then I'm all signed up, and the super-fit girl behind the counter shows me around, telling me not to hesitate if I need help with anything, which makes me feel a whole lot better. She's a personal trainer, and she's so encouraging and passionate about working out I'm tempted to sign up right here and now.

"What do you want to do today?" she asks.

"I was thinking of starting with cardio," I say with a shrug.

"That's a great place to start. We have an indoor track as well as the machines. I'll walk you over. The elliptical is popular with people just starting out. It's lower impact and doesn't feel as discouraging as when you start out wanting to run a mile."

"That makes sense. Yeah, I'll do that."

She takes me over and gives me a quick rundown on how to work the machine, which is pretty self-explanatory anyway. Then I put on my wireless earbuds and set up my phone, watching *The Vampire Diaries* while I work up a good sweat.

Half an hour later, I'm exhausted, and my legs feel like noodles. Wiping sweat from my brow, I get off the machine, wipe it down, and head to the track to walk a few laps as a cool down.

I almost don't see him, but he catches my eye at the last second, right before I go into the hallway that takes me to the track in the second level of the gym. He looks good in the athletic shorts and tank top—very good. His hair is pushed back in that sexy-messy way again, and even though I've seen him naked, I'm taken aback by how fit he is.

And then Dean sets the weights down and flashes that signature cocky smirk at some girl standing by a bench. She's wearing booty shorts and a sports bra and immediately makes me want to skip dinner. I don't think I'll ever be that thin.

He goes around her, helping her get the right stance before lifting weights. His hand lands on her lower back and she returns that cocky smile with a sexy grin, and a sick feeling bubbles up in my stomach.

"Doesn't matter," I mumble, wiping more sweat from my face. We had one incredible night together, and that's all it was and all it ever will be.

"Rory!" someone calls, and I internally wince. My face is beet red, and I know I stink. But hey—so do a lot of other people here. I've just made it up the stairs and am emerging onto the track. I turn and see Quinn walking next to a gorgeous blonde woman. Quinn is red-faced as well, with her hair up in a messy bun on the top of her head.

"Hey," I say, taking one of my earbuds out of my ears. "How are you?"

"Dying," Quinn says and looks at her phone. "I'm doing thirty second sprints and am supposed to be running for thirty and walking for thirty, but I'm struggling today."

"It's kind of dry in here," I offer, looking up at the heat vents. "It makes it hard to breathe."

"Yeah, maybe that's it." Quinn picks a lock of hair off her neck and wraps it around her bun. "This is Scarlet, my sister-in-law. And Scar, this is Rory."

"Hi," I say, still a little out of breath.

Quinn's phone buzzes in her hand and she throws her head back. "Dammit. I swear the *walk* seconds go by faster than the *run* seconds."

"You're wasting time," Scarlet points out, laughing. "Go run while I continue to walk at a leisurely pace."

"It would be rude to run away from Rory," Quinn tries, and we all laugh. "I need an extra thirty seconds. Then I'll run double."

"You'll regret that." Scarlet pushes her long blonde hair back.

"You're not running?" I ask her.

"I don't like to break a sweat. Walking is good enough for me. Though I do like yoga. Mostly because my husband likes to watch me do yoga."

"Gross," Quinn says, wrinkling her nose.

"Quinn said she had four brothers. I know Dean, and then two others own the bar, right?"

"Right," Quinn pants, putting her hand on her side. "Weston is my oldest brother, who Scar is married to. Logan and Owen are the ones who own the bar."

"That's a lot to keep track of," I say with a chuckle.

"Hah. Tell me about it. It was a lot to put up with as a kid." She looks at Scarlet. "Rory has three older brothers."

"I couldn't handle a fourth. I feel for you."

"My brother is younger than me," Scarlet says. "I miss that little asshole."

"Oh, I'm sorry."

Scarlet waves her hand in the air. "He's not dead, and he'll be home soon. Well, I hope. He's in the army."

"It's hard having a brother in the military. Mason, one of my brothers was a marine. He's an FBI agent now."

"Weston was in the army," Quinn says. "He's the oldest and I'm the youngest, but I still remember the day he left...and the day he came back after his first tour. We were all so relieved when he finished his second and decided to go into law enforcement here in town instead of going back again."

I bob my head up and down. "Mason is only a few years older than me, and it was so hard."

"FBI is cool, though," Quinn slows down, and the color is fading fast from her face. "Though I don't think all those FBI shows are that realistic, are they?"

I let out a snort of laughter, mind flashing back to the many times Mason went on a rant about how untrue those shows were...or how they hit too close to home.

"Not really...are you okay?" I ask, recognizing the look on Quinn's face. She's about ready to pass out. I quickly throw out my hand, catching her before she falters.

"Whoa, Quinn." Scarlet grabs her other arm and we help her to the side of the track.

"I'm...I'm...okay," Quinn pants, sinking down to her butt and leaning against the wall.

"Do you want me to find Archer? Shit. He's not here. Maybe there's another doctor."

"I'm a nurse," I tell her and find Quinn's pulse. Despite running, her skin is cool to the touch. "Do you have a history of low blood sugar?" I ask, gently opening her palm to see if her hands are clammy.

They are.

"Only when I'm—you've got to be fucking kidding me." Quinn's eyes fly open.

"What?"

"Only when I'm pregnant."

"Oh my God." Scarlet's hand flies to her face. "You've been feeling sick on and off for days."

"Your heart is racing, which could just be from running, or it could be from low blood pressure," I go on, looking at my watch and then feeling her pulse again. "Which is common in pregnancy too."

"It was really low last time around." Quinn brings her hand to her head and closes her eyes, and I notice her fingers are trembling.

"Take some deep breaths, and I'll find you something to drink. You need sugar and protein, and I have a protein bar in my bag." I get to my feet. "Stay with her," I tell Scarlet.

I hurry around the track, not stopping as I rush through the gym area to get to the lockers. I'm not even thinking about Dean as I breeze past him. I have exactly three dollars in my wallet—I never carry cash on me—and grab my wallet, the protein bar, and then sprint to the vending machine. I get a red Gatorade, leave the change, and run back up to the track.

Quinn has her head in her hands now, and Scarlet looks up as I sprint back over. An older woman has stopped as well to check on Quinn.

"Here," I say, twisting the cap off the drink. "Take a small sip. You don't want to overload your system, but once your sugar goes back up, you'll feel so much better."

"Are you diabetic?" the older woman asks, spinning her fanny pack around and unzipping it.

"No," Quinn replies, looking like she might throw up.

"I think she's hypoglycemic right now," I reply, gently taking Quinn's wrist in my hand to check her pulse. It's still racing, and the anxiety of feeling like shit isn't helping.

Quinn takes another small drink and leans back, resting her head against the wall. The older woman steps closer, and now that I'm wearing my nurse-hat, I'm not afraid to tell while you might mean well, you're not helping. Back the fuck off, lady.

But I'll say it nicer than that.

"Should I get someone from the front desk?" the older woman asks.

"No, she's a nurse," Scarlet tells her. "She's got this."

"Yeah, we should give her some space," I say.

"Okay. Take care." The old woman starts to power walk away,

and as much as her crowding bothered me, it bothers me more that three other people have passed us without asking if we need help.

"Deep breath," I tell Quinn, taking the Gatorade from her. I put the cap back on and open the protein bar. Careful not to touch it since my hands aren't clean, I hand it to Quinn, and she takes a tiny bite. I wait a few seconds and offer her more to drink. We repeat this slow process for a few minutes.

"I'm feeling better now," she says and starts to get up.

"Not so fast." I take her wrist again. "Your heart is still racing. I'm afraid you'll fall going down the stairs, and if you really are pregnant, that's the last thing we want."

"I'm going to get Wes," Scarlet says and springs to her feet. She jogs down the track and hurries down the stairs.

"I'm sorry," Quinn says, pressing the heel of her hand to her forehead.

"Why are you sorry?"

"For being a basket case."

"If possible low blood pressure and low blood sugar from a potential pregnancy makes you a basket case, then I'm just a hot fucking mess. Especially after you had to drive me home wearing your brother's clothes over open-toed high heels in the winter." I wrinkle my nose. "Talk about basket case."

"Nah, that just proves you're a fun, outgoing person."

"I'm anything but," I say with a laugh. I can tell Quinn is really embarrassed right now, and for some reason I think the best way to remedy it is by telling her something embarrassing about myself. You know, level the playing field and prove I'm just as human as the rest of them. "I don't go out much, and that was actually the first time I went out by myself."

"Really? You look like someone who'd go out and have guys fawning all over you. Sorry to judge."

"Hey, if you're judging me to be some seductive mistress of the night, I kinda like it."

Quinn laughs. "Now you sound like a vampire."

"That's even cooler."

She takes another small drink of Gatorade, and I move from crouching in front of her to sitting next to her.

"How are you feeling now?"

"The ground isn't spinning beneath my feet anymore."

"Good. You probably pushed yourself too hard given everything that could be going on. You should probably get checked out. Is Dr. Jones home?"

"Yeah, he got called in last night and was sleeping when I left."

"Did you drive yourself here?" I ask and she nods. "I don't think you should drive home. If one of your brothers can't drive you, I will."

"I'm sure they—speak of the devil." She tries to get up when both Dean and a guy who has to be Weston come running down the track. Like the other brother I saw at the bar, its obvious Dean and Weston are related.

Dean's eyes are on Quinn, brows furrowed with concern on his face.

"Rory," he rushes out, surprised to see me. Then he blinks and reaches for Quinn's arm, helping her to her feet. "You okay, sis?"

"Scarlet said you almost passed out."

"I'm fine." Quinn tries to swat Dean away, and Weston steps in, ready to pick her up if he has to.

"I have no way to know for sure," I start, "but she's showing signs of low blood pressure and low blood sugar. She's been taking small sips of Gatorade and a few bites of a protein bar, which will help hold the sugar levels steady. But she should go home and be properly checked out."

"Archer will check me out good and proper," she says, wiggling her eyebrows. Dean immediately makes a face.

"And she shouldn't drive herself home," I rush out before Quinn can insist she's good enough to take herself home.

"I'll drive you," Dean says right away. "And thanks, Rory." His eyes linger on mine for a few seconds.

"Of course." I smile, heart lurching in my chest. We walk together down the track, and Weston puts his arm around Quinn as we go down the stairs, holding her steady.

"I'm glad you were here," Scarlet says, walking with me to the lockers so she can grab Quinn's stuff. "And props for not mentioning her maybe being pregnant."

"It's not my place to tell."

Scarlet stops at her locker. "Does Quinn have your number? I'll have her text you and let you know how she's feeling."

"Yeah, she does. I think. She did at least. I still have hers. I can text her in an hour or so."

"She'd like that." Scarlet slips her arms through her coat and unlocks Quinn's locker next, grabbing her coat and purse as well. "It was nice meeting you, though I'd rather it be under better circumstances."

"Right?"

"Are you busy this weekend?"

"I am, actually. I'm driving up to Chicago to meet my brother and parents for lunch." I undo my combination lock and pull out my jacket, but I'm still hot and sweaty and don't want to put it on yet.

"Are you from Chicago?"

"No, I'm from a small town in Michigan, but my brother works at Rush."

"Oh, okay. I'm from Chicago. I do not miss it, though. I like the quiet and lack of crime here."

"I've only been to Chicago a few times, and I always did touristy stuff. Which is what I'm doing this weekend. I want to eat at the Cheesecake Factory."

"Please tell me you're getting cheesecake."

"Do you even go to the Cheesecake Factory if you don't get cheesecake?"

Scarlet smiles. "Thanks again for helping Quinn. She's my best friend and is more like my sister than my real sister is to me."

"I'm a nurse. I like helping people."

"We'll have to get together sometime when you're not busy."

I smile again. "I'd like that."

We both walk out of the gym, and I strip out of my coat as soon as I'm in my Jeep. My phone is at three percent, and as soon as I plug it in, a text comes through from Annie, the charge nurse at the hospital. All her text says is to call her when I can. I'm at my max for hours this week, so she can't be calling to ask me to fill in for a call off, so my mind immediately goes to me doing something wrong, though I can't think of anything.

I crack my window, needing fresh air since I'm still sweaty, and call Anne's cell. She answers on the first ring.

"Hey, Rory. Is this a good time?"

Oh no. I did do something wrong. Is she going to fire me? "Yeah. I just left the gym."

"Great. How do you feel about Miami?"

"What?"

She laughs. "How do you feel about Miami?"

"Um, it's nice? I've never been there."

"Would you like to go?" she asks.

"I'm not following."

"There's a medical convention there, and this year its main focus is on advancements in surgery. Several of our surgical staff have been selected to go, and one of the nurses who was originally going can't make it due to obligations with her children. To be fair, I put everyone's name in a pool to draw from, and you're my lucky winner."

I blink. "What?"

Anne laughs. "It's not as good as it sounds. You'll still have to pay for your own airfare, but the hotel and three meals a day are covered for you. Text me your email address and I'll forward you the information. Look it over, and if it's something you'd like to do, then let me know and I'll handle the scheduling. Since this is considered training, you will get paid for the hours you spend at seminars."

"Oh, wow. I'll look everything over, but I think I already know my answer."

"With that cold front moving in early next week, I think I know your answer too. I'll talk to you soon."

I end the call and text Anne my email address. I back out of my parking spot with the warm sun and ocean views on my mind.

CHAPTER 19

DEAN

"You are making a way bigger deal out of this than it needs to be." Quinn pulls her arm free from my hold, stepping into her house. "I'm fine."

"You don't look fine," I counter. "You're super pale, and I mean paler than normal."

Quinn glares at me, sinking down on the hall tree in the mudroom to take her shoes off. "I just overworked myself, that's all. I didn't get much sleep last night, and I didn't eat anything before working out today."

"That's a terrible thing to do." I step on the heel of my shoe and slide my foot out, and then do the same with the other. "You have to eat or you won't gain anything."

"I'm trying to lose weight, not gain muscle."

"You still need to eat." I extend a hand and help her up, going through the mudroom and into the kitchen.

"You're back early," Bobby, Archer's brother says, looking up from the kitchen table. He's sitting with the girls, playing with Play-Doh.

"Mommy!" Emma and Arya squeal.

"Look what I made!" Emma holds up something that slightly resembles a turtle.

"Shhhh," Bobby reminds them. "Your brother is sleeping in the living room."

"You got Aiden to nap?" Quinn goes over to the table and sinks down. Her cheeks are red, but the rest of her face is pale. I get a glass of water and open the fridge, finding something for her to eat.

My mind goes right back to Rory, and knowing that she not only took care of my sister but also that Quinn considers her more of a friend now isn't helping.

I tried everything to get Kara to hang out with my sister. Once Quinn and Archer got together—and I got my head out of my ass—I lost count how many times I suggested the four of us hang out.

"Here," I say, bringing Quinn a cheese stick and a glass of water. Not the best meal, but it's better than nothing. "You need to eat."

"You okay?" Bobby asks. He's a recovering addict, and it was because of him Archer and I got to be such good friends, actually. Our first year of college, Archer's parents had to fly out to Vegas over Christmas break and deal with Bobby, who'd overdosed.

Not wanting my roommate to have to spend Christmas alone, I invited him to come back with me. He fit right in with our family and became an honorary Dawson before break was over.

Archer wouldn't let Bobby around the kids until he got clean, and while he struggled a lot, he's going on a full year of sobriety now. He looks much better, and I know how much having a relationship with his brother again means to both Archer and Quinn.

"Yeah, I just got a little lightheaded while running."

"What does lightheaded mean?" Emma asks, giving Quinn a blob of play dough.

"Dizzy," she says and starts molding the play dough. "But I'm fine now."

"You need to go lie down?" Bobby asks. "I can stay."

"You wouldn't mind?"

He taps his phone to check the time. "I got about an hour before I have to leave. I can put in a pizza for the kids if you'd like."

"Yeah, that'd be great. Thank you." Quinn looks at me. "And thank you for driving me home. I would have been fine."

"Better safe than sorry," I say. "The roads are still a little slippery."

Quinn rolls her eyes and looks at her daughters. "You are so lucky your brother is younger than you."

"I wish I didn't have a brother." Emma sticks out her tongue. "Boys are gross."

"That's not a nice thing to say. Aiden loves you."

"I love Aiden," Arya says. "My brodder."

"He's a good little brodder," Quinn repeats, leaning in to give Arya a kiss. "Uh-oh." Quinn clamps her hand over her mouth and gets up, running to the bathroom, the distinct sound of her throwing up echoes through the house.

"Should we get Arch?" Bobby asks, making a face as he looks in Quinn's direction.

"Nah. I'd rather send her upstairs if she's sick. I don't have time to catch a stomach bug."

"You've already been exposed."

"I'm thinking positive on this."

"Can we have pizza now?" Emma asks, unfazed by the sound of puking.

"Sure." Bobby pats her on the head and gets up to preheat the oven. I bring the glass of water to the bathroom and pull my shirt up over my mouth and nose.

"Stop being so dramatic," Quinn moans, reaching for the water. "You were in the car with me. You would have gotten it then." She takes a drink and slowly gets up. "I am going to go lie down, though. Thanks again for driving me home."

"No problem, sis. I hope you feel better soon."

~

away from the TV to see the message. It's not from one of my contacts, but as soon as I see the out-of-state area code, I know its Rory.

Why is she texting me? Maybe she changed her mind after all and wants to come over. I grab my phone and open her text.

Rory: How's your sister doing? I didn't want to text her in case she wasn't feeling well or something.

Me: She seemed better once I left, though she might have a stomach bug. You were exposed.

Rory: Poor Quinn. And I think I'm fine. I don't get sick often.

Me: Thanks for helping her today.

Rory: You're welcome.

I stare at the phone, not sure what to say. I can't really fit a witty remark or find a way to flirt with Rory after a conversation about my sister throwing up. Three little dots pop up on the screen only to disappear, and then pop up again a few seconds later. She's typing...typing...typing...and now she's not anymore.

Fuck it.

Me: What are you doing?

Rory: Not coming over for a booty call

Me: You're no fun.

Rory: I'm lots of fun.

Me: Prove it.

Rory: Well...I do like role playing ;-) I get reeeaallllllyyyy into it too.

That was not the response I expected from her.

Me: Oh yeah?

Rory: Yeah. I love when it lasts for hours. Actually, the last

time I role played, it lasted days. We had to break it up into sessions, but the big finish was worth it.

Me: You're not talking about what I think you are, are you?

Rory: Unless you're thinking about role playing a half-elf sorceress who uses her magic to con people while avenging a loved one, then no.

Me: I don't know what to say to that.

Rory: I'd be willing to role play with you. You'd make a great dwarf.

She sends a picture of a Dungeons and Dragons character sheet along with a winking face.

Me: I'd rather be a Dragonborn. It's easier for me to get in character that way

Rory: OMG YOU'VE PLAYED?

Me: That would be a no. But if you want to teach me...

Rory: Nice try.

Me: What if I really wanted to play?

Rory: If you actually wanted to play D&D? Like for real? Then yeah, I'd teach you.

Me: Can we play naked?

Rory: And THAT would be a no. Goodnight Dean.

I set the phone down, and that same strange feeling comes over me. But this time, I know exactly what it is.

There's no way I'm going to keep Rory off my mind.

CHAPTER 20

RORY

I step back, looking at my sundresses laid out on the bed. It's Wednesday evening, and I've officially been signed up to go to Miami next week for work. To offset the days I've been missing, I worked a double yesterday and stayed over a few extra hours today when one of the evening-shift nurses was running late.

The weekend went by fast, and it was so nice to see my brother and parents. And then Lennon was here for her interview—which she nailed—and we got to hang out that evening.

Now it's business as usual, and with the promise of sunshine and beaches in the near future, I know this week is going to drag by.

"It's only a few days," I say to Figaro, who's batting a bottle cap around the floor. "But I'd rather have options than get there and regret not bringing more, right?" I nod to myself. "Right."

I put two dresses back in my closet and move the other to my "pack" pile, which is starting to get so big I'm not sure I'll be able to fit everything in my suitcase.

"Don't worry, Mrs. Johnson is going to take good care of you.

You might not want to leave when I get back. Which we'll have to talk about."

I pick up the bottle cap and throw it for Figaro to chase. The woman in the apartment above me is letting me drop Figaro off with her for the days while I'm gone. We've already introduced him to her cat, and after a few good hours of nonstop hissing at each other, the two cats seem to mildly tolerate each other now.

I pick up the agenda for the week and sink down onto my bed. Each day starts with breakfast, and then moves right into presentations. Some actually sound interesting, and others are being put on by medical and pharmaceutical companies trying to sell their products. Which could be interesting, yet if I can find a way to get out of one or two, I will. I'd much rather take that hour lying out in the sun than listening to someone talk about the different ways to sanitize surgical tools.

I'm a bad girl, I know.

"I only have one swimsuit, and I've had it for years." I pick up the bottle cap again and roll it across the room. Figaro bats it under the dresser. Instead of trying to get it, he looks at me. "I've created a monster."

I get the bottle cap back, wondering why I even bother with cat toys, and grab my laptop. After a few quick minutes of online shopping, I order two new swimsuits. The first one is a white one-piece with a deep V-neckline and high-cut sides. It's sexy while still holding onto a bit of modesty and will be perfect for my pool time after I've gorged myself at dinner.

The second is right there on the edge of my comfort zone, but I processed the payment before I had time to second-guess myself. It's a sparkly blue bikini, with cheeky bottoms and a rather skimpy top. I've always been on the thin side of average, but I'm by no means in good shape, and with only a week until the trip, there's no way I can get to my ideal body weight in that time.

"I'm fine the way I am," I say, looking myself in the mirror.

I've wrestled with body image my whole life and spend most days somewhere between *I need to change* and *I'm hot the way I am.*

Yawning, I close my computer and set it aside on my nightstand. My stomach grumbles, and I groan when I remember that I didn't go grocery shopping on my way home from work because I was tired. My plan was to nap and then head out before this snowstorm hit.

I ended up looking through my clothes instead, and now the snow is fluttering down. People still tend to panic whenever a bad snowstorm is predicted, and the store is probably picked over. This is what I get for putting things off.

Forcing myself up, I look out my window, watching the snow fall. While I complain about the cold and lament about how much I miss the sun, there's no denying the beauty in fresh snow.

There's something about the way it blankets the earth, softening everything and muffling harsh noises. It always made me feel safe too, because if someone was trying to get into my house, I'd see their footprints in the snow. It might be a weird thing to appreciate about snow, but it gave me piece of mind when I thought someone was standing outside my window at night.

If there were no footprints, then it wasn't a human at least. Which kind of freaked me out more at times, but I think I'd rather have a ghost spying on me than a real person who could kidnap and torture me.

Though that's not to say an angry spirit couldn't do the same…

Stretching my arms out over my head, I grab a sweater and pull it on. My hair is still in a messy bun from work, and I yank the band out, snapping a few strands of hair in the process. I quickly brush out the knots and then pull my hair into a braid over my shoulder.

Prepping myself to go out into the bitter cold, I put on a hat, scarf, and thick gloves.

"I'll be back in a bit," I tell Figaro. "Don't wait up for me." I shove my feet into boots, run back into the kitchen to get the reusable bag I almost forgot, and then go out into the cold.

~

I WAS RIGHT. THE GROCERY STORE IS PACKED, AND THE SHELVES ARE picked over. I'm able to get enough to get me through the week at least, though my preferred French vanilla coffee creamer was gone. I put the last few things in my cart and head to the front of the store to check out.

Right as I'm pushing my cart out of an aisle, Dean walks past. I've done a good job the last few days not thinking about him, and I've accepted that what we had was nothing more than a one-night stand.

No feelings.

No strings.

No regrets.

And when Quinn texted me the day after she got sick at the gym, I hardly thought of Dean as well. Hardly. But then I was busy with family and now looking forward to Miami, and I've kept my mind occupied.

But seeing him now is making my heart skip a beat and I want to reach into my chest and slap that thing around. He's a player and is good at the game.

I can't have feelings for him.

Coming to a dead stop with a heavy shopping cart on a floor that's slippery from melted snow is a bad idea. I lose my balance and the cart keeps going, jerking me forward. Dean probably wouldn't have noticed me if I'd just walked like a normal person, but someone fumbling through the store gets pretty much everyone's attention.

Dean catches my cart and stops me from falling flat on my face. I twist my arm as I break my fall, quickly straightening up and acting like nothing happened.

"Thanks," I rush out, feeling blood rush to my cheeks. I sweep my eyes over Dean and blood rushes through the rest of me. He's wearing dirty work boots and worn jeans, with flecks of paint or plaster on them. His *Carhartt* jacket is unzipped, showing off the flannel shirt he has on. It's day and night from the well-put-together Dean I've seen at the bar, and I really like this grungy construction worker look.

"You have a tendency to do that." He flashes a cheeky grin. "Good thing I've been around to catch you."

Hah. I wish. We both know what would happen if I really fell, buddy.

"The floor is slippery."

"Yeah, that tends to happen in the winter." He eyes my cart. "Don't tell me you're one of those people who loses their shit whenever it snows."

I raise my brows. "Oh, hell no. I told you I'm from up north. This little snowstorm is nothing."

"I know you're not from Canada," he replies flatly.

"I used to live in Michigan." I twist my fingers around the handle of the cart. "In a little town called Silver Ridge. Look it up if you want, it's real."

"I've heard of Silver Ridge."

"Really? People in the next town over haven't even heard of it."

Dean shrugs. "Sam mentioned it."

"Oh, right. I forgot you knew my brother. So see? I really am from Michigan."

Dean steps to the side, moving out of the way of busy shoppers, who definitely are freaking out over the snow. "Though I am curious what else you made up."

"Other than my name and being from Canada, nothing. Oh, my brother is in the FBI, not the Canadian police force." I swallow hard, noticing bits of dust in Dean's hair. Was he working on a construction site today? When he talked about

174

taking tile samples to his office and meeting with clients, I assumed he stayed mostly behind a desk and acted more like the boss.

There's something hot about a man who works with his hands.

"You really like archery?"

"Love it," I say with a smile. "And I really am good at it."

We stand there for a second, and my heart is beating faster and faster. I need to say something before the silence gets awkward and Dean walks away. Which is what he should do.

And what I should do.

Walk away. Go our separate ways.

"You have dust in your hair," I blurt, and Dean reaches up, running his hand through his thick locks, messing it up and reminding me how he looked when I woke up in his bed. I take in a slow breath, talking down my libido. "I thought you stayed in the office all day."

"I mostly do now since I'm preparing to take over once my dad retires, but I still go out and help out on job sites." He brushes the saw dust out of his hair and off his shoulders. "We were hanging drywall today. I went by to help speed things along so I could send my guys home before the snow started."

"That was very nice of you."

Dean shrugs off the compliment. "It's supposed to get nasty out there with a mix of ice and snow later."

"Ugh, I know. All I hope is we don't lose power. I don't have a fireplace, and I really wanted to binge TV tonight."

"I have a fireplace," he says matter-of-factly. "And a generator. You can come over and take shelter with me." His perfect lips pull up in a smirk again, and he knows exactly how good he looks right now.

I'm never one to turn down a snack when I'm starving, but I remember him giving this same exact look to that woman at the gym. Hell, he might have used this same exact line on her too.

"I'd rather take my chances at home."

"It can take a while for the power to come back on. Last year we got hit with a similar snowstorm and the power was out for two days in some parts of town."

"Oh no. How will I ever survive?" I roll my eyes.

Dean's smirk turns into a smile. "Did your survival class cover how to build an igloo?"

"As a matter of fact, it did," I snap, though by "cover" I mean we were given a piece of paper that I more or less glanced over.

"Well, you have my number. When the power goes out—which it always does after a snowstorm—call me." His phone chirps with a text and he digs it out of his jacket pocket, grinning at whatever someone texted.

I'm sure it's a woman, fawning all over his macho-man offer to keep them warm during a snowstorm. I blink and the image of us, naked on the couch while a fire crackles and pops in the hearth, flashes through my mind. My body reacts on its own accord, and I have to work hard to keep my resolve from crumbling and accepting his offer to ride out the storm together.

He lives closer to the hospital than I do. I could always run and grab a toothbrush and have what I need to get up in the morning and go into work.

All it will do is lead to more disappointment.

"Don't hold your breath," I huff and inch my cart forward. "I've been just fine on my own this far. I'm sure I'll survive."

"Hasn't anyone ever told you it's better to be safe than sorry? I proved last time I can take care of you in more ways than one during a power outage, didn't I?"

I roll my eyes. "Laying it on a little thick there, aren't you?"

"Only because you're so stubborn."

My fingers tighten around the cart again. "We had our fun, Dean, but now it's time for us both to move on. I know I'm hard to get over, but you've got to let me go."

He stares at me for a good few seconds and then laughs. "But how can I when I know how good it feels to have you in my bed?"

My eyes widen and the older couple whose cart is full of bread and milk slows, giving Dean a dirty look. Witty comebacks have never been my forte, and I usually think of the perfect thing to say hours—or even days—after the moment has come and gone.

So instead, I do what I do best, and just stare at Dean in awkward silence, lips parted as my brain turns like a rusty wheel as I try to come up with a response.

"That's what I thought." He flashes a cocky grin and takes a step back. "I'll keep my phone by me," he says with a wink. "Just in case."

And then he turns and walks away.

Never in my life have I been so turned on and so irritated by someone at the same time. Damn you, Dean Dawson.

⁓

"Perfect." I bring my bowl of soup into my lap and turn on the TV. I've been home from the store for a while now, and plugged in my laptop and phone, just in case. I even took a quick shower and turned on the dishwasher while it was only half full.

If the power goes out, I'm ready. *Take that, Dean.* I shake my head at my own thoughts and carefully crumble saltine crackers into my soup. The wind picks up, blowing icy snow against the glass. I'm already dreading the drive into work tomorrow morning.

Eastwood already closed down all of the schools, but there's no closing down the hospital. As long as the roads are open, I'm expected to go in. And even when the roads aren't open, I'm expected to go in. Though Anne seems much more reasonable than my last unit manager.

If I were at Dean's, my drive to the hospital would have been cut in half. Maybe I should go over there. You know…for safety reasons.

"Stop it," I tell myself and go back to my soup and Damon Salvator. I've already watched the entire series in full three times now, but *The Vampire Diaries* is one of those shows I can watch over and over again.

Along with *Charmed* and *True Blood*. Yeah, there's a theme going on, and I might still harbor some hurt feelings over never getting my letter to Hogwarts. Though I'm still holding out hope that I'll move into an old Victorian house and discover my powers as a witch.

The lights start flickering an hour or so later, and I take it as my cue to go to bed. I rinse out my soup bowl and fill up an extra bowl of water for Figaro. Then I pop two melatonin pills and climb into bed. I like to sleep in the pitch black, but have to leave the hall light on, which is weird, I know.

But that's what my sleep mask is for. I can whip it off if I think an intruder is in the house. I know…it doesn't make sense. It's not like being able to see the dark figure in the hall would make them run away. It's been my routine since college, which was my first experience being away from home for a long period of time.

I crank up the electric blanket and settle down into the pillows, telling Alexa to turn on my sleep sounds app. I had a long, busy day, and I should be tired. Yet my mind drifts back to Dean and that stupid sexy smirk. I push all thoughts of him out of mind and try to trick my brain into having a wonderful dream about Henry Cavill being my boyfriend and coming home to Silver Ridge with me, showing everyone who laughed and told me I'd never find a man that I can and did find an exceptional one.

But my go-to fantasy fails me, and I'm in that half-awake, half-asleep state, twilight dreaming about going home with a hot guy on my arm. Surprise, surprise, that guy is Dean.

CHAPTER 21

I hit send and then notice a typo in my email. Dammit. Oh well. It's not the first and won't be the last. I let out a breath and reach for the stack of papers on the table next to me. It's early in the morning and the roads are shit, and there is a police order to stay home unless necessary. While I could argue that our job is necessary, I'm not risking anyone's life just to get in a few hours of work.

I got up early just to start calling the guys on our crew, telling them to wait an hour or two and see how things are. The plows have been out all night, and I hear one rumble down the street in front of the house.

I've been up since dawn and should go back to bed, but as soon as I lie down and close my eyes, I see her face.

Hear her voice.

Taste her on my lips.

I can't remember the last time I felt this way about anyone—unable to get them out of my head. Except I do, and I don't want to admit it to myself, because those feelings led to a proposal, a marriage, and a house.

All built on fucking lies.

I flip a page in the estimate I'm going over before sending to a client and have to read everything twice. I struggled with obsessive thoughts after the divorce, replaying everything in my mind and putting the blame on myself.

This, though…this is different. Because Rory is different, and just thinking about her looking all flustered while trying to keep her shit together makes me smile.

Which is fucking stupid.

It takes me twice as long to finish proofing the estimate. Then I plug everything into a spreadsheet to send to the client, who should be pleasantly surprised their dream house is not only within budget, but fifteen grand under what I initially quoted them.

Needing more coffee, I get up, pour myself a cup, and then go look outside. Mrs. Rogers, my neighbor across the street, is struggling to shovel her driveway by hand. We got a good six inches of snow last night, mixed with some icy rain, making the snow heavy as shit.

Mrs. Rogers is in her sixties, whose husband left her for a younger woman several years ago. She's into all that new-age stuff and always wears a million gemstones and bangles around her wrists, and has told me more than once my chakras need to be cleared, whatever that means.

I feel an unspoken kinship to her, knowing what it's like to have the rug pulled out from under you. I suck down half my coffee and then hurry to put on the proper gear to go into the garage, firing up my snowblower.

I make a beeline for her house, plowing a path down my own driveway and through the piles of snow along the curb from the plow going by. Mrs. Rogers stops shoveling and waves to me, shouting something I can't hear over the sound of the snowblower.

I kill the engine on the plow so we can talk.

"I got this," I tell her. "Go in and get warm."

"Oh, honey, you are a lifesaver. This damp air is making my arthritis flare up. You sure you don't mind?"

"I wouldn't be here if I did." I motion toward her house. "Watch for ice on your way in. It's slippery out here."

"You're telling me." She smiles once more and goes back inside. I clear all the snow from her driveway and then go back across the street to do my own driveway. I'm sweating by the time I go in, and right as I'm about to go up and shower, the doorbell rings.

It's Mrs. Rogers, and she's holding a plate of cinnamon rolls.

"This is the least I could do," she tells me.

"They smell delicious. Thank you."

"Oh, thank you, honey. It would have taken me all day to shovel that driveway."

"Like I told you last winter, don't worry about it. I'll get it for you."

"You're a good guy, Dean," she says. "You're going to make a lady very lucky one day."

"Nah," I say as I wave my hand in the air, dismissing her comment.

"Why not? You don't like the ladies anymore? I haven't seen cars in your driveway lately."

That's because I haven't brought anyone home since Rory. And I'm not sure what to think about her taking notice of my escapades. "I still like them. But the whole settling down thing didn't work for me the first time around."

"So you're just going to give up and quit?" She lets out a laugh. "If I gave up after my first marriage failed, I never would have met my Henry, God rest his soul." She brings her hand to her heart and looks up. "I knew I'd never find a love like that again, but I gave it another shot and ended up with James." She narrows her eyes, and now I'm certain she's talking about her current ex-husband. "But he led me to Wyatt." She raises her eyebrows. "I'm

181

sixty-seven and still haven't given up on love. You're way too young and too good-looking to call it quits."

"I'll…I'll think about it."

"We're all damaged." She takes a step back toward the door. "Don't let it scare you into settling."

I see her out, making sure she doesn't slip on the porch steps. I've been given enough advice post-divorce to fill a fucking book, and usually I brush it off. I know people mean well, but it annoys me regardless. Though for some reason, Mrs. Rogers's words are hitting me hard.

It's nothing I haven't heard before. But before, I didn't know Rory.

~

My phone buzzes with a text, and then another, and another. I don't have to look to know the texts are coming from one of the two group messages I've been a part of for years. The most active group text is with my brothers, Archer included.

I pick up the phone and see the messages are coming from group number two, which also includes my brothers, but also Quinn and Mom.

Quinn: Do you guys want to come here for dinner tomorrow? Like sixish? I'm ordering pizza.

Logan: We'll be there, I have Friday off. So does Owen..

Weston: Us too, but I'm in the station until 6

Quinn: We'll wait until you're here to eat.

Owen: I guess I have to come since I can't pretend to be working now. That's a fucking lot, Logan

Mom: Owen, be nice. And yes, Quinn, we'll be there. We might bring Nana depending if she's not too tired from going out earlier in the day.

Logan: Warn Archer not to come in the house with his lab coat on again.

Owen: I think he does it on purpose. He likes getting hit on by Nana

Quinn: He told me he finds it flattering LOL but don't tell him I told you!

Owen sends a photo of a shirtless man listening to an old woman's heart with a stethoscope.

Me: It's disturbing how fast you were able to find that exact image.

Logan: He has them saved on his phone "for every occasion"

Owen: Always gotta be prepared!

Mom: This is not what I imagined being a mom of grown boys would be like

Quinn: Don't worry, you have me.

She sends an angel emoji and Mom responds with a bunch of pink hearts.

Weston: Some of us have actual work to do.

Owen has something saved for that too and sends an "officer buzzkill" meme in two seconds flat.

Mom: I'm putting my phone down now. Behave yourselves, and I'll see you all tomorrow.

The workday is technically over, but I'm still at the office. Dad is here somewhere as well, wrapping up a meeting with a client that got pushed from this morning. He called this build his "last official" project, but he said that about the other two "last" projects we took on.

As far as working with family goes, this hasn't been bad. Dad made sure not to give me any handouts, and I worked my way up to where I am now. Rubbing my forehead, I go back to another estimate I'm putting together and do my best not to think of Rory.

Fucking Mrs. Rogers and her hippy advice has been weighing on me all day. *We're all damaged.* It's so simple yet something I forget. I'm not the only one who's been screwed over, who's been burned by love.

Who's to say Rory hasn't? Though anyone who'd screw her over would be a complete idiot.

Maybe...maybe one date wouldn't be so bad.

I pick up my phone again, exit out of the group text and open up a new text to Rory. I don't give myself time to hesitate.

Me: Did you survive the blizzard?

She doesn't answer right away, and I go back to work, assuming she's still at work as well. I finish the estimate and am putting my paperwork in the filing cabinet when she texts me back.

Rory: I just barely survived. I was worried I was going to have to kill the meatiest person on my floor and feast on their flesh so I wouldn't starve once my provisions were gone.

I laugh, able to see the sarcasm on her face.

Me: I'm glad you made it. Things got dicey there for a while. The power flickered a couple times here.

Rory: I got you beat. It flickered a FEW times here. Everyone knows a few is more than a couple.

Me: Good point. I'm glad you survived.

Rory: Me too. Freezing to death in this little apartment is such a boring way to go.

Me: And since you did survive and are most likely nearly out of food...do you want to grab dinner tonight?

I look at the screen, waiting for her to say something—anything. Those little dots show up, and this time they don't disappear. She's just taking a long-ass time to reply, or is deleting and rewriting most of what she's written. Finally, she replies.

Rory: I had a really long day at work. I just want to go home.

Me: Tomorrow?

Shit. Tomorrow is dinner at Quinn's house. Oh well. She'd be all too happy to know I was taking Rory out on a proper date.

This time, the little dots come and go four times before I hear back from her.

Rory: I don't think that's a good idea. Like I said, we had our fun.

I let out a sigh and roll my eyes. And this is why I don't even bother.

CHAPTER 22

"My money is on another baby." Logan adjusts Henry in the baby carrier, careful not to wake the sleeping baby. We're all at Quinn and Archer's, and were surprised to see Archer's parents and Bobby here as well. Quinn brushed it off, saying the kids asked to have everyone over, but by the way Emma and Arya are glued to some princess pony show on TV, I don't think that's the real reason.

"Four kids." Charlie shakes her head. "I don't know how Quinn hasn't lost her mind. One is enough for us—for now," she adds quickly. "I don't want to think about having another until Olivia is two. She takes after her dad and is such a troublemaker. A cute troublemaker, at least."

"I like knocking you up." Owen wraps his arm around Charlie and kisses her neck. Charlie pushes him away, laughing.

"We're done with two," Danielle says, looking at their youngest. "I already have a feeling this one is going to be a handful."

Feeling out of place in this conversation, I go into the kitchen to get something to eat and see Bobby standing at the counter.

There's an open bottle of wine next to the fridge, left out by someone who wasn't thinking. Bobby has told us he doesn't want us to stop drinking when he's over. We can enjoy alcohol responsibly and shouldn't punish ourselves.

"Hey," I say, coming up behind him. "Want me to take that?"

Bobby pulls his sobriety chip out of his pocket and flips it around in his fingers. "No. I'm…I'm good."

"You sure?"

"Yeah. I think we all know why we're here, and another niece or nephew is good motivation. I…I missed the newborn stage with the other three. I'm determined to be there for the whole thing this time."

I clap him on the back. "You will be."

The front door opens and closes and Quinn calls us all to eat now that Weston is here. It's pure chaos getting all the kids to sit at the little table Quinn set up next to the formal dining room table, and two pieces of pizza are dropped, and one cup of milk is spilled.

Finally, we're all settled, and everyone digs into their food, looking at Quinn and Archer between bites, waiting for them to share their news. Quinn looks ragged again, cheeks pale with dark circles under her eyes. She's not eating, which is a dead giveaway that she's pregnant again.

"When are you due?" Owen asks, reaching for his drink. Charlie elbows him. "Oh, come on. Why else are we all here? Unless you're dying or something." He actually looks worried at the thought. "You're not dying, are you?"

"I'm not dying," Quinn quips. Archer takes her hand and smiles. "And yes, we are expecting again."

Archer takes a folded-up ultrasound photo from his pocket and Mom lets out a shriek, jumping up and racing around to hug Quinn.

"Twins! Oh my goodness, you're having twins!"

"We are," Archer answer, since Quinn is being smothered by our mother. "It was quite the surprise. They're not identical," he adds, knowing we're all wondering.

"These are our last," Quinn assures everyone with a laugh. "We wanted four but got a bonus baby."

The rest of dinner is spent talking about babies, and Mom telling Quinn—in way too much detail—about her experience being pregnant with twins. Quinn goes upstairs to lie down right after dinner is over, not feeling well.

Jackson begs me to go downstairs with him to play video games, and I take one for the team and skip out on helping clear dinner dishes. We're two rounds into Mario Kart when Archer comes downstairs, followed by Weston.

"Aw, man," Jackson huffs. "Is it time to go already?"

Wes takes the controller from me. "It's time for you to lose."

"Dad," Jackson laughs, looking up at his dad. The older he gets, the more he looks like Weston.

"Hey," Archer calls, motioning for me to come over.

"What's up?"

"I was supposed to go to that medical convention on Monday, but after Quinn's OB appointment today, I don't want to leave her."

"Is everything okay?"

"Her blood pressure is still low, and the morning sickness is hitting her hard already, even though she's been taking anti-nausea medication."

"Fuck. But the babies are okay?"

"Yeah. Nothing is abnormal," he assures me. "I can't leave her with three kids knowing she feels that bad, and carrying two babies instead of one is causing her to have a lot of round ligament pain."

"I don't know what that means, but it doesn't sound fun."

"It's not. But I already have my room paid for and can't get a refund. It's at a sweet hotel, and Quinn and I both thought you should go. Get out of here for a while."

A break from the cold sounds fucking fantastic.

"And I already called the airline and can transfer my first-class ticket to someone else for a small fee."

"First-class, you say? Twist my arm, why don't you. I'll go."

CHAPTER 23

RORY

I move to the back of the plane, rationalizing that I have the best chance of surviving a crash if I'm in the back. I know it doesn't really matter where you sit, but I'm a bit of a nervous flyer and I've never flown solo before.

I made it through security just fine, though, and found my terminal with no issues either. After a half-hour delay, we're clear for takeoff. I take a selfie and send it to Hilary, teasing her that I'm going to Miami while she's stuck at work. I felt bad, actually, being the newbie and getting randomly selected to go to the conference.

Though other than lying by the pool in between panels, I don't really know what I'll do. I'm alone in a big city I've never been to before. It's a bit intimidating, but just sitting here in the plane is empowering. It might be silly to some people who do stuff like this all the time, but to me, a solo trip to Florida is a big fucking deal.

Now if only we could get rerouted to Orlando and I'm able to make a quick stop to Disney...

My phone vibrates with a text, and I open it to find a group photo of everyone at work huddled together, pouting. We got more snow last night, which is what caused the backup with the flight. The temperature rose enough during the day to help melt the snow on the runway, but it's dipping back down tomorrow to the lower teens. I'm going to hate the cold even more when I come back, I know.

I get settled, stash my phone in my bag, and grip my armrest as we take off. I got a window seat, and watch the landscape pass us by for most of the flight instead of reading the first book in a new vampire romance series I bought specifically for the plane.

The rest of the flight is pretty smooth, with only a bit of turbulence here and there. The sun is shining, and I get off the plane smiling, ready to feel the sun on my skin. My bag is one of the last to come out, making me panic for a few seconds that it was lost.

It's early afternoon, and the dinner with the other conference attendees is optional tonight. I'm not one to sit and make pointless small talk, and I don't like what I call "fake friends". Maybe I'm weird to rather go through this conference more or less on my own than to glom onto a group of people I'm never going to see again.

All I want to do tonight is order food from the open-air café by the pool and end my night with a fruity drink before crashing in my bed. Warm, humid air crushes me as soon as I step out of the airport, and given the frigid cold I just came from, the clammy Florida air is most welcome.

It takes a while to go from the airport to the hotel thanks to traffic, but I'm once again mesmerized by my surroundings. I really need to get out of the Midwest more often.

I can smell the ocean as soon as I get out of the Uber, and I excitedly rush into the hotel to check in. My room has an ocean view that I'm dying to see.

Feeling giddy, I take my key card and smile the whole elevator ride up. I'm light on my feet, moving down the hall, looking for my room as I roll my heavy suitcase behind me. I pass by my room and quickly backtrack and stick the keycard in the lock. The little light flashes green and I open my door, expecting to see the curtains pulled back, showing off that gorgeous view.

What I see instead is a middle-aged woman standing by the bed in purple pajamas with curlers in her hair, sporting bright purple eyeshadow and red lipstick.

"Oh my goodness, I'm so sorry," I blurt and look at my keycard. "There must have been some sort of mix-up."

"Are you LeAnn?"

"No, I'm—oh, right," I say as it clicks in my head. LeAnn was the nurse who was originally going but had to back out when one of her kids made it into some sort of tournament. "I'm Rory. LeAnn couldn't come."

"Oh, that's a shame. We've been chatting online for months. I'm JoAnn," she laughs. "LeAnn and JoAnn!" She slaps her thigh, letting out a howl of laughter. "What a hoot, right?" She doubles over, laughing so hard tears roll down her face. "Come on in, dear!"

I have a roommate.

A roommate I don't know.

Who looks like she's ready to go to bed already…at three PM, To be fair, she could have flown a long way on an overnight flight or something.

"Where are you from, dear? I drove all the way from Tampa."

Okay, so no to the overnight flight.

"Eastwood, Indiana," I tell her. "The same hospital as LeAnn."

"Poor dear," JoAnn clucks her tongue. "She was looking forward to some time away from her kids. Do you have kids? No, you're much too thin and your breasts are fantastic. Mine looked like that once upon a time. Three kids and twelve years ago!" She laughs at herself again, loud and boisterous.

She likes to laugh, which is good. Maybe she's fun and I won't mind being stuck in the room with her.

"I'm about to tuck in for my afternoon nap. Do you like Judge

Judy? I keep it recorded on my DVR at home so I'm not sure what's on here." She gets into bed and pats the mattress next to her. "I brought corn chips. I'll share if you promise to be nice."

I step into the room and the door clicks shut behind me. "That sounds fun, but I was hoping to check out the pool."

"Ah, good idea. If I had a banging body like that I'd be out there too." She laughs again and turns on the TV, cranking the volume up. I stand there, rooted to the spot, not sure if this is real life or not.

Shaking myself, I put my suitcase on the bed to open it up.

"You know that thing is covered in germs, right? A girlfriend told me her cousin's husband's friend works at an airport in Texas and he said all the suitcases come back covered in urine."

"Why...why would they be covered in urine?" I shake my head. "Never mind. I'd rather not know." I pull my suitcase off the bed, shoving it between the bed and the wall. I undo the lock and get out my clothes, not feeling comfortable leaving my personal items out with a stranger in the room. I pull out my cosmetic bag, bikini, my sandals, and a new sundress I caved and bought off Amazon three days ago.

I lock my suitcase back up and dodge into the bathroom to freshen up and change. My hair has been in French braids since last night, and I shake out my locks and pull my hair back into a messy bun at the nape of my neck. I give myself a final onceover, very happy with my last-minute dress purchase, and go back out into the room.

JoAnn is asleep already and is snoring loudly. Instead of one drink, I'm going to need two, and a set of earplugs.

The next few days are going to feel like weeks.

CHAPTER 24

DEAN

I almost feel bad when I look around the suite. Archer told me he booked this big swanky room because he was planning on surprising Quinn at the last minute to have her come with him. He'd already arranged for his parents to watch the kids and everything.

Quinn has no idea, and it's going to stay that way. She'd feel guilty neither of them got to go, and she doesn't need that kind of pressure. She complains we're all too overprotective of her, but she's my baby sis. I'm always going to be overprotective.

I've been in Miami for nearly an hour already, and still have no fucking clue what I'm going to do. I should have gotten out of Eastwood a long time ago. Put space between myself and everything. Given myself time to clear my head.

I'm here now. And I still have to clear my head, because Mrs. Rogers's words are still haunting me. I pride myself on not having fears, of not letting shit hold me back. Yet here I am, all the way in fucking Florida because I can't get Rory out of my head.

I let my half-assed attempt to take her out to dinner be the end of it, not wanting to pursue her more out of fear of rejection.

"Fuck," I mumble. This is why I hate downtime. I get too introspective and then start feeling. I need a drink. And then maybe I'll...I'll...fuck. I have no idea.

But I'm starting with that drink.

~

I HAVE NO IDEA WHAT I'M GOING TO DO, BUT I COULD GET USED TO this view. The pool is in the back of the hotel, overlooking the ocean. A live band is set up near the pool, and women are walking around in skimpy bikinis.

It's every teenager's fantasy about what Miami looks like. And maybe mine too. I stop under an awning, looking out at the ocean. A woman walks around the pool, stopping at a lounge chair, and looks out at the ocean as well.

Her back is to me, and she pulls her sundress over her head and bends over, neatly folding it at the foot of the lounge chair. I admire her ass without being too obvious. Old habits die hard, and if she's alone, then I'm going over to talk to her and maybe we'll—

The woman turns, adjusting her towel like a pillow, and I catch a glimpse of her face. You've got to be fucking kidding me.

It's Rory.

And now I know why Quinn and Archer wanted me to go. Rory is a nurse at the hospital where Archer works. Of course he'd fucking know she was here. I take a step back, moving next to a palm tree, and look out at Rory again.

Fuck. Me.

Two guys in the pool are ogling over her, obviously pointing as they talk. Another guy gets whacked on his arm by his girl-friend when she catches him staring. Rory has no idea how fucking gorgeous she is, does she?

I watch, slinking back another step so she doesn't see me. She sinks down onto the lounge chair, stretching her long legs out in front of her. She lays her head back, smile on her face.

Rory is here, in Miami.

The fuck?

I blink, look away, and look back. Nope. Not imagining this. She's really here, and anger floods through me. It's easier to be pissed at Quinn and Archer than deal with how seeing her actually makes me feel. I pull my phone out of my pocket and send Archer a text.

Me: What the actual fuck?

Archer: I need some context here, man.

Me: You fucking know what I'm talking about. Was this the plan all along?

Archer: Still not following

Me: Is Quinn even pregnant?

Archer: Now I'm generally concerned.

Me: RORY IS HERE.

Archer starts typing, stops, and then my phone rings.

"Rory is fucking here," I hiss as soon as he answers. "This is just the kind of thing my meddling sister would do. But it's not fucking funny."

"Slow down," Archer says and I hear the theme song for some kiddie show in the background. "Rory is in Miami?"

"No, she's in fucking China. Yes, she's here! You knew, didn't you?" I demand again.

"No, I swear. The only people from the hospital that I knew were going, was an older nurse and two surg techs. They rarely work with me, so I didn't pay attention," he admits. "Why is Rory at the medical convention?"

"How the fuck should I know?" I snap. "She's here, looking hot as hell lying out by the pool."

"Are you...are you spying on her? Is that why you're whisper-yelling?"

"Yes!"

Archer laughs, and I'm tempted to end the call. "I didn't know she was going. I'll be at work in the morning and I can find out why she's there and not the other nurse."

"No, it's fine." I peek out from behind the palm tree, stealing another glance. Rory crosses her legs at her ankle and brings one hand up over her head, eyes shut and head resting to the side.

Fuck, she's gorgeous.

"Stop being a creep and go talk to her," Archer says.

"She's going to think I'm stalking her."

"If you keep standing in the shadows, she will."

"I'm not standing in—fuck, I am."

"Dude, calm the fuck down. Quinn has spent the whole morning throwing up, so I'm not even going to tell her Rory is there. She doesn't need to get herself all worked up."

"Right. And thanks."

"Shit," Archer grumbles.

"What?"

"Shit. Actual shit. I need to change Aiden's diaper. Put on your big girl panties and go talk to Rory. If you don't, someone else will."

The line goes dead and I pocket my phone, suddenly forgetting how to act like a normal human being. I spent the last year having women swoon and fawn all over me, and Rory is the first one to turn me down.

It's not the only reason I'm getting flustered thinking about going over and talking to her, and I know it.

Someone jumps in the pool, splashing Rory. She sits up, startled, and glares at the group of young men who are already drunk and acting like idiots. She grabs her towel and wipes the water droplets from her body. She stretches her arms out in front of her and stands.

I whirl around, not wanting to get caught staring.

"What can get you?" someone asks.

"What?" I blink and realize I'm standing right in front of a cabana-styled bar. "Oh, I, uh…" I can see Rory walking over out of the corner of my eye. "Jack and Coke," I blurt, going with my usual. It's what I came down here for in the first place.

"I'll be right with you," the bartender says to someone, and I don't need to turn to know that person is Rory.

"Okay, thanks," she says, and I'm so fucking thankful for the guy standing in between us. As long as he—dammit. The guy takes his drink and walks away. I hear Rory start to scoot out a stool. I need to turn. Act surprised. Say something before—

"What the hell are you doing here?"

Shit.

I turn. "Rory. Hey."

"Seriously. What are you doing here?" Her green eyes widen. "Are you stalking me? For real?"

The bartender, having heard, comes back over. "Is he bothering you?" he asks Rory, who's looking at me in disbelief.

"I…I'm not sure."

"Archer couldn't come," I rush out before I get security called on me. "He gave me his reservation."

Rory holds up her hand, still shaken up. "Why couldn't he come?"

"Quinn is pregnant with twins and has been really sick."

Rory looks at me, unblinking, for several seconds. Then she lets out a breath and turns back to the bartender. "It's fine. And I'd like something strong without tasting like alcohol, please. Surprise me."

The bartender smiles at her and gives me the side-eye. I'm not a bad guy, but I'm grateful he's on top of things.

Rory pulls the stool out and perches on the edge. Her dress is folded over one arm and she looks so fucking amazing in that blue bikini.

"You look good," I say, never shy to compliment someone.

She looks down at herself, as if she's just now remembering she's wearing a swimsuit. Her cheeks, which are a little red from the sun, flush even more. Her mouth opens and closes, unable to find the words to say.

"Is…is Quinn okay?"

"Yeah. She's had bad morning sickness with all of her pregnancies and something about round ligaments are bothering her."

"Ohh, poor Quinn. But twins, wow."

"Yeah. It's crazy to have two sets of twins in the family. Hers aren't identical like our brothers, though."

"They're gonna have five kids." Rory's eyebrows go up.

"That's a lot of kids," I laugh. "They both wanted a big family."

"I'd like two. Maybe three," Rory says, tipping her head. "All girls if I have my way. Then one day, I'll die under mysterious circumstances and destiny will awaken their powers as the chosen ones to defend the world against demons and evil forces."

"I'd be happy with one kid that is perfectly normal. Though having powers would be pretty sweet."

"Right?" Rory tips her pretty face up to me, and I realize I'm still awkwardly standing here. I scoot a stool over and sit next to Rory.

"I didn't mean to startle you," I say. "I was pretty shocked to see you too. I thought Quinn tried to mastermind this whole thing, actually, but Archer insists they didn't know you were coming."

"He probably doesn't know," Rory says, and the bartender brings me my Jack and Coke. "Another nurse was going to go and had to back out like a week ago. I was randomly chosen to go in her place."

Random means this was all up to chance, and I'm getting the feeling something bigger is at play here.

"Wait, why would Quinn mastermind you coming to Miami?"

"She knows you've piqued my interest."

"Piqued your interest?" Rory repeats. "So she'd want you to come all the way to Miami for someone you're interested in?"

"She's always trying to set me up with someone and she knows I like you."

There I said it. Both to her…and out loud to myself.

"Does that matter, though?" The bartender set some sort of frozen pink drink in front of Rory. "Ohhh that looks good. Thank you!" She takes a sip and looks at me, waiting for an answer.

"Does what matter?"

"If you like me or not. You said you're not *into relationships* or whatever. So what does it matter if you like me or not?"

"Because I'd like to take you out."

Rory takes a sip of her drink. "I'm confused. What do you want from me?"

"I want you to give me a chance."

She takes another drink, brows pushing together. "I'm gonna be honest here. My last boyfriend broke up with me because he decided I wasn't worthy of committing to. So, sorry if I'm a little leery."

We're all damaged.

"No need to apologize. And let's start slow. Have a drink with me?" I hold up my Jack and Coke.

"Sure. Can we move into the sun first? I almost forgot what warmth feels like."

I laugh and get out my wallet, paying for both our drinks despite Rory's protests, and take our drinks onto the patio by the pool.

"Why don't we live here?" Rory leans on the railing and looks out at the ocean.

"We like torture?"

"I think so. I never thought I'd be able to leave Silver Ridge because the thought of leaving my family was scary. But then I took the job in Eastwood and I regret not getting out of that town sooner."

"Why did you want to get out of town?"

She takes a slow drink and looks up at me. I'm having a hard time not checking out her ass, which is bent up in the air a bit from her leaning over. She really doesn't have a clue just how fucking hot she is, and it makes me all the more attracted to her.

"This might shock you," she says sarcastically, "but I wasn't one of the popular girls in school, and the mean girls never lost their, well, mean girl mentality."

"How were you not popular?" I ask.

"Let me guess: you were?"

I shrug. "I guess so. I was on the football team and—"

"That's all you have to say." She looks back out at the ocean again. "I liked nonconventional things, so I didn't fit in, but I think the fact that I didn't want to fit in bothered the bullies the most."

"You were bullied?" High school was years ago, but the thought of someone bullying Rory makes me angry.

"Yeah. Amber McMillan was the crux of it, and she still lives in Silver Ridge and is just perfect. Don't worry, I'm not carrying around ten-plus years of baggage, but it's nice being in a new town where people don't refer to me as Weird Rory."

I playfully nudge her. "What if I like Weird Rory?"

"Then I would think you're much cooler than I gave you credit for."

"We're all weird. How much you show it depends on how comfortable you are in your own skin. Amber McWhat's-her-face was probably jealous you were able to be you."

"My mom says the same thing," Rory laughs. "But yeah...I can't imagine not being me."

"Like I said, you made an impression on me."

"No, Blaire did," she says seriously and we both laugh. A few minutes pass by before either of us speaks again, but the silence isn't awkward. It's peaceful.

"Can I take you out?" I ask her. "Tomorrow."

She smiles. "I have panels to sit in on, but I'll be free around five."

"It's a date then."

Her smiles grow, "What are you going to do all day? You're not going to pretend to be Dr. Jones and lead a discussion on surgical techniques, are you?"

"I wasn't, but that sounds fun now."

She laughs and stirs her drink with the straw.

"I'll probably do nothing," I tell her.

"That sounds nice."

My brows furrow. "Maybe. I haven't done nothing in...in a while."

Rory twists her body toward mind, eyes meeting mine. "Because of work?"

I lower my gaze, wrestling with the words inside. "Partially, but also because..." I look up, breath hitching when I meet her beautiful eyes again. "My wife cheated on me and I walked in on her with another man. After the divorce, doing nothing was when I'd remember how fucked-up my life was."

"Oh, I'm...I'm so sorry, Dean. You mentioned being married, but I didn't know you still had feelings for your—"

"I don't," I interrupt. "Things were over between us long before they ended. We were both too stubborn to admit it then, and I'm not ashamed to now admit there was part of me that didn't want to face the truth. I'd rather ignore it than say I'd messed up and ask for a separation even though it crossed my mind multiple times." It's the first time I've admitted that to anyone. Archer knew a little about the issues Kara and I had, but I didn't want to burden him with a secret he had to keep from Quinn.

So I kept it all to myself.

"And in hindsight, we should have split shortly after we got married. I'd ignored the signs. I did what I was supposed to do, but not what I wanted to do. We dated, I proposed, and we got married. I wanted to stick with the marriage. Make it work." I shake my head. "Doing nothing forced me to think about how much grief I could have saved myself—and my family—if I'd followed my heart all along."

"Well," she starts. "It's never too late to start over, right?"

"Right."

I look her over, cock jumping and heart skipping a beat in my chest. She's so fucking sexy, but there's more to her, and it hits me right then and there that I'm going to do whatever it takes to prove to her that I want more than just one night.

CHAPTER 25

RORY

I roll over, pulling the pillow down on my face. JoAnn has been snoring for hours, making it impossible to sleep. I already feel uncomfortable falling asleep with a stranger in the bed next to me, and the constant, loud snoring is driving me up a fucking wall.

Knowing I had to get up early tomorrow, I tried going to bed early. And now that I can't fall asleep, the anxiety of being tired and falling asleep during the panel is making me too wired to sleep. I need to get up and get out of this room before I snap and pull the Bible out of the nightstand drawer, chucking it at JoAnn.

It's going on one AM, and a quick look down at the pool area lets me know the nightlife is going strong. I go into the bathroom and pull on the sundress I wore this evening. I rake my fingers through my hair, don't bother with makeup, and grab my shoes and purse. After double-checking I have my room key, I quietly sneak out and pad down the hall, letting out a breath of relief when the elevator doors ding.

I'm not really sure what my plan is but sipping on another strawberry daiquiri while listening to the ocean sounds so nice right now. I cross through the lobby and head to the bar by the pool.

Dean walks in right as I get to the door. He looks tired, and I think about what he said before. I feel for him, and understanding what he's been through explains why he's reluctant to start a new relationship again.

"Hey," he says, slowing to a stop. "Going out to party?"

"I wish." I run my hand through my hair, wishing I'd brushed it. "I have a roommate who, well, I'll just say she isn't someone I'd be roommates with. She's friends with the nurse who was originally coming. Sorry, I'm rambling. I've never met someone who snores louder, and it was either come out here or be arrested for murder in the morning."

Dean laughs. "You made a wise choice. Want some company? I couldn't sleep either."

"Yeah. Is the bar still open?" I rub my eyes. "I'm already tired, so I'm hoping a drink will be what I need to fall asleep despite the snoring."

"You're welcome to crash in my room."

Heat rushes through me at the thought of getting in bed with Dean again. "Seriously?" I ask, after taking a second to remind myself to calm my tits. He just admitted to liking me and now he's trying to get me to sleep with him again.

I should have known better.

"I have a suite with a pullout couch in the living room. I'll take that and you can have the bed."

"Why do you have a suite?" I ask, buying myself more time before I answer. I'm more comfortable with Dean than I am with JoAnn, who I know nothing about. I don't completely trust Dean's intentions, but I know he's a good guy.

He's not going to smother me with a pillow in the middle or the night.

"Archer got it with the intention of bringing Quinn as a

surprise. I don't know why they needed such a big room, but that's kind of what they do."

"Must be nice."

"Yeah. The room is impressive. I even have a mini kitchen. There's nothing in it, though." He brings his hand to the back of his neck. His demeanor has changed, and this time, he's not trying to seduce me in any way. He's just being nice.

"I'd really like that, then. I'm exhausted and just the thought of chugging another sugary drink just to fall asleep makes me feel sick."

He holds out his arm for me to take. "Then let me take you to my room."

"It'll be seven hundred for the night," I say loud enough for a group of young twenty-something's to hear. "Plus an extra hundred to let you call me Mommy."

Dean laughs. "It'll be the best eight hundred bucks I've ever spent." We go back into the hotel and get in an elevator. "Do you need anything from your room?"

"My jammies. And my clothes for the morning."

"Let's stop there first. I want to hear how bad this snoring is."

"You'll hear it from the hall, I promise."

I hit the button to go to my floor. Dean walks with me to the door, and JoAnn's snores can really be heard from the hall. Dean snickers and stays outside while I dash in to grab what I need for the morning. I stuff it all in my carry-on bag and lock my suitcase back up.

"Tick-tick." Dean taps his watch when I come back into the hall. "If I'm paying by the hour, I want to get my money's worth."

"Ohhh, there's a rush fee too."

"I don't think you know how this works." He hits the *up* button for the elevator.

"And you do? From experience, right?"

"I have never paid for sex," he says right as the elevator doors open. We step inside and go up three more floors. The exhaustion I was feeling before is starting to turn into jittery nerves.

I don't trust Dean's intentions, but I trust Dean. Does that even make sense? He said he's going to sleep on the pullout couch, and I know that's where he really will sleep.

Is he still trying to get in my pants? I'm sure. In fact, if I suggested we have sex he'd be all over it. I know my own limits and refuse to sleep with him again unless something more transpires between us.

Dean opens the door to his room and steps aside, letting me in first.

"Wow. You weren't kidding. This is a nice room." I'm standing in a small foyer, looking into a living room. There's a kitchen off to the side, and it's bigger than what I have in my apartment. "And the view!" I cross the room, going to the balcony.

"There's another balcony off the bedroom," he tells me, coming up behind me. I set my bag down on a chair and put my hands on the railing. We're only one floor away from being on the top of the building.

"I could live on this balcony."

Dean stops just inches from me, and I can feel his body heat coming off in waves. Everything inside of me begs me to lean back into him, to let him wrap his arms around me. I'd spin in his arms, and one kiss is all it would take for us to stumble into the room. He'd carry me into the bedroom, and we'd make love before passing out in each other's arms.

And then I'd wake up, feeling like we're going to be together forever, and he'd tell me he's meeting someone else for lunch.

Nope. Not doing it.

"I should get to bed," I say, and my words physically hurt me. I turn too fast and smash myself right up against Dean. He shouldn't be allowed to feel this good.

"Right. Me too."

A fresh ocean breeze blows my hair over my face and Dean

pushes it back. His fingers hover on my neck, and he leans in. My heart speeds up and I've lost all willpower to move away.

Kiss me.

His eyes close and his lips part.

Kiss me, now.

Then he inhales and steps bad. "Goodnight, Rory." Turning sharply on his heel, he disappears into the hotel room. I let my eyes fall shut and exhale heavily.

I knew I should have brought my vibrator.

~

"Shut up," I groan, reaching for my phone to silence my alarm clock. I hit snooze, and I swear, only two seconds later, the stupid thing goes off again. Once I finally fell asleep, I slept peacefully. I left the balcony door cracked so I could hear the sounds of the ocean. And this bed—holy crap, this bed! It's so comfortable and the sheets are impossibly soft. I would stay in here all morning if I could.

But, dammit, I get to go sit in a conference room and listen to someone talk about surgery. I stretch out, smiling when I remember last night. Dean was a perfect gentleman, but I don't want to read too much into it.

Giving myself one more minute, I finally get up and drag myself out of bed. I take a quick shower, get dressed, braid my hair, and put on just enough makeup to look put together.

I smooth out the sheets and comforter on the bed and gather up my stuff, putting it all in my carry-on bag again.

"Dean?" I whisper, stepping into the living room. He's on the pullout couch and kicked off the blankets in his sleep. He's only wearing boxers, and while I've seen him naked before—and had that gorgeous cock inside me twice—I feel like I'm stealing forbidden glances as I look him over. The air conditioning was running all night, making it a little chilly in here. I pick up a fleece blanket and drape it over Dean before heading out.

I send him a text when I get into the elevator, thanking him for letting me sleep in his room for the night. I left my agenda in my room, and I debate going to get it or just winging it. I'd rather wing it and not miss breakfast. I'm starving.

I have to sign in and get a name badge before I can go get my food, and the smell of bacon is calling to me. The line to sign in is long, and I don't want to miss any food. Finally, I'm signed in and make a beeline to the breakfast buffet.

"Rory!" JoAnn calls, standing up and waving. Her hair is fluffed to the heavens and her eyeshadow is bluer than the ocean. I've just filled my plate and am looking for a place to sit. "I saved you a seat, dear!"

Forcing a smile, I go over and sit between her and another woman who looks like they exchanged makeup tips.

"Where were you this morning?" JoAnn asks. "With a man?" She wiggles her drawn-on eyebrows.

"I actually ran into a friend," I say and take a bite of bacon. It's just as good as it smells. "I crashed in his room."

"His. Ohhhh."

"We're friends," I press. "Though I think he might want more." I shake my head. "I don't know."

"What do you want?" JoAnn nudges my arm.

"I don't know either," I say, finding it easy to talk to her. After these few days are up, I'll never see her again. "He's very easy on the eyes and is a good guy. But he went through a divorce like a year ago and seems reluctant to commit, and I'm the type of person who loves commitment." I lift my shoulders up and down in a shrug. "And I also get attached easily. I don't want to get hurt, that's what I want."

"But if he would commit, you'd bed 'em and wed 'em?"

I stifle a laugh. "Yeah, I mean, in time, but I don't want to get ahead of myself."

"Smart girl," the woman next to me says. "I believe you're talking about what my daughter told me is the *friend zone*, right?"

"Yeah," I say, not wanting to explain the weird nature of my relationship with Dean. We had hot, raunchy sex within hours of meeting each other, and now I'm refusing to entertain the thought of his lips on mine...even though I really, really want his lips on mine.

Be strong, Rory.

"So, tell me about work! I've been with the same podiatrist for twenty years. We separate a lot of webbed toes. You are a nurse, correct?"

"Yes, and I've been in general surgery for a few years now," I tell her, wanting to stop talking so I can snarf down the rest of my food before the first panel begins. "I like it. We, uh, do a lot of appendectomies."

"RN and cosmetic surgery here," the other woman says, raising her hand. "We do a lot of breast implants."

JoAnn has the rest of the table go around and talk about what we do for a living, and I barely get all my food down before it's time to go. I don't mind JoAnn so much—while we're awake. I'd still prefer to sleep in Dean's room tonight, but this time I'll take the pullout couch and he can have the bed.

My mind drifts to him throughout the first presentation, and I wonder what he's doing. Having a day to literally do nothing but soak up the sun would be amazing.

I'm distracted the entire morning, but at least I don't fall asleep. We break for lunch and are given an hour to get something from the provided buffet or go out and buy from the hotel or one of the nearby restaurants. I check my phone when the presentation is wrapping up and smile when I see a text from Dean, asking if I want him to get me something for lunch.

"Texting your non-boyfriend?" JoAnn loudly whispers, looking over my shoulder.

"Maybe. I'm not sure what he's doing or where he is right

now," I whisper and tell Dean I'll be able to grab something here, but thanks. I eat with JoAnn and Brenda again, and this time we sit next to a surgeon who spent last year traveling to third world countries, offering free training. Her stories are so inspiring and make me want to spend a summer in Africa, lending my nursing skills to those who need them.

Then it's back to business, and by the time the day is winding down, I'm tired and having a hard time staying awake. I text Dean on my way up to my room, needing to get a new dress. My makeup bag is still in Dean's room, but my curling iron is here.

I get my hair all curled before hearing back from Dean.

Dean: Sorry, I was on the beach and get shitty cell service.

Me: That's okay. I'm almost ready, but I need to get something I left in your room.

Dean: I'm headed up there now. I need to shower before we go out.

Me: Okay. I'll head up there now.

Dean: You can stay again if you want.

I bite my lip. I don't want to say yes, but I don't want to say no either. I really don't want to sleep next to a stranger again, though I did spend the day with JoAnn. I don't think she's a psycho murderer anymore.

Me: Let's see how dinner goes.

I send the text before I realize how it sounds. Whatever. I put everything back in my suitcase and debate just taking it up with me. Deciding to leave it, I grab clothes for the morning along with my toiletry bag and go up to the third floor.

Dean answers on the first knock.

"You look beautiful," he says, eyeing me up and down. My heart flutters. There's something about being told you look beautiful as opposed to hot or sexy.

"Thank you." I step in and he shuts the door behind me. I pause, eyes meeting his, and I'm pretty sure the same thoughts are racing through his brain. We could go out to dinner and actually see where this leads.

Or we could rip each other's clothing off and know we'll have a good time.

"I still have to shower," he says apologetically. "I didn't want to get in and have you come to the door and then me not answer."

"That's fine. I'm going to go through your bags and look for incriminating evidence while you're in the shower. And then I'll probably sneak in, take some nudes, and blackmail you for a lot of money so I don't post them on the internet."

"There are already nudes of me on the internet. For free."

"Dammit."

He chuckles and runs his hand through his hair, looking over my body as if I'm already naked. And now I know he's most certainly thinking about ripping my clothes off. We're going about this backwards, having started with primal sex and now trying the whole dating thing.

"Go shower," I say. "I'm hungry."

"Me too. I made us reservations."

"Where?"

"It's a surprise." He grabs the hem of his shirt and pulls it over his head as he walks way, knowing what the sight of his half-naked body will do to me.

Wrong felt right the first time around, but the second time... though I'm willing to test that whole *two wrongs don't make a right* thing.

CHAPTER 26

RORY

"This view is amazing," I say, setting my fork down. Dean and I just finished a shared appetizer. We're on a rooftop balcony in downtown Miami, and I'm pretty sure I'm never leaving.

"Someone canceled their reservation seconds before I called," he says. I can feel his eyes on me as I look out at the city, and my heart skips a beat—again. This feels like an epic first date, but then again, so did the first night we spent together.

There's a good chance Dean is just trying to wine and dine his way into my pants.

"Oh, wow." I turn back, meeting his gaze. "It's like fate."

His lips curve into a smile. "I think so too."

The table is cleared, our wine is refilled, and we're told the main course will be out shortly.

"Is that your phone?" Dean asks, eyes going to my purse. "I hear something buzzing."

"You have good hearing." I get my purse out. "It's your sister."

"What does she want?"

I unlock my phone and show Dean a picture of a litter of kittens. "She thinks I should take one."

"You're not a crazy cat lady, are you?"

"I crazy in general and I like all animals. Does that count?"

Dean laughs. "I suppose. Quinn has a million cats."

"She told me. I just have one. He keeps me company. It can get a little lonely living on my own."

"Yeah," he agrees and gets a distant look in his eye that he blinks away in just a few seconds. "I've considered getting a cat. I'm not home enough for a dog. I'd feel bad leaving it alone all day."

"Same here, either a Golden Retriever or a German Shepherd."

"Logan, one of my brothers who owns the bar, has a German Shepherd. He's a nice dog."

"We always had pets growing up."

"Us too, and as crazy as Quinn is about cats, our mom is about dogs. She has four right now."

We talk about our past childhood pets until our food comes, and there isn't a lull in our conversation until we stop to look over the dessert menu. We decide to split a big piece of chocolate cake.

"Okay," I start, drinking the rest of my wine. "What about the best piece of advice you've ever been given?"

Dean thinks for a moment. "Ask for forgiveness, not permission."

"I said best," I laugh and he nudges my foot with his under the table.

"Fine, I'm kidding. The best advice came recently, actually. Someone told me not to settle out of fear of failure."

"I like that." I smile, feeling my heart do that stupid fluttery thing for the million time this evening.

"What about you? Best advice you've been given?"

"Don't be afraid to be myself." I tuck my hair behind my ear. "And I'll admit I've struggled with that."

"Why?" Dean asks sounding genuinely curious. "You seem pretty damn amazing."

"Like I said yesterday, I'm not conventional."

"That's not a bad thing."

My cheeks flush and I wish I had more wine to distract myself with.

"What's your dream job?" Dean asks, continuing my little question game. "You get paid a million dollars a year to do this."

"That's easy. I'd feed baby manatees. You?"

"Jellybean taste tester."

"Ohh, good one. Unless it's the gross Harry Potter flavored beans."

"I expect to have some gross ones thrown in there. Gotta keep my day interesting."

"If you could have any animal for a pet, what would you have?" I fire off another question.

"A wolverine. You?"

"Sloth, and he'd just hang around my neck all day."

"Don't they stink?"

"I've never been privileged enough to smell a sloth."

"I'll see what I can do about that. Maybe I can make some calls."

"Don't get my hopes up, Dean Dawson."

"I'd never. Not on purpose at least."

The cake comes, along with more wine, and we eat every last bite of what has to be the best chocolate cake in the world, while continue the little Twenty Questions game. The waiter comes over, asking if we're ready for the check now. It's only then we realize we're the last ones on the restaurant. We've been talking and laughing and time just slipped right by. I only took one drink of my second glass of wine, and I pick up the glass as Dean hands the waiter his credit card.

"I'll leave a big tip," he says. "I didn't notice anyone leaving. Or being here, for that matter."

"I'm good company to keep." I take a gulp of the sweet red wine.

"You are." The waiter brings Dean's credit card back, and I catch a glimpse of the tip he leaves, following through with his word of tipping much more than necessary. Having waited tables in college, I definitely appreciate thoughtful customers like this.

Dean takes my hand as we leave the restaurant, and we slowly walk down the street in the direction of our hotel. We took an Uber over here, and it's quite a walk to get back.

It might take us an hour at this leisurely pace. Yet I have the feeling Dean doesn't mind one bit, and I know I don't at all.

"Do you have a full day of panels again tomorrow?" he asks after we go a few blocks in silence, enjoying each other's company.

"I do." I wrinkle my nose. "I wish I could skip. I probably could and no one would notice, but I'm getting paid to go learn, so I'd feel bad if I didn't go."

"Yeah, you probably shouldn't skip. Aren't other people from the hospital here too?"

"Yeah. I saw them yesterday, but we don't work together so we didn't hang out. My roommate kind of adopted me."

Dean laughs. "You had no idea you were going to have a roommate?"

"Nope. She seems nice and all. It's just weird sleeping in the same room with someone I don't know."

"Stay with me again," he says with no hesitation. "Same arrangement."

"I can take the pullout. That bed is comfy. You should have it."

"The pullout couch isn't bad, and I can nap during the day. Take the comfy bed."

I give his hand a squeeze. "Thanks." We pause at a crosswalk and I look up at him, admiring his sky blue eyes. A large group comes up behind us, and Dean steps closer. I can feel his body heat coming off in waves, and I have to turn and look away, reminding myself to stay strong.

"Can I take you out again tomorrow?" he asks.

"Let me check my schedule, but I should be able to pencil something in. Dinner again?"

"I do plan to eat," he says and my mind immediately goes to the gutter. Yes, I'd love for you to eat again too. "Though, correct me if I'm wrong, but I have a feeling you'd like the zoo. I don't think the Miami Zoo has manatees though."

"I'd love that! I haven't been to a zoo in so long."

"I took Jackson, my oldest nephew last summer. It was the first time I'd been in a while and I'll admit it was fun."

"That's sweet of you to take him."

"He's a good kid."

Dean tightens his hold on my hand and we cross the street, falling in step with another large group.

"Do you need to get anything from your room?" Dean asks when we get back to the hotel lobby.

"I already grabbed what I need."

He raises his eyebrows. "Really?"

"I like to be prepared."

He just pulls me close, fingers dancing along the curve of my hip. There's no way I'm going to resist him tonight. I don't want to, and caving into my physical desires sounds so fucking good.

"It's late. You should get to bed. You got up at what, seven yesterday?"

"Yeah, and I barely made it down for breakfast. Whoever thought starting at eight was a good idea must love cruel and unusual punishment."

Dean laughs and pushes the button to the elevator. It's late, and there aren't too many people in the lobby at this hour. We're the only ones in the elevator, and I'm all too aware of, well, everything about Dean right now.

He smells good and already has a light tan from just one day out in the sun, which is totally unfair but looks good on him. He makes me laugh. I can carry on a deep conversation with him. He's close with his siblings and seems to really value family. And I can see myself becoming good friends with his sister.

If only he wanted something more serious, I'd be at risk for falling. Though who am I kidding? I'm already walking a dangerous path.

I drop my purse and take off my shoes as soon as we're in the room, and turn toward Dean.

"Want to look out at the ocean with me?" I ask. "It looks even bigger at night, which sounds silly, I know."

"I know what you mean. It does." Dean takes my hand again and we walk to the balcony. "Like it's holding back secrets."

I rest my hands on the balcony railing and Dean steps up behind me, hand landing on my waist. A breeze comes in from over the water, blowing my hair back. Inhaling, I turn, coming face to face with Dean, our eyes lock and my heart is about ready to jump out of my chest.

Everything in me wants him, and this time, I don't hesitate. I stand on my toes and kiss him. Dean wraps his arms around me, crushing me to his chest, and kisses me back with fervor. His tongue pushes into my mouth and we stumble back into the hotel room, clumsily moving to the bedroom.

As soon as we get to the threshold, Dean breaks away. His eyes are wide, and I can tell it's taking everything he has to stop kissing me.

"What are you doing?" I pant.

"I said I wanted a chance to prove you're more than just a hookup." He grabs the door and starts to close it. "Good night, Rory."

CHAPTER 27

RORY

Mom: I haven't heard from you in over a day. Did you get kidnapped? I saw on Dateline human trafficking is bad in Miami.

Mason: Leave the crime stats to me. (But it is bad.)

Jacob: Rory can take care of herself. Calm down.

Sam: I knew I should have gone to that convention. It's cold as tits up here.

Mason: What kind of cold tits have you been feeling?

Mom: UGH but Rory, please let us know you're okay.

I laugh, reading through the conversation I missed while sitting through the last panel. Dean is waiting for me in the hotel lobby, and we're going to dinner again tonight.

We spent yesterday evening at the zoo and Dean cut me off mid make-out session again. I slept alone on that king-sized bed, and JoAnn teased me throughout the panels today, laughing hysterically at me still insisting Dean was a friend.

I'm starting to trust his intentions more and more, but I still need to be careful. Because I'm fairly certain I'm starting to fall for him

"Can you pick me up and act like you're kidnapping me?" I

ask Dean. We're walking along a wooden path in the sand. "And I'll find someone to take our picture."

He raises an eyebrow. "What are you planning on doing with that picture?"

"Send it to my mom because she's been convinced I'm going to get sold into human trafficking."

Dean's blank stare makes me laugh.

"As a joke, of course."

Dean shrugs. "Sure." He dives forward and picks me up, throwing me over his shoulder with ease. I laugh and push my hair out of my face.

"I didn't find anyone to take my picture yet."

He turns fast, spinning me around. "Excuse me sir," he calls, going up to an older man. "Could you take our photo?" He turns around so I'm facing the old man.

I'm laughing to hard I can hardly get the words out. But the guy takes the phone, giving us a weird look as he snaps photos. I really ham it up, reaching and doing my best to look terrified.

Dean sets me down, hands lingering on my waist, and we lock eyes. Everything fades away and I have to shake myself back to reality.

"Thank you," I tell the confused old man. Dean puts his arm around me and looks through the pictures with me.

"That one," he laughs.

"I like it too. I'm impressed with my acting skills." I send the picture in the group text, snickering.

"Is that a chat with your mom and brothers?" Dean asks.

"Yeah. It's kinda lame, isn't it?"

"I don't think so. I'm in an ongoing chat with my brothers, Quinn and our mom too."

"We're cool kids," I laugh. Only a few seconds later Mom replies.

Mom: Not funny, Rory.

Sam: Good one, sis.

Mason: What's concerning is how no one around you seems to notice

"You should probably send another. You know, prove I'm not actually kidnapping you."

I bump my elbow into Dean's side. "You afraid you're going to get arrested or something?"

"Your brother is an FBI agent."

"Fine." I put my head next to Dean's and snap a picture.

Me: I'm willingly going with this guy. He said he has kittens and ice cream in his van.

Dean laughs and slips his arm from my shoulder to my waist. I put my phone back in my purse before I see anyone's responses to the photo I sent. Sam probably recognizes Dean and will wonder why he's in Miami with me.

"I never asked you," I start. "How were you able to get off work on such a short notice?"

"Everyone was rather eager to get rid of me," he laughs. "I usually take a vacation in January and hadn't since the divorce."

"So it sounds like they knew how much you needed a break because your family cares about you."

"Fine, if you want to get all sappy." We get to the end of the path and stop. "What time is your flight?"

"Eight-thirty."

"That's early. Mine's not until noon." He flashes a smug smile. "And it's first class."

"Ohhh, nice. I've never flown first class."

"I hadn't either until this trip. Too bad I didn't know you were going. I probably could have gotten Archer to transfer Quinn's ticket into your name too."

"I couldn't accept that."

"You could. First class is fucking sweet."

I laugh. "I'm not fancy enough for first class. I feel like someone would call me out and tell me to go back where I belong."

"I kind of felt that way too, standing in line behind some lady dressed in head to toe designer clothes. Or at least I think it was designer." He shrugs. "I don't really know." We sidestep away from the path, moving out of the way of the other tourists. I tip my head up to the sun and groan.

"I'm not ready to leave this. Have you looked at the weather at home yet?"

"No. How bad is it."

"It's snowing."

Dean makes a face. "It's going to feel even worse coming from here."

"I know. Seriously. Why do we live in the midwest?" I laugh.

Dean tugs me forward, and I stumble over the uneven boards. He wraps his arms around my waist and brings his face to mine, lips just inches away. My heart is in my throat again, but he turns his head instead of kissing me.

"So tomorrow night," he starts.

"I'm working midnights."

"That's awful."

"I know," I groan. " I don't know why I agreed to do it. My schedule got all shuffled around so I could come here, and at the time, an early flight, sleeping during the day, and then going in for a midnight shift didn't sound bad. Now it sounds awful."

"It does. You don't have to work the day after that, do you?"

"Thank goodness no."

"The night after you work midnights then." Dean takes one hand from mine and grips my waist. "Can I take you out on another date?"

"You can." I'm smiling ear to ear, heat rushing to my core. Fuck, I want him. "Or you can come over and let me cook for you."

"You did mention your father owned a restaurant. I'm going to have high expectations."

"In that case, I will have to pick up something and pretend

that I made it," I laugh. Dean pulls me closer and I snake one hand up over his shoulder. "When do you get off work?"

"I can leave the office by five most days. If it's any later, I'll text you."

"Okay. You know where the super upscale, luxury apartments in Eastwood are, right?"

"We have those?" he raises his eyebrows.

"Oh yeah. Top of the line everything. You do know where they are though, right?"

"Yes. Quinn and Archer lived there while their house was being built, so I'm pretty familiar with that complex. It needs updating, but it's nice."

"Yeah, I can't complain. I figured I'll stay there for a while until I get things sorted out."

He tucks my hair behind my ear. "Makes sense." We turn around and head back to the hotel to get dinner before spending our last few hours soaking up every last second of Florida heat we can at the hotel bar.

We've enjoyed each other the last few days. There's no mistaking Dean's attraction to me, and it's obvious how my body reacts to his.

Yet...I have no idea what we're doing. He said he wanted to prove that I'm more than a piece of ass to him, but then what? I hate confrontation of any kind, and it would be easy to keep doing this—whatever it is—than to ask about it and make things weird.

But I have to know.

Because the more time I spend with Dean, the more I like him. The more I feel, and the more I want...which puts me at an even bigger risk of getting hurt. So tonight at dinner, I have to lay it out there.

He might tell me he doesn't see this going anywhere, but at least I'd know.

"Rory!" someone calls as soon as we step to the side after giving our name to the hostess.

"That's my roommate," I whisper to Dean. "We can pretend we don't hear them."

"She looks like Drew Carey's mother."

I laugh. "I know. She's really nice though."

"I think they want us to join them. We can."

"You sure?"

He shrugs. "Why not? It's at least a thirty minute wait until we get a table anyway."

Dammit. How am I going to talk to him now?

"Hi," I say, stopping by their table.

"Join on, dear! We have the room."

"You don't mind?" I ask, though it's not like she's going to say no now."

"Of course not! This must be your friend." JoAnn's eyebrows, which are drawn on higher than yesterday, hike up past her poofy bangs. "The one keeping you busy all night."

"This is Dean," introduce, sitting in the chair Dean pulled out for me. "And Dean, this is JoAnn and Brenda. They're both nurses as well."

JoAnn leans over. "Now that's what I call a man." She bats her lashes and flashes Dean a smile.

"What do you do for a living, son?"

"I'm a contractor," Dean tells her, taking a seat next to me. "And co-owner of my family's company."

"And you two knew each other previously?" JoAnn slathers butter on a slice of bread.

"Yeah. We've, uh, hung out before," I say, taking the cloth napkin and spreading it out in my lap.

"So you traveled together?" Brenda asks, looking at Dean like she wants to take the butter from JoAnn, slather it all over Dean and eat him like a snack.

"I didn't know she was going to be here," Dean says and puts his hand on mine. I'm still unsure what's going on between us, but he sure is acting like we're a couple, a couple who keeps things annoyingly PG.

"But I'm glad we ran into each other."

"Me too," I say, heart flutter once again. "I really don't want to go back to Indiana. It's so cold."

"I'm from Santa Fe," Brenda says. "I'll happily trade you for some of our heat."

"I'd take you up on that offer if I could," I laugh, as the waitress comes over and takes our order. Both Brenda and JoAnn are fascinated with the snow, having never seen it before, and ask us questions about a midwest winter until our food comes. The night isn't going as I planned, but I can't say that I am not enjoying myself.

Dinner is wrapping up, and JoAnn is trying to get us to go to karaoke with her once we're done. That's the last thing I want to do—being in front of a group of people is my idea of torture, and I can't carry a tune in a bucket—yet part of me wants to say yes.

I have a history of getting to a point in a relationship where I think everything is going along perfectly and then shit falls apart at my feet. If Dean and I never get to the point of having a relationship, then—fuck—I don't know. We do this song and dance long enough for it to become our routine?

No, that's awful.

My chest starts to tighten and I'm regretting eating my entire side salad along with the penne pasta. I moved from the only home I'd ever known to get a fresh start, to keep things simple, to really give myself a chance to establish *me* and to finally become one hundred percent comfortable in my own skin. Am I screwing everything up by looking for something that's not really there? This could very well be some vacation fling…though if Dean wanted a fling he could have women lined up outside his door.

My insecurities come rushing back and I sink my teeth into my bottom lip, tapping my foot against the floor. I've worked hard not to let them get to me anymore, but I'm human, and right now I'm feeling like there's no way Dean would want to be with me.

He was married, betrayed, and divorced. I get why he doesn't want to settle down again. Why would little old me be the one to change his mind?

"Rory?" Dean says in such a way I know it wasn't the first time he called my name.

"Yeah, sorry." I shake my head and force a smile. "I'm spacing out."

"What are you thinking about?" He flashes a look letting me know what he's thinking about. Maybe I should relent to him, letting him ravish my body one more time before we part ways, awkwardly avoiding each other when we no doubt cross paths in our small town.

"How much I don't want to go back to work," I blurt. "Or the cold. Maybe I'll stay here forever."

"Just make sure you let your FBI agent brother know it was your choice and I didn't actually kidnap you."

"Ohhh, that just gave me an idea. We can live an exciting life on the run."

"I need to get a seventies muscle car and biker boots first."

I laugh. "I like your style."

"So," JoAnn claps her hands together. "Come sing with us?"

"I promised Rory we'd walk along the beach and look for shells," Dean blurts. Neither of us have any idea if we'd even be able to find shells on the shore.

"You two have fun." JoAnn gives a big wink. "I won't wait up for you."

"I'll probably grab my suitcase before we head out," I say, wrinkling my nose. "I have an early flight tomorrow."

"Well get over here and give me a hug!" JoAnn opens her arms and I lean over and am swallowed by her embrace. "Are you on the Facebook?"

"Yes. I have Facebook."

"I'm going to find you and send you a friend request! My profile picture is of Dudley, my puggle. We'll have to keep in touch. And I'll be watching for that status change." She gives a big wink.

"Okay," I say, smiling again. "It was really nice meeting you both."

Dean comes with me to get my suitcase, and then we really do go to the shore, wanting to feel the sand between our toes one last time before we have to trade our sandals for snow boots. The low tonight is seventy-two, and some of the locals have on sweatshirts and pants, making us both chuckle.

Slowly, we go down the wooden path and then emerge onto the beach, walking close to the water. The night is alive with the energy of the city, yet it's still so peaceful by the ocean.

My heart is in my throat, wrestling with the words that want to come out, but die from fear before they reach my lips. And then I remember the advice Dean shared earlier. *Don't let fear make you settle.*

I think I see a shooting star, which is probably just an airplane, but I take it as a sign to buck up and stop being afraid. I'd rather know the truth than live in lies.

"What are we doing?"

"Walking along the beach." Dean looks at me with that stupid, sexy smirk.

"That's not what I mean." A cool breeze comes in from the over the ocean, making me shiver. "And you know it."

"I...I don't know." He slows, plowing his hand through his hair. "I like being with you."

"I like being with you too." I wait, and he doesn't go on. I bring my arms in, crossing them over my body. Biting my lip, I look out at the dark water again. The sound of waves crashing on the shore echoes around us, and the sand is still holding onto a bit of warmth from the sun.

"Hey," he says and brings his hand to my face, cupping my cheek. The rough skin of his palm feels so good against me. "We don't have to think about it. I like what we have going on now." He moves closer and his other hand lands on my waist, fingers pressing into my side.

I wish I could let it go completely and enjoy this moment right here. Because the setting is perfect, and the man in front of me is everything I ever wanted…only he doesn't want me in the way I need to be wanted.

CHAPTER 28

DEAN

What the fuck is wrong with me?

I told Rory I wanted her to give me a chance to prove she's more than a one-night stand. To prove *we* could be more because I want there to be more between us.

And when the perfect opportunity was laid out in front of me, I fuck it up. If I sat down and let myself think about it, I'd know I'm still letting my shitty baggage to weigh me down, but this time, it's dragging Rory along with it.

I've wanted nothing more this whole fucking trip than to slam Rory up against the wall and kiss her until she's breathless. I want to carry her to bed and fuck her until she's screaming my name, coming so hard she sees stars and can't form a coherent sentence from all the pleasure.

From the moment I met her—even when I thought she was Blaire—I knew there was something about her.

Something different.

Something I couldn't get out of my head.

I don't want to lose her. It wasn't a lie: I *do* like what we have. Rory is smart, funny, sassy and sarcastic at times, but ultimately sweet and caring. She's not afraid to be herself and we just get each other. Being around her feels natural. I spent the last year trying to fill a void that's been there all along, before the divorce, before my marriage started to crumble at my feet.

The moment my eyes met Rory's the wind didn't echo painfully through the hole in my chest. It's not the first time I've felt like this, but with Rory, it's different somehow.

And it scares the shit out of me. I haven't known Rory for that long. I can't be falling in love with her already.

But, fuck, I know I am.

I should have told her the truth. I have feelings for her and it's scaring the fuck out of me.

I sink down on the pullout bed and bring my head to my hand, rubbing my forehead as I look at the closed doors of the bedroom. It's late, and Rory went right to bed since she has to be up early in the morning to catch her flight.

It's not too late to tell her how I feel; to put it all out there on the line. She'll either take me or leave me, but I'll know one way or another. Yet...*fuck.* I let out a heavy sigh and get up, stripping down to my boxers. I brush my teeth and gather up some of my stuff and shove it in my suitcase.

I pace over to the closed bedroom doors and pause outside, listening. Everything is quiet, but that doesn't mean she's asleep.

"Rory," I call quietly, hoping to hear her stir and get out of bed. "Rory," I try again. I wait a beat and put my hand on the doorknob, slowly twisting it. If she is sleeping, I don't want to wake her up. I inch the door open and peer inside the room. She left the bathroom light on, with the door cracked to let in a little light. The balcony doors are open as well, and the crashing of the waves echoes through the room.

She's snuggled up in bed, with a pink unicorn sleep mask on her face.

"Rory?" I whisper. "You awake?" She's lying on her back, with one arm up on the pillow above her head, and doesn't move. "Night, Rory." I step back, silently closing the door, and go into the living room. I get into bed, throwing my head back into the pillows.

It'll be a fucking miracle if I can fall asleep tonight.

"Shit!"

My eyes flutter open at the sound of something clanging to the floor. Rory is rushing around the room, and in her haste, knocked a metal vase over.

"You okay?" I ask, sitting up. I didn't fall asleep until the sun was creeping up on the horizon.

"No," she says, sounding panicked. "My alarm didn't go off and I need to be at the airport like now."

"Oh, fuck." I spring out of bed, and Rory pauses, flicking her eyes up and down my body. Then she shakes her head. "I'm so flustered and can't find my wallet."

"You put it on the counter," I remind her, pointing to the kitchen area. "So you wouldn't forget it."

"Thank you." She grabs it and spins around. "I feel like I forgot something."

"If you did, I'll find it. It's not like I'll never see you again." I take a few steps toward her. "In fact..."

"Fuck. My Uber is here already."

"Go. I'll check the room and make sure you got everything," I assure her.

"Okay, thank you." She shoves her wallet into her carryon bag and hikes it over her shoulder. Time is of the essence here, and I can't blurt out everything I was thinking last night.

But I can't let her leave like this.

"Rory," I say, hurrying over. She stops at the door and whirls around. She's stressed about missing her flight, and I don't want to add to it. So instead of wasting time with words, I cup her face in both my hands and kiss her. She lets her bag fall to the floor. I push her up against the wall, and deepen the kiss, pushing my tongue into her mouth. She hooks her arms around my neck, and my cock jumps when she presses her hips into mine.

"You...don't want to...miss your...flight," I say between kisses. Holding Rory in my arms like this is the best fucking feeling in the world.

"Right," she pants and rakes her nails down my back. "I...should...go."

I put my mouth to her neck and bring one hand up, balling up the hem of her dress. Her phone vibrates, and she groans, pulling away only to give back in. We kiss again and I muster every ounce of control I have to stop kissing her. I rest my forehead against hers.

"This isn't goodbye," I say with a smile. "But I'll miss you."

"You will?"

The question in her voice kills me. "I will, Rory. I meant it when I said I like being with you." The words are right there on the tip of my tongue, wanting to come up and tell her exactly how I feel. If only there was more fucking time.

I run my hand over her hair, smoothing it out. "Can I be lame and ask you to let me know when you're home safely?"

Nodding, she smiles. "Yes, but I want you to do the same."

"Okay, I'll text you so I don't wake you up."

"Ugh," she groans. "I forgot I have to go home and sleep before work."

"I do feel for you." I kiss her once more and then pry myself away. "I'll see you tomorrow."

"Right. Dinner tomorrow." Her eyes linger on mine for another few seconds, and then she rushes out the door. I stand there, rooted to the spot, looking where she was just standing.

Tomorrow cannot come fast enough.

CHAPTER 29

"Hey girl!" Jane waves to me from behind the desk in the nurses' station. "How was Florida? Did you have fun? You look tan. Ugh. I hate you."

I take a big drink of my coffee—which is cold by now—before I can answer. "It was a lot of fun." My mind goes to Dean, and I get confused all over again.

One moment he's the same player he was the night he took Blaire home from the bar. Then another he's the real Dean, joking and laughing along with letting me see past his walls. And then he's back to giving me mixed signals.

It's infuriating, really, and I stewed it over the whole plane ride home. I like him, but I'm not going to sit around waiting for him to get his head out of his ass and leave his baggage at the claim. He was hurt before, and I can't even imagine the pain and humiliation that would come with walking in on your spouse in bed with someone else.

If he's not ready to move on, fine. If he never wants to date someone ever again, fine, but don't fucking tell me to give you a chance to prove yourself and then nothing happens.

Though maybe it did? Ugh. I'm running on too little sleep to think about this right now.

"And educational," I add. "There have been a lot of advancements in surgery just over the last year."

"Yeah, I'm sure. How were the beaches?"

I tell Jane everything I can without giving away any details about Dean, and it helps the first slow part of the night shift go by just a hair faster than a crawl. There are no scheduled surgeries overnight, and when we get a lull like this, it means one of two things: we're going to have a relatively easy shift or shit is going to hit the fan at any second.

Of course tonight, the latter happens and we have two emergency surgeries come in at the same time. Dr. Weiss is already here, and the on-call surgeon is paged to come in ASAP.

I start prepping one of the patients for surgery, doing my best to smile and be calm, helping to ease the sixteen-year-old girl's nerves. Her appendix needs to be taken out *now*. She'd been feeling stomach pain for over a day and ignored it, not wanting to miss a party one of the popular kids invited her to.

"Being popular in high school is overrated," I tell her, wiping her skin with an alcohol swab. "I know it doesn't seem like good advice coming from an old lady like me, but trust me, you'll move on to bigger and better things."

"Were you popular?" the girl asks, teeth chattering.

"Not at all. I was the epitome of nerd."

"You don't look like it. You're pretty."

"I was a late bloomer." I feel for a vein to insert her IV needle into. "And I'm still just as nerdy and weird as I was then." She looks away as I start the IV. "I always felt bad for the popular kids," I say, only telling half the truth. I was in her shoes once and would have done anything to go to a party and be accepted by the it-crowd. "It would be exhausting being that fake."

"I never thought about it like that." She closes her eyes, wincing when the needle pops through her skin. "But it would."

The girl's mom comes back into the room and bombards me with questions. We move in a whirlwind from there to get the girl into the OR. The surgery takes longer than average, but it's successful in the end, and I'm by her side when she wakes up in the PACU. I do my assessment, talk to the mother again, and then go out to let Dr. Weiss know his patient is awake.

"Hey, Rory," Dr. Jones says when I go back to the nurses' station. He's sitting at the desk looking over files. "How was Miami?"

I open my mouth only to snap it shut and consider my words. "Do you want me to answer as the nurse who works with you, or the chick who spent the last few days with your friend?"

Dr. Jones looks up from the chart, smiling. "Both," he admits. "While we're here, be the nurse," he adds quickly as Jane comes back to the desk, setting a notebook down.

"Here are her vitals," she tells Dr. Jones, who looks them over and then writes out a few orders.

"Oh, Rory," Jane starts, grabbing a red piece of paper from the desk. "Did you see this? It's a fundraiser we do every year. You can buy roses and send them to people. It's fun, and today is the last day to put in an order!"

"Ugh, I hate those," I say without thinking.

"You do?" Jane almost looks offended.

"I guess I don't anymore, but I used to. I never got any roses when our school did those."

"Aww, that's so sad. I'm sending you a rose for sure." She gives me a wink. "You're not supposed to know who it's from, though."

"Thank you. I'll send you one too." I take the red paper and write down the names of everyone I usually work with. It's for charity, and I don't want anyone to feel left out.

Putting the paper back, I go around the desk and sit at the computer next to Dr. Jones to get ahead on my charting.

"How's Quinn feeling?" I ask once Jane has gone back to the PACU to do rounds. "Dean told me she's having a rough time."

235

"The nausea is worse this time around than any of her other pregnancies."

"Poor Quinn. Oh, and congrats."

"Thank you," Dr. Jones says with a smile. "Two babies instead of one was a shock, but we're really excited. This was going to be our last, so we're going out with a bang."

It's weird sitting here talking to Dr. Jones like this. I feel like I have inside information on his family and I shouldn't be privy to it. I wonder what Dean has told him about me, if he's even said anything at all.

"I'm going home. Hopefully I won't see you until the next shift."

"Yeah," I laugh. "Tell Quinn I said hi."

"Will do."

I finish my charting, check on my patient, and sit back down, resting my head in my hands.

"Want to take your lunch now?" Jane asks, startling me.

"Yeah." I rub my eyes, thankful I didn't put mascara on before I came in. "Please tell me there's coffee in the break room."

"There always is at night."

"Good. Want to start an IV for me?" I hold out my arm.

"Ohhh, you have nice veins." Jane grabs my arm and runs her finger over my arm. We joke about the weird things we notice as nurses, and then I go in and heat up my Ramen noodles, downing a cup of coffee in the process.

I'm dead on my feet by the time I leave the hospital, so exhausted I'm a little worried about driving home. I make it unscathed and move in a fog, feeding Figaro, stripping out of my clothes, and then collapsing in bed.

I sleep soundly until one PM and wake up groggy. I roll back over and stay in bed for another half an hour. Then I get up, shower, and do a speed clean of my apartment, including changing my sheets.

Taking a break, I scroll through Pinterest, looking for something to make for dinner. I go back and forth between doing something easy or pulling out all the stops. I don't mind cooking; I mostly hate cleaning up after I cook.

I almost settle for tacos, but then change my mind. Picking my phone back up, I call Dad.

"Hey, sweetheart!" he answers.

"Hey, Dad. What's the recipe for that chicken you made the night Mom was going to break up with you but then decided not to because the food was so good?"

Dad laughs. "That's the story your mother told you?"

"Many times."

"I'll text it to you."

"Thank you," I say, letting out a breath of relief. "What do I make with it?"

"Pasta is always good. And it pairs well with red *and* white wines."

"I have soybean spaghetti. Will that work?"

"Soybean spaghetti?" Dad echoes. "Why in the world do you have soybean spaghetti?"

"I'm trying to be healthy. It has more protein than regular noodles."

"You kids and your health trends. Are you making this for a man?"

"Dad? Can't I make good food for myself to enjoy. I'm going to share with Figaro."

"Sharing with the cat, I'll believe. But making *Don't Leave Me* chicken makes me wonder."

"Hah. So it was the chicken that made Mom stay with you!"

"Yes," Dad says dryly. "That's the only reason your mother married me, had four children with me, and is still married to me forty-five years later."

"Well, you never know." I look at my tiny kitchen and bite the inside of my cheek. I am cooking for a man, and but I don't know if this chicken is going to be enough to keep him from leaving in the morning. "It's pretty easy to make, right?"

"If you can follow a basic recipe, yes."

"That's debatable."

"You assist with surgery. That's a scary thought."

"Helping cut people open is way more fun."

"You cut them open, Sam puts them to sleep, Mason hunts criminals, and today Jacob told me he had his arm elbow-deep in a horse's ass."

"When you say it like that, we sound really cool."

Dad laughs. "You know how proud your mother and I are of you."

"You did a pretty good job raising me."

"It was mostly your mother," he laughs. "Enjoy the chicken tonight."

"I will. Thanks Dad. Love you."

"Love you too, honey."

I end the call and wait a few minutes for Dad to send me the recipe. I make a grocery list, twist my damp hair into a bun, and pull on a hat. Eastwood didn't get the snow that was predicted, but after spending my days in eighty-degree weather and full sun, I'm freezing. I speed through grocery shopping, wanting to get back home with plenty of time to do my hair and makeup before needing to start dinner.

Sticking the two bottles of red Moscato that I grabbed at the store in the fridge, I go into the bathroom and spend way too much time doing my hair and makeup. But I look good at least.

I left my phone on the kitchen counter and missed a text from Dean.

Dean: My last clients had to reschedule their meeting. I'll be wrapping things up at the office soon. Are you up? I can bring you coffee.

Me: I'm up and I've had enough coffee to kill a whale already. Be here in forty-five minutes? I'll have dinner ready :-)

Dean: Half an hour? I miss you.

I can't help the stupid smile that comes over my face.

Me: I suppose I can let it slide. I'll start cooking now.

I set the phone back down and run around like crazy, vacuuming and hiding my pile of dirty laundry in the closet. I light my favorite peony-scented candle and put lemongrass oil in the diffuser in my bedroom.

"I am not trying too hard," I tell Figaro. He's sitting on the table, tail swishing back and forth. "Keep up that sass and you are not getting the fat trimmings from the chicken." I pull out all the ingredients I need and read over Dad's text with the recipe. "Besides, I'm still not sure where things are headed," I go on. "I like him, and I'm really hoping he spends the night, but…" I let out a sigh. "I just don't know."

Figaro jumps up on the counter when I start trimming the chicken. I push him off with my elbow and he comes right back. I give up, quickly wash the raw chicken germs off my hands, and lock him in the bathroom until I'm done. He comes running, leaping onto the counter as soon as I let him out.

"If Dean sees you all over the counter, he's not going to want to eat anything I make him, you know." I pick up the black-and-white cat and set him down by his food bowl, showing him the little pieces of chicken I saved.

I turn on music and pour myself a small glass of Moscato as I cook. The chicken is almost done when Dean knocks on the door.

"He's here!" I whisper to Figaro, who's sleeping on the couch and doesn't so much as bat an eye. I give the counter a frantic wipe down, smooth out my hair, and take a deep breath.

Then I open the door, smiling as soon as I see Dean.

"Hello good sir," I say, suddenly donning a British accent.

"Good morrow, my lady." He dramatically bows and I laugh. "Dinner smells good."

"Thanks." I take his coat from him and hang it up in the little closet at the front of the apartment. Figaro will lie on it if I put it over the back of the chair in my living room. "It's one of my favorites, but I haven't made it myself in, well, ever."

"Should we order a pizza as backup?" he teases.

"Way to have faith," I shoot back. Dean follows me to the kitchen, and I go right to the fridge to get out the wine. "How was work?" I ask as I get out two glasses. "Do you want some? I didn't think about getting anything else. I don't really know what else to get."

"Sure, and work was fine. I had a lot of office work to do today, catching up on what I missed. It was nice to have my last meeting moved today. I meant it when I said I miss you." I hand him a glass of wine and he takes a drink, making a face. "This is really sweet."

"It's how I like my wine. I don't like the taste of alcohol, like at all," I tell him. "Which might have to do with my excessive partying I did in college."

"You were a party-girl?"

"Hardly. I don't hold my liquor well, and I still can't stomach even the smell of tequila after one fateful night that involved jello shots, Taco Bell, and an hour hanging over the toilet there, crying and swearing I'm never drinking again."

Dean laughs. "I've had a few of those experiences too."

"I'm way too old to wake up hungover now." I take a small sip of the sweet wine and check on the chicken. The cheese is nice and bubbly and needs just another minute to brown up a bit.

"I remember being able to stay up all night, have beer with breakfast, and hit the gym at noon and feel fantastic," Dean laughs.

"I never did that, but I used to pull a lot of late nights staying up reading until three or four AM. Now I need a full eight hours of sleep or I'm in a fog all day."

"There's nothing like getting old. Once you cross thirty, it's all downhill."

"I'm only twenty-eight," I say, batting my lashes. "A spring chicken compared to you, old man."

He laughs. "I'm only thirty-four."

"Yep basically dead, have you checked out nursing homes yet?"

"My grandma is at East Meadows and she says the nurses there are very gentle when they wipe her butt. And I mean she actually said those exact words. She has no filter at all anymore."

"She sounds fun."

"That's one way to put it. She's gotten mean in her old age too, but now her memory isn't what it used to be." He frowns. "Though she always hits on Archer at family gatherings. It's disturbing but hilarious at the same time."

"That would be awkward, but I'd be laughing in the background for sure. I only have one grandparent left, and mine has become quite unfiltered too. I hope I have her spunk when I'm in my eighties."

The oven timer goes off, and I take the chicken out. It's done now, and I let it cool in the pan for a few minutes before cutting into it and dishing it up. Dad always insisted that's one of the most important things to keep the flavoring at its best.

I dish up the food and we sit at the table. My heart lurches in my chest when I look at Dean. He's so handsome, and it's so easy to sit here and talk to him. We talk and laugh throughout dinner, and we take dessert into the living room, along with the bottle of wine.

Sitting close together on the couch, we search through Netflix, finding something to watch, though I don't think either of us is too interested in anything on TV.

"Can I find a live cam of a beach somewhere?"

"And pretend we're back in Miami?"

"Yes. I miss the sun."

"Me too." Dean puts his arm around me, pulling me to him. I

lie back, stretching my legs out. "Though I did see the high on Monday is fifty-three. Followed by snow on Tuesday."

"Winter lasts a year in the Midwest."

"It feels like it." I rest my head back against his chest. "What about this? Have you seen it?" I ask, highlighting a popular scary show.

"I haven't, but Quinn and Scarlet are obsessed with it."

"I've only made it through one episode."

"Too scared?" Dean teases.

"Hah. No, I had a list of other shows to watch, and I'm weird and rewatch the same things over and over."

"You know what you like. There's nothing weird about that." He slips his arm under mine, fingers resting right at the hem of my shirt. I dressed up without being obvious, wearing my favorite jeans and tight black top.

We watch a few minutes of the show, snuggled up together. Then Dean sits up a bit and pulls me to him. I move onto his lap, arms locking around his neck. His eyes meet mine, and my emotions burn inside my chest.

It hits me that this is my last chance to pull away, to break his gaze and move out of his arms...which feel so fucking good around me. Dean gathers my hair in his hand, moving it over my shoulder.

If he kisses me, I'm done for. There's no way I can resist what's to come—which will be me, multiple times. But more importantly, I don't want to resist him.

And tonight...tonight I'm not going to.

CHAPTER 30

RORY

"**M**orning," Dean mumbles, voice thick with sleep. Weak sunlight comes in through the window, illuminating the room in a muted gray glow. He's had his arm around me all night, and waking up in his embrace is everything. He moves closer, spooning his body against mine. "I'm liking the heated blanket more than I thought I would."

"Told you it's nice," I say, eyes still shut. We're both naked and my bed has never felt more comfortable than it does with Dean next to me. He has to get up and go to work, but right now I'm not ready to let him go.

"It is." His lips brush against the back of my neck as he talks. "And so is this." He gives me a squeeze. "I want to wake up next to you tomorrow. And the morning after that…and every next morning in the foreseeable future."

My eyes fly open and I spin in Dean's arms. I put my leg over his and he plants his lips to my forehead. "Dean Dawson, are you implying what I think you're implying?"

"That we should have sex every single night and wake up naked next to each other? Then yes, yes I am."

I laugh. "I do like the sound of that. But waking up...with me..."

"Yes," he says, answering the question that I haven't yet asked. "I don't want anyone else." He puts his lips to mine, kissing me gently, and then lifts his head back enough to look in my eyes. "I think I'm falling for you, Rory. And it scares the shit out of me, but I want you and only you."

My heart flutters in my chest and my lips part, but words fail me. I lift my head off the pillow and kiss him. "I want you too," I whisper.

"Good. Because it would be really fucking awkward if you didn't."

I laugh and pull him on top of me, feeling his cock start to harden. And then his alarm goes off. Groaning, he rolls off me and grabs his phone, turning the alarm off.

"Can you pretend you're sick?" I ask when Dean settles back on top of me. I run nails up and down his back.

"You're making me seriously consider it."

"I know you really can't," I say, splaying my fingers over his shoulders. "But I can make you breakfast."

"You don't have to do that."

"I know. I want to. I got bacon last night and I really want some."

"So making it for me is just a ruse."

"Pretty much." I splay my fingers over his shoulders, missing him already. "How do you like your eggs?"

"Scrambled."

"Me too." He kisses me once more and pries himself off me, looking for his clothes we discarded somewhere on the floor on the way to my bedroom last night.

Dean gets in the shower and I get up, pulling on underwear and a fuzzy sweater. I go to the kitchen, loading the dishwasher while breakfast cooks. I'm not a morning person even after years of getting up for early shifts as a nurse. But right now...

right now I'm on cloud fucking nine and I never want to come down.

"Now this is a view I could get used to."

I turn, seeing Dean standing in the threshold of the kitchen with only a towel around his waist.

"Likewise."

"I think this needs to be a thing." Dean comes up behind me, wrapping one arm around my waist. "No pants when you cook."

"Can this thing go both ways?" I stir the eggs and set the spatula down, twisting around in Dean's arms. "You don't wear pants either?"

"I don't think we'd ever eat a damn thing then." He brings his large hands to my ass, gripping my cheeks. "Well, I'd eat."

"I really don't want you to go to work, and it's not fair you have to work on the weekend. Especially when I'm not working on the weekend this week. I work every other weekend, in case you were wondering how that works."

"That makes sense. And I usually don't, but with the spring home tour coming up, I'm meeting with the town Board of Trustees." He makes a face. "It's going to be fun."

"You have lunch to look forward to." I stand on my toes and kiss him. "And if you're a good boy, I'll bring you dessert."

Dean gives my ass another squeeze. "You know, I'm suddenly feeling sick. Too sick to go to work."

"I know I should be a responsible adult and not encourage this kind of behavior, but dammit, Dean, I want you to play hooky too."

"You're a bad influence, Rory Harris."

"I'm the worst." He brings his head down, pressing his forehead against mine. And then bacon pops and hot oil splatters my butt.

"Ow!" I yell and jump, hand flying to my bottom. "Maybe cooking with no pants isn't a good idea," I laugh.

"Yeah, that could be dangerous."

I flip the bacon once more and grab plates. "How do you take your coffee?"

"Black."

"Really?"

"Yeah. Sometimes I'll add a little sugar."

"I don't like the way coffee tastes. I probably drink more creamer than actual coffee, but I need caffeine. I get a headache if I don't have at least one cup of coffee in the morning."

"You're addicted."

"I have been since my first year of college."

"There are worse things to be addicted to."

I laugh. "Good point. Now go sit. Breakfast is ready."

"I'm sorry," I say to Lennon, pulling into a parking spot in front of the Dawson Contractors main office. "But that doesn't mean you didn't get the job."

"I haven't heard anything," she repeats. "No request for a second interview. None of my references contacted. Nothing. Ugh. This is the fourth year I've been trying to get a principal job."

"You will get one, I know it."

"I hope so. And I'm super bummed I won't be by you. It would have been so cool, and I know you don't like being alone."

"I'm totally alone here."

"You know what I mean. I'm better than any new friends you could make anyway. Right?"

"Right," I laugh. "But I'm kind of dating someone now."

"Shut up! When did this happen?"

"This morning."

"Who? Tell me everything!"

"Remember the hot guy I was supposed to go on a blind date with but ended up sleeping with anyway?"

She laughs. "How could I forget—no fucking way! You said he wasn't a relationship kind of guy."

"One night with the old Royster and he changed his ways."

"Don't ever refer to yourself as *Royster* again," she says. "You sure you're dating and not reading into casual sex?"

"Yes. Long story short, he was in Miami and—"

"What? I need to hear the long story, and why didn't you tell me?"

"I didn't want to make it a thing in case it didn't turn out to be, well, a thing." I shut off the Jeep's engine and unbuckle my seatbelt. I tell Lennon about what happened in Miami and everything that's transpired since.

"Go bring your new man his lunch," she says. "I'll call in a panic over switching careers later next week, I'm sure."

"Don't quit. You love being a teacher."

"Today I didn't."

"It's Saturday," I remind her.

"Exactly my point. Love you, Ror."

"Love you, too, Len." I end the call, check my makeup, and scroll through social media, wasting another few minutes before going into the office.

Since it's Saturday, the secretary isn't sitting at the front desk. I slowly walk down a hall, looking at the names on the doors. Dean's office is right across from Harold Dawson's, who I assume is Dean's father.

I can hear voices coming from a conference room at the end of the hall, and since the door to Dean's office is open, I go inside and sit at one of the chairs in front of his desk. I log onto a Dungeons and Dragons message board that I used to frequent and read through the posts. There used to be a thread to find local players. Maybe I'll find a group who plays around here.

The meeting disperses, and a few minutes pass before Dean walks down the hall. He's not headed to his office, but he turns as he passes, looking right in at me. The biggest smile takes over his face when our eyes meet.

"Rory," he says, and the man walking next to him looks in too. "Dad, this is Rory. Rory, this is my dad."

I get up, and Dean and his father come into the office.

"It's nice to meet you," Mr. Dawson says. "I hope you weren't waiting long. I didn't know we had any client meetings this afternoon or else I would have wrapped up that meeting sooner."

"Rory isn't a client, Dad." Dean strides across the room. "She's meeting me for lunch because we're dating."

Mr. Dawson's eyes widen, and he smiles. "Well, it's nice to meet you, Rory. I'm Harold." He holds out his hand for me to shake.

"I'm Rory," I say and internally wince. "Which you already know."

Harold chuckles. "Whatever you brought smells delicious." His eyes go to the cloth shopping bag I set on Dean's desk. "Enjoy your lunch," he tells us both. "It was nice to meet you Rory. Maybe I'll see you again."

"You will," Dean says confidently, and I do my best not to smile like a goon. The beginnings of relationships are always the best, and this time, I don't have a sense of impending doom like I have with almost every other relationship I've had.

"You weren't waiting too long, were you?" Dean asks.

"Not at all. I kept myself busy looking at a D&D site to see if I could find any local players. I'd crash their party. In costume."

"You said you're a sexy half-elf who wears those degrading slutty leather outfits, right?"

"Aww, you paid attention."

"There was a slight chance of actual role playing. Of course I paid attention."

"But you added in the slutty costume part."

He tips his head to the side. "I can dream, right?"

Laughing, I move into his arms. "I wouldn't have thought Elven warriors were your thing."

"If you're dressed like it, anything is my thing."

"I do have a few costumes. I might bust one out tonight if you're lucky."

He laughs and kisses my forehead. "Don't tease me now."

"I take my costuming very seriously."

"Wait," he says and picks up the bag of food. "You were looking for strangers to play D&D with?"

"Yeah. I haven't played in a while, and since we talked about it, I've been wanting to play again."

"I'll play with you."

"Really?"

"I don't know how good I'd be. You have to talk in character, right?"

I narrow my eyes. "Are you sure you haven't played before?"

"I haven't," he laughs. "But I have seen it played on The Big Bang Theory and I thought it looked kind of fun. I like fantasy-based video games."

"You'd probably like it. It takes a few sessions to get acquainted, but it's not all that hard. We can't play with just the two of us, though."

"Quinn would play. Scarlet probably would too. And if they are, we can get Weston and Archer in with us, and I'm pretty sure Logan would join in as well. I'm not sure about his wife, though, and Owen would be terrible to play with. Wait, you haven't met them yet, have you?"

I shake my head. "Logan and Owen are the ones who own the bar, and one of them is married to someone who owns a bakery, right?"

"Yep. That's Danielle, Logan's wife. Owen is married to Charlie. She's a lawyer."

"And they all have kids?"

"Yeah."

"That's a lot of family to keep track of."

"It is," he agrees. "It's easier once you can put faces to the names. Well, except Logan and Owen are identical twins."

"Just adds to the confusion," I laugh and look around Dean's office. "This isn't what I imagined your office would look like." Everything is clean and modern. Dean's college degree is hanging on the wall behind his desk, along with a framed photo of his entire family at Quinn and Archer's wedding.

"What did you think it would look like?"

"I don't really know. But this is very...very professional."

"That's what I'm trying to go for. We updated the entire building last year. Presentation is important when people come in here, unsure if they want to hire us to take on projects costing hundreds of thousands of dollars."

"That is a good point." I step over to the adjacent wall, looking at black-and-white photos of buildings in various phases of construction. "These are cool."

"The first one is my house," he says.

I tip my head up, looking at the photo of his house back when it was just the framing. "That's cool."

Dean moves behind me, hand landing on the small of my back. I lean against him, taking my time looking at the rest of the photos.

"You built that double staircase?" I point to a photo in the middle.

"Yeah. That's Quinn and Archer's house."

"Holy shit."

"That's the general reaction." He slides his hand to the curve of my hip. "Their house is huge." He points to another photo. "This is Owen and Charlie's house, and the next few are from the renovation my dad did himself on their current house."

"Their house looks amazing."

"It's a century-old farmhouse. It was a dump when we moved in."

"I bet it looks gorgeous now."

"It's very nice. You'll have to see it sometime," he says, not really thinking as he slides his hand down toward my core. Then he suddenly stops. "Eventually. I'm not saying you need to come meet my parents or anything."

He's getting flustered, and it's so freaking cute. I turn, wrapping my arms around his shoulders. "I've already met your dad, you sister, one sister-in-law, and one brother. Plus, I work with Dr. Jones. Isn't that like half your family?"

He smiles. "Pretty much. In that case, do you want to come to dinner with me on Sunday? We always have dinner at my parents' on Sunday."

"I would very much like that."

Dean closes the distance between us, hands traveling all over my body. Warmth rushes between my legs and I tighten my arms around his neck. I'm wearing flats today, and stand on toes to kiss him. He tightens his hold on me, and takes a step back, bringing me with him.

We stumble back together, taking clumsy steps so we don't have to break apart. Then Dean picks me up, taking me to the opposite side of his office. He shuts the door with his foot and slams me against the wall, kissing me harder than before.

My legs are fastened around him, and his cock starts to harden against me. I drag one hand down his chest, untucking his shirt. He sets me down and I undo his belt, pulling it through the loops and dropping it on the floor.

I think we're alone in the building, but I'm not sure. And right now, I don't care. I want Dean, and he wants me too. My heart is all fluttery, and I'm fueled with primal desire. I pop the button on Dean's pants and press my hand over his erection.

Then I drop to my knees, inching his pants down, and take him in my mouth, flicking my tongue over the sensitive tip of his dick. Dean groans and throws one hand out, bracing himself against the wall. I wrap one hand around his thick shaft, moving it up and down along with my lips, sucking him hard.

"Fuck," he pants, reaching down and urging me up. He side-steps, taking me with him. Then he spins me around and pulls my sweater dress up, exposing my ass.

He gives it a slap and pushes me down. I grip the edge of his desk, pussy aching to have him inside me. I spread my legs, eyes fluttering shut when he reaches around, fingers slipping inside my panties.

He strokes my clit, and I'm already so wound up, it doesn't take long before I'm right there, about ready to come. He plunges his fingers inside me, finding that sweet spot right away, and rubbing against it before pulling his fingers out and rubbing my clit again.

I clamp my hand over my mouth, muffling a moan as I come, knees threatening to buckle. My pussy is still spasming when he pulls my underwear down and lines his cock up with my entrance. Both of his hands go to my waist, and he enters me, moving slow at first and then speeding up his movements.

I cry out, unable to help myself as Dean fucks me. He brings one hand back between my legs, gently stroking my sensitive clit. I know he's close, holding off on his own pleasure until I come again.

Sometimes, the pressure to have an orgasm would ruin the mood for me, but right now, I don't think I could stop it if I tried. Dean plays my body like an instrument, and only a few minutes later, stars dot my vision and I start to fold over onto Dean's desk. He wraps a strong arm around me, holding me up as he buries his cock in me. A groan escapes his lips, and he pushes in balls deep, cock pulsing as he comes.

"Holy shit," I pant, knowing I'll fall right to the floor if Dean lets me go. My legs are shaking and my ears are ringing. Dean and I awkwardly sidestep, keeping his cock inside me, until he can reach a box of tissues. I quickly wipe myself clean and pull my underwear up.

Still panting, I turn, perching on the edge of his desk. "I think this should be a thing too," I say, still breathless. "Along with cooking naked, I should *bring you lunch* at least once a week."

Dean pulls his pants up and strides over, taking me in his arms. "It's definitely going to be a thing."

CHAPTER 31

DEAN

Mom: Who's all coming over tonight? I need to know how much to make.

Logan: We'll be there.

Me: I'll be there. I'm bringing someone. Don't be weird.

Mom: Rory?

Me: ...

Owen: One-night stand Rory?

Me: ...

Mom: I don't need to know these details, boys. And Dad said Rory is a lovely lady. Are you, Charlie, and Olivia coming?

Owen: Yes. Charlie wants to know what we're having for dinner.

Mom sends three emojis: a chicken, an eggplant, and a wedge of cheese.

Logan: On second thought, we're not coming over for dinner.

Mom: Why? Quinn requested I make it.

Owen: Quinn requested you make chicken dick-cheese?

Mom: Why on earth would you think that? I'm making chicken with eggplant parmesan.

"What's so funny?" Rory asks, coming back into the living room after using the bathroom. It's Sunday afternoon, and she's been here since last night. We fell asleep after making love, and when she said she was going to head home and would meet me back here to go to Sunday night dinner, I told her to stay. She has to work in the morning and won't be staying the night again tonight.

We're taking things slow, but I really fucking like where this is headed.

"Read this." I hand her my phone and she cracks up. "They're going to be weird too, just to warn you."

She pulls the blankets back up over herself. "Then I'm in good company." I drop my phone to the floor and put my arm around Rory. We're watching reruns of *The Office,* and doing nothing together is really fucking nice.

We both end up falling asleep, waking with just minutes to spare to make it to my parents' on time. Everyone but Owen, Charlie, and Olivia are here, which is pretty typical.

"They can be pretty loud," I forewarn. "Especially the kids."

"Yeah, because they're kids," she laughs. I take her hand on the way to the house. The dogs all come running, and Rory crouches down, letting them sniff her so they stop barking.

Everyone but my parents and the kids are crowded around the island counter, and a dozen or so whiskey bottles are in front of them. Quinn is sitting on a barstool, looking both nauseous and annoyed she can't partake in whatever drinking game is going on.

"Hey!" Archer calls when I walk in. He raises a shot glass in the air, and I can tell he's borderline drunk already. He doesn't drink often, since he's on-call a lot. We've all had fun giving him hell about turning into a lightweight in his old age. "You're just in time to—Rory, hey!"

"He's drunk. It'll be entertaining," I tell her, giving her hand a reassuring squeeze. I know she thinks it's a little weird to hang out with her boss in a social setting like this. But Archer is a good guy and wouldn't make her feel awkward at work or anything.

"Guys, this is Rory."

"Hi," Rory says, reaching down to pet one of the four dogs that are bombarding her. Quinn smiles and slowly gets up, coming over to greet Rory. "How are you feeling?" Rory asks her.

"Like shit." Quinn puts her hand over her stomach. "I think the babies hate me already."

"Babe, they don't hate you." Archer fills his Glencairn whiskey glass and takes a drink. "They can't form emotions yet."

"You can't form emotions," Quinn snaps and Archer takes another drink.

"You all right, sis?" I let go or Rory's hand to give Quinn a hug.

"Other than the nonstop puking, being the only one here not drinking, and the fact that my babies hate me, I'm fine."

"She can be a tad dramatic," I whisper to Rory. "And pregnancy makes her emotional."

"Dramotional," Rory laughs. "That's what my brothers call me. I can be emotional and dramatic like the best of them. And I don't think your babies hate you. You're way too cool to hate."

Quinn's eyes fill with tears and she nods. "I'm not, but thank you for saying that. I've always been a nerd."

"Me too." Rory gives her a smile. "I was actually just telling Dean I'd love to find some people to play Dungeons and Dragons with me, and he thought you'd like it."

Quinn smiles, doing a one-eighty from the mood she was just in. "I'd really like that. I don't have to be pregnant in the game, do I?"

"You don't have to be a woman. Or human."

"Great."

Archer pours whiskey in two glasses and hands one to me and

Rory. "Tell us what you think. We're sampling whiskey for...for something."

"For the bar," Logan says. "And it's nice to meet you. I'm Logan. This is my wife, Danielle."

"Hi," Danielle says.

"Hi." Rory gives her a small wave. "You own the bakery, right?"

"Right."

"I haven't been in yet, but I'll definitely stop by sometime."

"Ask for me when you go in. I'll sneak a few extra cupcakes in your bag before you leave."

"Ohhh, I'd love that! Thank you."

I lace my fingers through Rory's again and we join everyone at the island. "Where are Mom and Dad?" I ask.

"Downstairs with the kids," Danielle answers. "*All* the kids."

"I still say we make a run for it," Scarlet jokes.

"Drink!" Archer tells me, pulling the cork out of bottle of whiskey. He goes to pour more in his glass and misses, spilling it on the counter.

"Hands of a surgeon, that one," Quinn huffs. "Though he really is good with his hands, among other things. If he weren't, I wouldn't be pregnant for the fourth fucking time."

"Gross, Quinn," I say, and she rolls her eyes. Rory brings the Glencairn to her nose, smelling the whiskey before taking a tiny taste. She wrinkles her nose and shakes her head.

"You don't have to drink," I tell her, knowing she doesn't like the taste of alcohol.

"I'm not." She sets the glass on the counter and looks at Quinn. "I can explain D&D to you, and we can start creating your character if you want."

Quinn's face lights up. "Okay!"

Rory takes a step forward, following Quinn, and I grab Rory's hand, pulling her back for a kiss. My brother's catcall and I hold up my middle finger.

"I like her," Scarlet says once Rory has left the room.

"I do too." I toss the whiskey into my mouth and pull out a stool at the island.

"She seems really nice," Danielle tells me, and I try not to think about how many times I heard my sisters-in-law tell me they liked Kara.

They never did.

"And she and Quinn have a lot in common," Archer says, swaying on his feet a bit. I pull out another stool and he sinks down. "Quinn keeps talking about her, and no, I didn't tell her about you guys spending a few days together in Miami."

"What?" Scarlet asks, leaning forward. "She was in Miami?"

"Fuck." Archer shakes his head. "I forgot no one else knew."

I roll my eyes. "Don't scare her off, okay?"

"So you really like her?" Logan asks carefully.

"I do," I say, unable to keep the smile off my face.

"That's how it works." Weston finishes the sample of whiskey in his glass. "Love finds you when you least expect it."

"Or," Scarlet starts. "When someone tries to con you out of everything you own."

Weston laughs. "You had to be sorely disappointed I had nothing to steal."

Scarlet loops her arm through Weston's. "Just your heart."

"Gross," Logan huffs, "Did he ever tell you why you got hired?"

Scarlet shakes her head, blonde hair falling in her face. "It wasn't for my impressive resume?"

"Nope," Logan laughs. "Owen and I picked the hottest nanny on the site."

"Oh, well, duh," Scarlet laughs. "Though now that I'm happily married with a couple of kids, I'm considering letting myself go."

"Please." Danielle gives Scarlet an endearing look. "You couldn't let yourself go if you tried."

"That is true," Weston tells her, setting his glass down and taking her in his arms. "You've been hitting the Oreos pretty hard and you haven't gained a single pound."

"True," Scarlet laughs, and then rounds on me. "So you like Rory? Like really like her?"

I hold up my hands. "We're taking things slow, but yeah. I do. She's...she's everything," I say, unable to control the words coming out of my mouth.

"And we like her," Weston adds. "I know what it's like to be married to a...a..."

"Cunt?" Danielle supplies. "I was there the day she tried to kidnap Jackson, remember?"

"I'm forever grateful you acted as fast as you did," Weston tells her, brows pushing together. My older brother has been a no-nonsense kind of guy since the day he was born. He's always serious, doesn't get excited easily, and is the first to bring down your buzz.

But he has no shame in showing his emotions when it comes to the ones he loves. If anyone in my family understands what it's like to have your world crumble around your feet, it's Wes.

The stakes were higher with him. His wife left when they had a newborn. Daisy leaving hurt Jackson as well as Weston, and here he is, happily married with another kid.

Could I have that too?

Fuck, I want it. And if anyone can be my happily ever after, it's Rory Harris.

The garage door opens again, and Charlie comes in, followed by Owen with Olivia in his arms. She starts crying when the dogs rush her, and Owen rolls his eyes.

"She's still scared of the dogs?" Logan asks jumping up to pull them back.

"What happened with the dogs?" I ask.

"They knocked her over," Charlie says, bending down to pet Rufus, the biggest of the bunch. "So now she thinks all dogs are out to eat her."

259

"But not Dex," Logan interjects. "She loves him."

"She thinks he's a big stuffed animal," Charlie says with a smile, taking off her coat. "I'm not positive she's aware he's an actual dog."

"He's a good dog," Logan agrees, talking about his German Shepherd. "Some creep came to the door yesterday when Dani was home alone with the kids. Dex scared him off."

"Why didn't you call me?" Wes asks, going into sheriff mode.

Danielle waves her hand in the air. "It was just some guy going door-to-door selling things."

"You live in the middle of nowhere," Archer counters. "More so than we do. Though as long as he wasn't selling cats, I'd be okay with it."

Everyone laughs and I look through the kitchen into the living room at Rory. She's sitting next to Quinn, phone in her hand. Owen comes up next to me and follows my gaze.

"That's your new flavor of the week?"

"She's more than—" I cut off, looking at the name tag on his shirt, which reads *Hello! My name is: Owen, the good-looking one*. "Seriously?"

"I told you to take that off!" Charlie tries to pull the name tag off Owen, but he moves Olivia, using their daughter like a shield.

"I'm trying to make things easy for the newbie."

"She's not going to have any trouble separating you two." Charlie rolls her eyes, trying hard not to smile. "Though I will apologize on his behalf," she tells me.

"She has three older brothers. I think she can handle us." I can feel everyone's expectant gazes on me. "We're taking things slow," I remind them. "Go easy on her, okay?"

"Okay," they say collectively. The timer on the oven goes off, and Danielle goes around us to check on the food. A few seconds later, Mom comes rushing up the basement stairs.

"You're all here!" she says, giving me a hug. "Did you bring Rory?"

"Yeah," I tell her. "She in the living room with Quinn."

Mom's eyes brighten, and I know she's thinking about how Kara never put in the effort to befriend Quinn even though my sister tried. "Bring her in here! I want to meet the woman who's captured your heart."

"Mom," I press. "It's not like that, okay? We're just dating. It's not serious." The words feel like a lie the second they leave my lips, but I have to keep it at this.

Nothing serious.

We're taking things slow, and I like the direction they're heading.

"I'll get her."

Mom waves her hand in the air. "Wait until dinner. I need to warm up the breadsticks. Why don't you go downstairs and help your father with the grandkids?"

"Sure," I say and go to the finished basement, spending the next ten minutes getting the kids to go potty and wash their hands. Finally, we get them all upstairs and seated at the kid table, and Rory holds Henry for Danielle as she fills her plate.

My heart lurches in my chest when I see Rory with my youngest nephew in her arms, baby-talking and pulling faces to make the kid smile. A strange feeling comes over me, unsetting and welcoming at the same time.

Rory fits in, but she doesn't know us. She has no idea that Owen and Charlie dated throughout high school only to break up in college and finally get back together years later. She doesn't know about Daisy and the shit she put our family through. She has no idea we painfully watched Logan try to get out of the friend zone with Danielle, and is clueless to the month-long feud between Quinn, Archer, and I.

She doesn't know the controversy over being Team Cat instead of Team Dog. She doesn't know why Archer became so close with all of us, and why it felt like a betrayal when he and Quinn started dating in secret.

She wasn't the one assuring me I wasn't being irrational— though now I know I was—and she'll never get how hurt I felt to find out the one person I trusted more than anyone kept a secret from me.

She doesn't know my past…but she can learn. It'll take time, I know, just like it will take time for me to fully get to know her. But if fucking scares me how easy this has been so far, and it's almost like I'm doing something wrong because life isn't supposed to pass by this smoothly.

Life hurts.

Love is complicated.

Nothing is ever what it seems, and right when you think you got your shit figured out, things fall to pieces at your feet.

CHAPTER 32

"It was so nice meeting you." Mrs. Dawson pulls me into a tight hug, and her perfume is overwhelming and nauseating…just like my mother's. It's oddly comforting.

"It was nice meeting you too." I pat her back and try to pull away but am trapped for another few seconds.

"Mom," Dean says, and his mother finally releases me. "It's late and Rory has to be at the hospital in the morning."

"Oh goodness," Mrs. Dawson says and lets me go. "Go home and get some rest."

"I plan to," I say and flick my eyes to Dean. We won't be spending the night together, well, unless he decides to come and stay with me. I have to leave the house at six-thirty AM, and he doesn't get into the office until eight. I'm fine leaving him in my apartment, trusting him enough to lock up.

But it makes more sense to go our separate ways and meet up later. My Jeep is at his house, and the current plan is to drive to Dean's house, say a quick goodbye, and then for me to go home, sleep, and get up in a few short hours.

"I'm sure I'll see you again," I tell Mrs. Dawson, taking the Tupperware full of leftovers she insisted I bring home with me.

Dean and Owen got one as well. I say bye to Weston and Scarlet, who are the last ones besides us here.

Quinn and Archer left soon after dinner. Quinn got sick, and I spent a good half an hour sitting in the bathroom with her, holding her hair back as she puked up everything she had for dinner. She said she got this sick with nearly every pregnancy, making me question my desire to have a baby.

Logan, Danielle, and their kids left after they did, followed by Owen and his family. Weston and Scarlet hung around for a while after that, since Violet had fallen asleep on the couch. It was pure chaos when she woke up, but now that they're gone, it's just Dean any myself.

I love the energy of the family. The nonstop chatter. How disorganized and chaotic everything it while at the same time it feels like it's exactly how it's supposed to be. It reminds me of my own family—minus all the babies, of course—and I feel comfortable around all the Dawsons.

"Oh, I better. Take care."

"I will." I smile and take my coat from Dean, slipping my arms into the sleeves. Dean goes to the kitchen window, looking out at the driveway, and remote starts his truck. "Thank you for dinner and everything tonight," I say as I put my shoes on. "My parents do dinner on Fridays and I miss it."

"You are welcome anytime, my dear," Mrs. Dawson says.

"She'll be back," Dean presses, eager to get out of the house. "I'll see you next week, okay?"

"Okay," Mrs. Dawson hugs Dean goodbye and tries to send him off with all the leftovers from tonight's meal, along with what she's already packed him. He takes out two Tupperwares full of leftovers, just to quiet his mother, and we set out, driving back to his house, where my Jeep is.

"Do you want to come in?" Dean asks, pulling into his garage.

I gasp, bringing my hand to my mouth. "Are you trying to take advantage of me, Dean Dawson?"

He wiggles his eyebrows. "Is it working?"

I unbuckle my seatbelt. "It is. And yes, I want you to fuck me in the kitchen," I say as a joke, though I really mean it. We've had sex on the living room couch and his bed, and that's it for his house.

"That can be arranged." Dean kills the engine and hurries out of the car, opening my door and carrying me inside. And—holy shit—he fucks me good and proper, and I'm too tired to drive home. We shower together and collapse into his bed. I set my alarm for half an hour earlier than normal, giving myself enough time to run home, feed Figaro, and change into scrubs.

I fall asleep in Dean's arms and do my best not to disturb him as I rush around to leave in the morning.

"I'll call you later," I say, kissing him. He's half-asleep but kisses me back. Then it's a mad rush to do everything I need to and get to work on time.

I yawn my way through shift change, but I've made it, mind drifting to Dean and how perfect things seem between us. My shift starts with an emergency surgery followed back-to-back by a scheduled gallbladder removal. I'm more than ready for a break when the time comes to finally take one. Yawning, I head to the hospital cafeteria to buy myself a hot lunch and some coffee. I scroll through my phone as I eat, not thinking too hard over the fact that Dean hasn't replied to my texts yet. He's working as well, and I know he has a busy day at the office.

My allotted time for lunch ends too quickly, and I go back to the OR, dragging my feet the whole way.

"More roses came," Hilary says, picking one up and smelling it. "Thank you."

"You are most welcome," I tell her with a smile. "Who are those for?" I ask, looking at the dozen or so roses left on the desk.

"You," she says and wiggles her eyebrows. "From some guy named Dean."

"What?" Shaking my head, I hurry to the desk and pick up the little card.

Rory-

Anyone who didn't send you a rose before is a damn fool. You are perfect the way you are. I can't wait to see you tonight.

-Your half-elven admirer (aka Dean)

I'm smiling ear to ear. How the hell did Dean know about this silly fundraiser?

Right. Dr. Jones—Archer—is best buds with Dean. He heard me say I never got anything like this sent to me when I was in high school and mentioned it to Dean.

"I thought you said you two weren't serious." Hilary plucks the note from my hands.

"We aren't," I counter.

"This seems serious to me." She beams and gives the note back. "He did good, girl. Jeremy didn't even send me a single fucking rose."

"He probably didn't know," I say, reading Dean's note over again.

Hilary waves her hand in the air. "I purposely left the flyer about this on the table. Three times."

"He shows you he loves you in other ways, right?'

Hilary rolls her eyes. "Sometimes."

An emergency surgery comes in, and we don't have time to talk about Dean or relationships anymore. It's nonstop until shift change, and I leave the hospital exhausted. I call Dean on my way, but his phone goes right to voicemail.

He didn't plug his phone in last night, having left it on the island counter when we went upstairs together. His house in on my way home from the hospital, and I plan to swing by and see if he's home before going to my place. I want to invite him over for the night.

My phone rings as I near Dean's neighborhoods, but it's not

him. The number comes up as unknown, and I only answer because I recognize the area code.

"Hello?"

"Rory?"

"This is her."

"Hey! It's Michelle, from Silver Ridge General."

"Oh." I blink a few times. Why is my old nursing director calling me? "Hi."

"I know you're wondering why I'm calling, so I'm going to cut to the chase. We got some additional funding from the higher ups, and I was given the green light to hire a handful of nurses back who were cut. You're at the top of my list."

"Oh, uh, wow," I say, slowing to a stop at a red light.

"But not only that, I'm looking for a unit manager."

I pause. Exhale. Inhale. Exhale again. "You want me to be a unit manager?"

"I do. The job comes with a significant pay raise to what you were making here before as well."

"Wow," I repeat, and my mind flashes to Dean. "I...I don't know. I really like what I have going on here."

"It's a lot to consider, I know, and this is out of the blue. How about I check back in with you tomorrow after you've had time to think things over?"

"Sure," I blurt, though I already know the answer. It's a big fat no. I've established a life here, and more importantly...Dean is here.

I would have jumped at the opportunity to go back to Silver Ridge before. But now...now I know my life is here in Eastwood.

CHAPTER 33

I flop back down in bed, pulling the covers up over myself. I'm cold without Rory next to me, and I almost feel guilty to go back to sleep knowing she's on her way to work.

But I'm so fucking tired.

My eyes fall shut, and I'll pulled back into a peaceful sleep, dreaming of times when Rory is here, in bed with me. We're both naked, and of course my dream leads to us fucking like animals. I'm right at the good part of my dream, where my cock is buried in Rory, when I'm pulled from my sleep.

My eyes flutter open, and my cock aches, hard from the dream I was having. I roll over and bring my hand to it, stroking myself. I'm in that weird half-sleep, half-wake stage, not really aware of what I'm doing.

All I know is that I miss Rory and long to have her here next to me. I wouldn't be rubbing one out, but could spread her legs and push my cock inside of her, coming at the same time she does.

The thought of her sends a jolt to my dick, and I roll over, imagining her here with me as I quicken my movements, jerking

myself off. I'm almost there, about ready to come when the doorbell rings.

The fuck?

Rory has the garage code. Why is she ringing the doorbell? I
open my eyes, squinting at the clock. She should be arriving at
work right about now. Maybe the doorbell didn't really ring and
I imagined it?

I turn on my other side and reach for the pillow Rory was
using, pulling it to me. It smells like her conditioner, and my
heart aches missing her.

And then the doorbell rings again, and this time, there's no
mistaking it. I sit up, blinking, and shake myself. The doorbell
rings again, and now I'm irritated. Who the fuck comes to the
door at this hour? I pull on boxers and the pajama pants and then
storm down the stairs.

Someone is standing on my porch, and I open the door, ready
to tell them to fuck off. Shooting back the deadbolt, the words
are right there, burning on my tongue. But when I open the door,
my words die in my throat.

"Hi, Dean."

I blink, staring down the woman on the porch.

"Kara?" I ask, breath clouding around me. "What the fuck are
you doing here?"

"I'm sorry," my ex-wife blurts. "I know this is a shock, but
please, hear me out." She holds up her hands.

"Why should I?"

"Because it's really cold and it took me a while to find where
you'd moved to." She smiles, eyes meeting mine, and everything
moves in slow motion.

She doesn't look much different than she did the day I left. Her
hair is the same shade of dark blonde, and I got her the coat she's
wearing three Christmases ago. She took a job in Newport only
months after the divorce was final, and I haven't seen her since.

"There's nothing to say." I take a step back, ready to close the door.

"There is." She throws her hand out and my heart lurches in my chest. She doesn't look any different, and I get a flashback to a few days before I walked in on her in bed with another man.

We'd been arguing over something stupid, something so small I can't even remember what now. I didn't want to fight anymore, so I grabbed her hands and made her dance with me.

We fell asleep tangled together after making love, and I remember feeling hopeful…that we could work things out and be happy again.

Hah.

"What?" I deadpan and take a step back, letting her in the house. It is cold, and I don't have a shirt on. "What do you have to say?"

She closes the door behind her. "I'm sorry." She lets out a breath. "I'm so, so sorry." Her eyes fill with tears and a voice in the back of my mind tells me to comfort her, like I have before.

But she's not my wife anymore. I have no commitment, no obligation to her.

"I forgive you," I say with a huff, running my hand through my hair. "If that helps you move on…know that I forgive you."

"Thank you." She unzips her coat and my stomach flip flops, hating the way she's looking at me. It's foreign and familiar at the same time. "I miss you, Dean."

"Kara, don't," I say, rubbing my forehead. My eyes fall shut and I can't believe this is happening.

"You look good," she says, stepping closer.

"I have a girlfriend," I rush out, but it does nothing to stop Kara from advancing.

"You had a wife."

"Yeah." I let my hand drop to my side. "And you cheated on me."

Silence falls over both of us for a moment. I look Kara up and down, and I finally get why people say it feels like they saw a ghost when something startling happens. Because that's exactly what Kara is: a ghost of my past, coming back to haunt me.

"Do you love her?" Kara asks.

"What?"

"Your girlfriend."

"That's none of your business," I say, though her words burn deep inside. I'm not sure I'm able to love anyone anymore. I want to, but I've put up so many walls they may never come down. "Kara," I start, and her name feels weird coming from my lips. How many times have I said it before?

"How is everyone?" she asks tentatively. "I follow Quinn on Instagram. Seems like she and Archer are doing pretty well."

"She's pregnant," I say, words spilling from me like vomit. It's early and my mind is getting confused. Kara had been part of my life for so long, it's strange having to remind myself she's on the outside now.

"And Danielle had a baby, right?"

"She did. A little boy named Henry."

Kara smiles, brown eyes meeting mine. She's familiar; she's predictable, even.

But that doesn't make this right.

"I have to go to work," I say. "Like I said before, it's time for you to leave."

"I don't have anywhere to go," she blurts, stepping forward and reaching for me. "I…I didn't tell my family I was in town."

"Why not?" I ask. She's always been close with her family.

"They were mad at me after we split…and I don't blame them. I was wrong, Dean. Wrong and stupid, and I've never regretted anything more in my life." Kara blinks back tears. "I've spent the last year trying to better myself."

"That's…that's good." I plow my hand through my hair. "I want you to find peace."

"I want peace with you." She steps forward and grabs my

hand. "I miss you, Dean. I messed up, I know. I was stupid—so stupid—and I'm sorry."

"I told you, I forgive you. We both made mistakes, Kara. I wasn't perfect either."

Tears stream down her face, and it hurts me to see her upset. "I wish I could go back…go back and redo everything. You were so good to me, Dean, and I miss you."

"You should leave," I repeat and put my head in my hands. This is really happening, isn't it? I squeeze my eyes closed and open them again. Dammit. This nightmare is actually around me.

"Please, Dean," she cries, and her bottom lip quivers. Her eyes fall shut and more tears roll down her cheeks. I get hit with another flash, and it takes everything I have not to reach out and wipe away her tears.

How many times have I done it in the past?

Kara and I were together for years. We dated. Got engaged. I loved her enough to get married. To fight for our relationship when I thought it was damned.

I look at Kara, and my words leave me. I want to be angry. I want to scream and yell and tell her to get the fuck out of my house, but all I do is feel sorry for her.

She says she's sorry and I believe her. Her regret is tangible, and part of me wonders what would have happened if I'd stayed for dessert that night instead of coming home early.

I wouldn't have found Kara in bed with another man.

Would she have kept on cheating? Wised up and come clean? Cut the guy off cold turkey, buried her secret and played the part of dutiful wife?

"I hate that I hurt you." She wipes her eyes with the back of her hand. "I would do anything to go back and do things differently."

"You would?" I swallow hard. We left with so much unsaid. I didn't want to hear her excuses. I wanted things to be over as quickly as possible, and the wounds I thought were healed are being ripped open again. "What would you do differently? Make sure you didn't get caught?"

"No," she says and starts crying again. "I was stupid, so, so stupid. You were so good to me, Dean, and I don't know how we fell so far. We were in love once...don't you think we could be in love like that again?"

My throat starts to feel thick, and a sick sense of déjà vu starts to set in.

I did think we could be in love again. If I didn't think we could fix things, I never would have left dinner early. I would have stayed at my parents', listening to Quinn complain about the end of pregnancy while Danielle cried over what a miracle it was she got pregnant so easily the second time around.

I would have gone outside with Logan and Owen, drinking expensive whiskey and bullshitting about something—anything—while enjoying life.

But I came home with an armload of leftovers, ready to tell Kara I was sorry for the distance. I was prepared to step up, to be the one to mend the holes in our relationship.

"We took vows," Kara goes on. "I broke mine, and I will forever be sorry for that." Her bottom lip quivers. "It's asking a lot, I know, but I can't live with myself if I don't try." She wipes away more tears, smearing her makeup across her cheeks. "We were family once. Can we be family again?"

"Kara," I start, heart pounding. I miss what we had, but I don't miss her.

I miss being married.

I miss having someone in my bed every night.

I miss thinking about starting a family...only we never quite got there.

But there's no going back. No starting over. It's too late now...isn't it?

"I have to go to work," I repeat. "Figure out somewhere to go and then go."

"Is the garage code your birthday?" She smiles and I hate that we have all this history together and she knows me.

"Yes. Don't be here when I get home. There is nothing left to say. We're over, Kara."

CHAPTER 34

RORY

T he smile hasn't left my face since my shift ended. I called Dean on my way to my car but got his voicemail. He told me he was going to be on a job site this morning, and after a quick stop home to feed Figaro and change, I'm on my way back to Dean's.

He told me last night to come over after work, using the garage code to get in if I got here before he did. The dozen roses he sent me at work are still on my passenger seat, and in hindsight I should have taken then into my apartment and put them in water.

Now I get to bring them in with me, admiring them and thanking Dean—with my body, of course—a dozen times over. There's a car parked on the street in front of his house, and I pull up behind it. I'm pretty sure Dean took the truck today, but I don't want to block the wrong spot of the garage just in case he didn't. I gather up the roses, hike my purse up over my shoulder, and hurry to the garage. It's warmed up a bit today, but it's super windy and I'm afraid the wind is going to blow the petals right off the roses.

I punch in the garage code and dodge inside once the door is up. Shivering, I hurry in, hit the button to close the big door, and watch it go down before opening the door that leads into the mud room.

"Hello?" a female calls from inside the house.

I freeze, mouth opening but words escaping me. If someone was breaking and entering, they wouldn't yell out hello, would they?

"Dean?" the same voice calls. Okay…so I doubt it's a burglar if they're calling out Dean's name. It's not one of his sisters-in-law, is it? The voice isn't familiar. "Dean, is that you?"

"No," I say, voice thin. "It's not."

"Oh." A woman appears in the hallway, stopping short when she sees me. "Sorry. I didn't mean to startle you."

"It's okay," I say, not moving. Is it okay? Should I throw the roses at her and make a run for it? "I wasn't expecting anyone to be home."

"I came over unannounced," she says, forcing a half-smile. "Are you his girlfriend?"

"We haven't really discussed titles yet, but yeah. I am. How do you know Dean?"

"I'm his ex-wife."

I blink and almost drop the roses. His ex-wife—who cheated on him? What the fuck?

"Oh. He, uh, he didn't mention you were here."

"I don't blame him." She blinks back tears, and I can tell she's been crying. I swallow hard and don't know what to do. This is awkward as fuck, and I'm not entirely convinced this woman isn't here to try to murder me.

"Why are you here?" I ask slowly and set the roses down on the bench of the hall tree, not taking my eyes off this woman. Mason would be proud.

"I wanted to talk to Dean," she says, voice thinning. "Fucking up my marriage will always be the biggest regret of my life. I came back to see if Dean would try and work things out."

The fuck? Is this why he hasn't spoken to me all day? I'm a reasonable person. I know he can't control when his ex-wife pops up in town. I can't get mad at him for her giving it her all, begging and pleading for him to take her back.

But not telling me what's going on and not even answering the phone…it makes my stomach flip flop.

"I'm sorry. I know that's the last thing you want hear since you two are together now. Or are you? You said you haven't discussed titles yet?" She pushes her light brown hair back. "That's so unlike him. He's a relationship kind of person. He asked me out less than twelve hours after meeting me."

I blink, not sure how to respond to that. "Oh, well, he's changed."

"I'm sure he has."

"Does he know you're here?"

Kara smiles. "Yes, I came into town unexpectedly and surprised him. He had to go to work but let me stay here."

Nothing about this seems right. Why would Dean let his ex-wife stay here? Did they hook up or something? No, I doubt it. Dean isn't that kind of person to go back to someone who hurt him like that.

And we're together.

"I'm going to call him." I take a step back toward the door, thinking I'd rather be in my car than in the house with this crazy lady.

"No need." Kara points to the door. "I think I hear the garage."

"Oh, yeah. I do too." I put my phone back in my purse and move to the side so Dean won't whack me with the door when he comes inside.

"Rory," he says, eyes flitting from me to Kara.

"Hi, Dean." Kara puts on a pretty smile.

"What are you still doing here?" he asks her. "I told you to leave."

"We need to talk," Kara insists. "And finish our conversation from this morning."

I tip my head up to Dean, chest tightening. "What is going on?"

"Nothing," he says. "Nothing you need to worry about."

"Are you sure?"

"Yes." He looks at Kara. "Can you give us some space?"

"Of course." Kara walks away and Dean steps out of the mud room, looking into the kitchen to make sure Kara isn't lurking behind the corner.

"She just showed up this morning," Dean tells me. "It threw me off guard and I thought she would have left and gone to her sister's by now."

"It's not your fault she showed up." I force a smile. "She wants you back, doesn't she? I mean, you are quite the catch."

"Yeah." Dean's brows pinch together, and he looks conflicted. Didn't he tell me he didn't have feelings for her anymore? I think his exact words were *it was over before it ended* or something very similar at least.

Is seeing her again bringing up those old feelings?

"Do you want her back?" I ask slowly, feeling like I'm sinking underwater in slow motion.

"No," he rushes out. "I don't. Seeing her again is reminding me why I've sworn off relationships. They're all damned."

My brows furrow. "What?"

He closes his eyes, wincing at his words. "I didn't mean it like that."

"How did you mean it?"

"I...I don't know."

"What?" And now I'm slipping under water. How did things go from cloud nine to a shallow grave so fast? Dean casts his eyes down, slowly shaking his head. "Dean," I repeat. "How did you mean it?"

CHAPTER 35

DEAN

This is a defining moment for us, and I know it. The scales could tip either way, and I'm fucking terrified of them coming apart at the hinges and falling into a rusty heap at my feet. I told Rory I want more, that I like waking up with her by my side. I didn't promise marriage, but I let her know I want her in my future.

And I do.

Yet standing here, with the woman I used to love behind me, and Rory in front of me fucks with my head. Nothing can fall apart if I don't put it together. I'm attracted to Rory. She's attracted to me. We get along great and the sex is a-fucking-mazing.

"I don't know." The words feel like a lie the moment they leave my lips. Because I do know what I want, and it terrifies me more than anything.

I don't want to get hurt again.

And I don't want to hurt her.

What if I'm not good enough? What if it was my fault things fell apart the first time and history is damned to repeat itself, that I'm the issue.

I can't bring myself to say it. Because everything came rushing back. The disappointment. The betrayal, the feeling of sand rushing out from under my feet no matter how hard I fought to keep my footing.

And in that moment, I don't want to damn Rory to a future of pain.

"I thought you liked being with me."

"I do."

"I'm confused." She brings her hand to her face, pressing her fingers to her forehead. "So you like being with me but feel like all relationships are damned to fail?" Her lips part and she shakes her head.

"No…I don't know."

She looks up, lips parting, and tears fill her eyes. "I…I guess… I'll…I'll…" Her eyes flutter shut, and a single tear rolls down her cheek. Her lips press together in a smile as she tries to hold it all together. "I guess I should go."

And then she turns and leaves.

The second Rory walks out the door I know I made a huge mistake. My heart sinks to the bottom of my chest, going to a place so low I didn't know it existed.

She's everything I've ever wanted, and everything I need. I don't want to lose her.

I can't.

I won't, because there's no use denying it. I am in love with her.

I rush forward, needing to go after her.

"Dean!" Kara catches my arm. "Don't go!"

"Stop," I say and pull my arm back. Kara tightens her hold on me and then hurries forward, grabbing my face and kissing me. Her lips are familiar, and she's still wearing the cherry lip gloss she wore before. I know exactly what to expect, what to feel.

And it does nothing for me.

Doesn't spark anything inside of me. Doesn't make my heart

skip a beat or cause desire to flood through my veins like it does with Rory.

"What the fuck?" I spit, pulling away. I hold Kara at arm's length. She fights against me, breaking free, and comes right back, hands going to my belt.

"Stop!" I yell brow furrowed, "What the fuck are you doing?" I swat her hands away.

"I want you," she says biting her lip. "And I miss you. I miss you so much, Dean. Don't you miss me?"

"No," I say, and the word reverberates through me. I don't miss *her*. I thought I missed what we had, but it hits me hard and all at once: what we had was an illusion. "I don't, and I don't know what you're doing or why you're still here. I told you to go."

"I can't," she says, tears falling from her eyes.

"Why not?"

"Because…because I'm pregnant," she blurts and looks up at me.

Silence hangs in the air and my lips part, a sharp breath leaving my lungs. "You came here, trying to get me to sleep with you." Dizziness crashes down on me, and I feel like I might throw up. "You were going to lie and tell me the baby was mine."

"You always wanted to be a father, and you'd be a good one."

"Yeah, to my own kid." The shock is wearing off and I'm pissed. Really fucking pissed. "You were going to manipulate me into getting back together. Do you think I'm stupid, Kara? Don't you think I'd realize the timelines didn't match up and I'd know it wasn't my child?"

"I don't know," she cries. "All I know is I miss you, Dean. I want a family. With *you*, I still love you."

"No, you don't. You need me, because you know I was always there. I carried my weight. I wasn't perfect, but I tried." I swallow my anger. It's not worth it. Not anymore. I raise my hand and point to the door. "Leave."

"Dean."

"No. I'm going to call your sister and tell her to expect you. Go. Now."

Kara sucks in a breath. "I'm sorry. For…for everything."

"Just go."

I watch Kara put her shoes on, sobbing as she ties each lace. Finally, she's out of my house, and I lock the door behind her.

"Motherfucker," I say through gritted teeth, balling my hands into fists. I storm back into the kitchen and pick up my phone, calling Rory.

The call goes to voicemail.

I call her back and she ends the call after one ring.

I call once more and this time her phone doesn't even ring.

Closing my eyes, I lean against the cabinet, needing to keep my cool. Several minutes go by and I try Rory again. Her phone is either off or she blocked me.

But it's not too late. I have to make this right.

CHAPTER 36

RORY

My bottom lips quivers and I barely hold it together on my way down the driveway. I have no idea how things went from fucking perfect to falling apart in three seconds flat.

I thought I was enough. I thought Dean cared about me the way I cared about him. My heart hurts, and I feel so stupid.

I'm crying as I start the Jeep, tears falling like rain. I yank my seatbelt into place. A small part of me hoped Dean would run out, telling me he made a mistake and he does care and want to be with me.

But he doesn't.

I drive out of the neighborhood, and my phone rings. Expecting it to be Dean, I'm hit with disappointment when I see that it's Michelle from Silver Ridge again.

I go to decline the call, hitting the red button on my screen display in the Jeep, but accidentally answer instead. I suck in a breath, trying to calm myself.

"Hello?"

"Hey, Rory! Sorry to bug you again, but I'm scheduling interviews and I'd really love to have you back. Would you be able to come in tomorrow?"

"Um," I don't work tomorrow, or the next day. And I don't see a reason for staying in Eastwood right now, especially when I'll get a promotion if I go back to Silver Ridge. It was my plan all along. Be a unit manager and continue to work my way up to director. If Dean wasn't in my life, Id' say this was fate.

I'm getting exactly what I wanted career-wise. "I think so. What time are you scheduling interviews?"

"Could you be here in the morning? I have an opening at ten."

"I'm about five hours away. But yeah…I think I can drive up there tonight, crash with my parents and be there by ten."

"Great! I have to conduct interviews, but between you and me, it'll be informal. I know you and I still have your resume on file from when I hired you last time."

"I'll see you at ten."

"Great! It'll be so nice to have you back, Rory!"

"Yeah." I'm struggling to hold it together. "Thanks for calling me about this."

"I said I would. See you soon, Rory."

"Bye." I end the call just in time. A sob escapes my lips. I cry as I drive, tears rolling down my face. I pull into my spot at the apartment and give in, ugly crying until someone walks by and taps on my window, asking me if I'm okay.

I'm struggling to breathe; heart aching like it's been split in two. Dean was everything I wanted…only he didn't want me. I don't know what's worse: losing him or feeling like I'm not enough for him to commit to.

I swallow another sob and nod, then mop up my face and call Mom, ignoring the missed calls from Dean. I'll call him back, but not yet. My heart can't take it.

"Hey, honey!" she says, answering on the second ring. "Is everything all right? You never call."

"Yeah," I say, putting on a fake-ass smile, forgetting she can't see me. "One of the nursing directors from the old hospital called me and offered me a job. She asked if I can come interview tomorrow morning."

"Back here in Silver Ridge?"

"Yeah. As a unit manager."

"Oh my goodness, that's wonderful! But what about your job in Eastwood?"

"I'd make more as a unit manager," I say, though I don't know if it's true. I got a big pay raise at Eastwood since the hospital is better. "And it's what I wanted, remember? Be a manager and then the director. Are you not happy to possibly have me back?"

"Of course I'm happy to have you back. I thought *you* were happy where you were, and that's the thing I care about most: seeing you happy. What about that handsome man you were seeing?"

My throat feels thick and tears stream down my face. My lips part but I can't form any words. "It…it didn't turn out to be what I thought. Dean—" I cut off, feeling overwhelming pain when I say his name. "He wanted to keep things casual, and that's just not I want."

"Oh, honey. I'm so sorry."

"It's fine." I grip the steering wheel and put another terrifyingly fake smile on my face. It's far from fine, and my heart is breaking into smaller and smaller pieces as time goes on. I let my guard down, trusted and believed him when he said he wanted something more.

I'm so stupid.

"Since the interview is at ten," I start, speaking slowly to hide the emotion in my voice. "I'm going to drive up tonight."

"It's not too late?"

"Cars have this crazy new concept called headlights."

"I'm aware," Mom deadpans. "Drive safe. Love you, Rory."

"Love you too."

I end the call and lean forward, crying so hard my eyes hurt.

My heart is a mangled mess in the bottom of my chest, and my poor mind isn't in much better condition.

I can't think straight, so I focus on leaving. On driving, putting more miles between me and this stupid place. I should never have come to Eastwood. Whoever said it was better to have loved and lost than to never have loved at all obviously never got their heartbroken.

I kill the engine and run inside, feeding Figaro a can of food and overfilling his bowl of dry kibble. I quickly rinse out his water bowl, refill it, and grab stuff a duffle bag full of everything I need for tomorrow, not putting much care into picking out my interview outfit.

Then I'm out the door and on my way home.

Only…it doesn't feel like I'm *going* home. It feels like I'm *leaving* home.

CHAPTER 37

DEAN

uck you, Kara. I bring my fist down on the counter, hard enough to cause pain to ripple through me but not hard enough to do damage to anything. Then I rush into the garage, desperate to get to Rory. I open my truck door and get in, only to realize I don't have the keys.

My mind is a fucking mess, and it takes me nearly ten minutes to find the keys, which I left in my jacket pocket. I jump back into the truck as soon as I have them and speed to Rory's apartment. Her Jeep isn't in the parking lot, but I'm not giving up just yet.

I park the truck and run to her door, knocking. She doesn't answer. "Rory?" I call, knocking again. "Are you home? Please, Rory let me explain."

I wait several minutes before retreating back to the truck. My stomach hurts, and that sick feeling is back. Where else would Rory go? I have no fucking idea, but I'll wait here until she gets back.

Then I can tell her I love her and she's the only one for me. I do want a relationship with her. When I think of my future, she's in it.

My phone rings, and I scramble to answer it. But it's Weston and not Rory.

"Hello?" I say, blowing out a slow breath.

"Hey. You'll never guess who I pulled over."

"Kara."

"Yeah," Weston says. "So I take it you've seen her?"

"Yep. She showed up at my house early this morning. And was still there when Rory came over after work."

"Fuck."

"Yeah." I pinch the bridge of my nose. "And now Rory left, and I have no idea where she is."

"Whoa, what?"

Squeezing my eyes closed, I tell Weston what happened. "Rory will come home eventually. I'll stay here until she does."

"Don't sit outside the apartments like a creep," Weston says. "Go home."

"I have to talk to her."

"She'll talk to you when she's ready. Getting the cops called on you for looking like a stalker isn't going to help your case. Go home and call her again in a few hours."

He's right, but it's still hard to pull out of the parking lot, and even harder to go home and do nothing.

Rory is everything. The one person in this big fucking world I don't want to live without. I'll do anything to prove it to her…if only she'll give me the chance.

"Hey, Rory, I'm getting worried. Just let me know you're all right please. We can talk whenever you're ready, but let me know you're safe."

I end the message and put my phone down, head in my hands. I'm back home and have been sitting at the kitchen island for over two hours now, just waiting.

Time is crawling, but every passing minute makes me feel like Rory is slipping farther away. I want her back in my arms. I want to kiss her and hold her and tell her I love her.

After I apologize for being an idiot, of course.

Another twenty minutes go by, and finally, she sends me a text.

Rory: I'm okay.

Me: Can we talk? Please?

Rory: Later. My old boss called and offered me a job as the manager of my old unit. I'm on my way there for an interview.

I blink, glad I'm sitting down or else I'd fall over from the sense of dizziness. She's leaving Eastwood? Taking a job back in Silver Ridge? No. She was so happy to get out of the town that harbored memories of her being teased and bullied.

Eastwood is her home now.

Me: Rory, I'm sorry. I didn't mean what I said.

I stare at the screen, waiting for her to text me back. She doesn't. I put my head in my hands again, chest tightening. My phone rings and I jerk up, thinking it's Rory.

It's Quinn, FaceTiming me. I answer the call and see the top of Emma's head.

"Hey, Emma."

"Uncle Dean!" she exclaims and brings the phone right under her nose. "What you doing?"

"Just hanging out," I tell her. "Does your mom know you have her phone?"

"I dunno."

"You should probably go find her and give the phone back."

"Okay." Emma walks through the house, telling me about some Barbie TV show she was watching. "Mommy, I found your phone."

"Found it?" Quinn grumbles. "You took it. Emma! You called someone?"

"It's just me," I say, and Quinn takes the phone from Emma. "You don't look too good, sis."

"Right back at ya, but at least I have an excuse. What's yours?"

"I think I broke up with Rory."

"What?" Quinn sits up. "Why the hell would you do that?"

"Kara showed up."

"Oh, hell no. I might have spent the day puking, but I will come over and cut a bitch."

"Aren't your children around you and within earshot?"

Quinn purses her lips. "They'll learn from a young age that you always have your family's back."

I half-smile. "Thanks. And she's gone."

"So Kara showed up and you broke up with Rory? What is wrong with you?"

"I don't know." I close my eyes, chest hurting again. "She wants more, and I'm scared I can't give that to her," I admit. "What if things go to shit again?"

"What if they don't?" Quinn's expression softens. "You like her, don't you?"

"I do. A lot...I think I'm in love with her."

"Then go make things right, you idiot!" Quinn orders, narrowing her eyes again.

"She got offered her old job in Silver Ridge back along with a promotion. She's on her way there. She wants to leave Eastwood." The words hurt, making me feel sick at the same time.

"Then go! Stop her. Tell her you're a dumbass and want her back."

"I don't know where she'll be."

"I'm assuming the interview isn't until tomorrow since it'll be late by the time she gets to Silver Ridge. So she'll stay with either her one brother that lives there or more likely, her parents."

"I don't know where they live."

"I'll find out and will text you her address."

"You can do that?" I stand, already going to put my shoes on.

"Are you going to hack into something to get her parents' address?"

"No. I'm just going to ask Sam."

"Oh, right."

"Now go," Quinn says, holding the phone up so she can glare at me. "I like Rory. Don't fuck this up."

≈

≈

GRAVEL CRUNCHES UNDER THE TRUCK'S TIRES, AND I DOUBLE-check the address on the GPS. It's late at night, and the whole town was asleep as I passed through. Silver Ridge is even smaller than Eastwood, and just got a fresh dusting of snow.

Rory's parents live in a Craftsman-style house with a large, frozen pond in the front yard. It's set back from the road, with a little section of yard carved out from a wooded hillside. Rory's Jeep is parked in the driveway, and my heart lurches in my chest.

She's here, just inside.

And I hope to God she'll let me talk to her.

I send her a text, not wanting to have a gun shoved in my face when I knock on the door in the middle of the night.

Me: Come outside.

Rory starts typing something back right away only to stop again. I put the truck in park and shut off the engine. She starts and stops typing several times before sending something through.

Rory: I'm not home.

I get out of the truck and slowly walk toward the front porch.

Me: I know. Come outside.

A light upstairs turns on, and I see her go to a window, looking down into the yard. Her eyes meet mine and her lips part, shaking her head. Then the light goes out, and the entire house is still, holding its breath.

Time passes slowly, and I think that this is it. That I fucked things up beyond repair and I'm never going to see Rory again. Pain ripples through my entire body, and I think it would feel better to dive to the bottom of that frozen lake than to realize Rory wants nothing to do with me.

But then the front door opens.

"Rory." I rush up the cement porch steps. She's standing in the doorway, wearing sleeper shorts, a baggy sweatshirt, and fuzzy socks. Her hair is a mess and her eyes are red from crying.

"Dean? What…what are you doing here?"

"I want you, Rory," I rush out. "I want to be with you tonight, tomorrow, and every day after that because I love you. I tried not to fall, but I did, and the moment you walked out the door, I knew I made the biggest mistake of my life by letting you walk away."

Tears fill Rory's eyes and she crosses her arms over her chest, shivering from the cold air.

"I'm sorry," I say. "I'm an idiot and got scared. I don't want to get hurt again, and I don't want to hurt you. You are so much more than I deserve, and the thought of disappointing you fucking scares me," I admit. Damn, it feels good to tell her exactly how I feel with no holding back. "I don't want you to move back here. I want you to come back to Eastwood…to come back home. With me."

Her bottom lip quivers and tears mar her pretty face. I bound up the rest of the porch stairs and take her in my arms.

"I love you, Rory."

She wraps her arms around me, blinking away tears. "I love you too, Dean."

CHAPTER 38

I shut the door and take Dean's hand, leading him inside. I'm shivering, but my heart is bursting with so many emotions. Dean came all this way to tell me he loves me.

"I love you," he repeats, cupping his large hands around my face. I slip my arms around his waist and let him kiss me, feeling warmth and desire flood through me.

"Dean," I pant, breaking away. He rests his forehead against mine. "Are you sure this is what you want?"

"I've never been so sure of anything in my whole life. The second you walked out the door, Rory, I knew I couldn't lie to myself. I was scared, but losing you terrifies me more than anything in this whole fucking world."

Tears spill out of my eyes and Dean wipes them away with his thumbs. "I love you too."

"Come home with me, Rory."

My head bobs up and down, and a light upstairs flicks on. Oh, right. I'm at my parents' house. Everything faded away, until there was only Dean—only the man I love—in front of me.

"Rory?" Dad asks. "Is that you down there?"

"Yeah, it's me."

"Is someone here?"

"Yes."

Dad hurries down the stairs, pausing when he gets to the landing. By the way Dean and I are holding each other; it's obvious he's not here to rob us or something.

"This is Dean. Dean, this is my dad, David."

"It's nice to meet you," Dean says, holding out his hand to shake. Dad takes his, confusion taking over his face.

"David, what's going on?" Mom calls from the top of the stairs.

"Someone named Dean is here."

"Dean!" Mom gasps and comes down the stairs. "Here, now?" She stops on the stairs next to Dad.

"I'm sorry to intrude," Dean goes on. "I took a wrong turn and had to backtrack, making it take longer to get here than I expected."

"Rory, what is going on?" Dad asks, glowering at Dean. I haven't told him anything about Dean yet, and all Mom knows is that we were dating and it sizzled out.

"I love your daughter," Dean says, looking back at me. My heart flutters and I lock my arms around his waist. "And she needs to know just how much she means to me. I couldn't let her leave and take the job here without telling her that."

"Can we have some privacy?" I ask, tearing my eyes away from Dean for a moment. "Please?"

"Yes," Mom says, tugging Dad back up the stairs. I take Dean's hand and we go to the living room couch. I'm shivering and Dean's not wearing a coat. He pulls me close to him and I cover us both up with a blanket. Before either of us can say anything, Dean kisses me, pushing his tongue into my mouth.

"I'm so sorry, Rory," he breathes between kisses. "I never should have let you walk away." He runs his hands through my hair.

"No, you shouldn't have." I smile and kiss him again. "I love you, Dean, but I need something to be clear."

"Okay."

"I want a relationship that has the potential to turn into something more. Marriage. A family. I'm not saying I want it soon, but I need you to know that is my end game."

"It's mine too," he confesses. "It's always been my end game, and it didn't work the first time, but it was because I wasn't with the right person. You are the right person. My person. I've never felt this with anyone before."

I'm smiling again. "I do like being your first."

He pulls me onto his lap, adjusting the blanket. "Come home with me, Rory? I mean Eastwood. I know this is your home."

"I grew up here, and my childhood home will always be special, but it feels...wrong. I know where I'm meant to be, and that's in Eastwood. With you."

≈

"Everything good?" I ask, rolling over. Dean and I are squished together in my old twin bed in my childhood bedroom.

"Yeah. It is." We fell asleep in each other's arms last night, and his work alarm just went off. He texted his dad, briefly explaining why he's in Michigan, hence him not being able to go into work. "What are you going to do about the interview?" he asks, spooning his body around mind.

"Is it shitty to call off at the last second?"

"I think it's better to cancel than to waste someone's time with an interview when you're not going to take the job."

"True. But is it shitty to text Michelle instead of call her?"

Dean chuckles. "It's not the most professional."

"Dammit." I roll over, facing Dean. A huge weight has been lifted off both of us, and despite how painful yesterday was, everything is perfect.

I'm in Dean's arms.

I love him.

He loves me.

No one knows what the future holds, but we're going to go into it together.

"Fine. I'll call." I tear myself out of Dean's arms and grab my phone. My pulse quickens and I thankfully get Michelle's voicemail. I leave her a message saying I just can't leave my current job…or current life in Eastwood. I hang up and go back into Dean's arms. We stay tangled up together a while longer, until the smell of coffee and bacon fills the house.

"We should get up," Dean grumbles, not making any attempt to let me go.

"I'm hungry."

"Me too." He kisses my forehead. "And I'm looking forward to getting back to your place. We need to have makeup sex STAT."

I laugh and put my lips to his. "There's a make-out spot a few miles from here. We can pull off the road and do each other in the car like horny teenagers."

"Don't tease me, Rory." He runs his hands up and down my body. "Are you tired? We have a long drive."

"Ugh," I grumble. "In separate cars."

"Let's get up and get it over with." He presses his lips to my forehead and we both get up and go downstairs. Dad is at the stove, making breakfast.

"Honey," Mom calls from her office. "Can I borrow you for a moment? You're about the same size as my client and I need someone to try on this dress."

"Yeah," I tell her, knowing half her needing me is so Dad can talk with Dean. I take a sip of coffee and then go to Mom's office. She's holding a pale pink ball gown.

"Is everything okay?" she asks, helping me into the dress.

"It's perfect."

"He must really care if he drove all this way in the middle of the night."

I smile. "He does. I love him," I say, smile widening.

Mom fluffs the skirt, beaming up at me. "Are you two able to stay for another hour or so?"

"Yeah, we'll stay for breakfast but then should head back to Eastwood. Figaro probably misses me."

"I texted Sam about Dean." Mom bends down and pins the hem of the dress. "He said he likes him and thinks he's a good guy."

"Mom, seriously?"

"I thought you'd be happy your brother likes your boyfriend. Out of the last few guys you've dated, none of your brothers have been a fan."

"That is true. I should have dated Sam's friends a long time ago."

Mom stands back and has me spin, making sure the dress swirls the way she wants it to. Satisfied, she helps me out of the heavy dress, and I put my pajamas back on. "You're glowing." She takes my hands in hers. "I have a good feeling about this, Rory."

I beam. "I do too."

CHAPTER 39

DEAN

FOUR MONTHS LATER...

"I lean across the bar, showing just the right amount of cleavage, and ask Tomlin if he'll let me have a room for one gold piece instead of five." Rory looks at me, giving me a wink. "He finds me very hard to resist."

Quinn pushes her little pewter game piece next to Rory's. "And I stand behind her, causally running my finger over the blade of my dagger."

Rory nods. "My friend and I would really like a room. We're quiet and will tidy the place when we leave."

"Tomlin's resolve is strong," I say, looking down at the guide. "Two gold pieces and the room is yours."

"Thank you, kind sir," Rory says. "I pay for our drinks and go up to the room in the inn."

The oven timer beeps, and I get up, putting the Dungeons and Dragons game on hold. Quinn, Archer, Weston, and Scarlet are all here, and we've made D&D an almost weekly thing. It took a while for us all to get into it, but now we're all slightly addicted.

"And I have to pee." Quinn puts her hand on her stomach. "Help me up."

"Of course, babe." Archer stands and helps Quinn to her feet. Quinn is finally feeling less nauseous but now has a lot of back pain. They found out recently they're having girls, making Aiden the Quinn of the family with four sisters instead of four brothers.

Rory goes to the stove and takes out the cookies she put in right before we started our games session.

"That smells good," I say, snaking my arms around her waist. "I want one."

She stands on her toes and gives me a kiss. "You'll get my cookies later." She wiggles her eyebrows and I kiss her hard.

"Can we end the game now?"

"We haven't even left the tavern!"

"I want to take you to the tavern."

"Ohhh, I like when you talk nerdy to me," she coos.

"You have work in the morning, right?" I ask.

"Yeah," she groans. "It's a full moon tomorrow too. It's going to be crazy."

"Poor babe. I can meet you for lunch."

"If I get a lunch." We kiss again before she turns to take the cookies off the sheet, putting then on a cooling rack she then carries to the table. We resume the game, playing for an hour and a half before putting it on hold again until the next time we're able to sneak a few hours away from our adult responsibilities.

As soon as I close and lock the door, I make a rush at Rory, picking her up and throwing her over my shoulder. "You've been kidnapped by orcs," I say, putting my Dungeon Master hat back on. "But you are insanely attracted to him."

Rory laughs, trying to squirm out of my arms. I carry her upstairs and toss her down on my bed.

"The only way to escape my clutches is through the power of seduction," I go on and Rory laughs, but looks at me with lust in her eyes at the same time.

"Well, in that case…" She pushes up on her knees and grabs my hands, pulling me down onto the mattress with her. My heart swells in my chest, and I look at Rory, falling in love with her a bit more and more every day. And every day, I think it's impossible to love her more than I already do.

EPILOGUE

DEAN

A YEAR AND A HALF YEAR LATER...

"Hey!" I say, stepping into the kitchen of my parents' house. It's Sunday night dinner, and the whole gang is here. It hasn't happened too often lately, with scheduling issues and Emma and Jackson busy with extra circulars.

"Oh my goodness, how cute!" Rory drops her purse on the ground and goes over to Quinn, who's sitting at the kitchen table with both babies in her arms. They're dressed the in Elsa and Anna dresses we got them for Christmas. "Dean, look!"

"They finally fit." I smile at my nieces.

"I was so excited," Quinn tells us. "Thanks again for getting these for the girls."

I wrap my arm around Rory's waist and plant a kiss on her cheek. We went to Disney World a few months ago and Rory and I had fun buying stuff for our many nieces and nephews. It turned out to be way more expensive than we thought though to buy everyone a shirt or outfit, but it was worth it seeing the excitement on their faces.

Owen, Charlie, and Olivia come in the house next, surprising everyone.

"You're on time?" I bring my hand to my chest, faking shock.

Owen takes Olivia's coat off and motions to Charlie. "Being ridiculously early for everything is part of her nesting."

Charlie puts her hands on her stomach. "This little guy has me wanting to organize and prepare everything. I keep panicking about having two kids." She looks at Quinn and shakes her head. "How are you still functioning with five?"

"I'm not," Quinn laughs. "Though having a nanny and house-keepers help."

"Must be nice to be rich," Owen quips, teasing Quinn. "The rest of us have to take care of our own children and wash our own dishes."

"You wash dishes?" Charlie puts her hand on her hip.

"Hey, I'm a good housekeeper."

Charlie gives us a look and we all laugh. Olivia takes Owen's hand, dragging him to the backyard so she can play outside with the other children.

"Want to outside?" Rory asks, looking through the window at Archer, Weston, my parents and all the kids. "It's so nice out."

Of course." I pull out a chair for Charlie, who slowly lowers herself down, and take Rory's hand. We run around with kids for a while, and Rory gets winded easily.

It's a little humid out, but that's not why she's not feeling like herself.

"Come with me," I tell her, motioning to the covered glider. I wrap my arm around her and gently push my feet against the ground, bringing the glider back.

"This is nice," Rory says, resting her hand on my shoulder. "And my rings look so sparkling in the sunlight."

I laugh, taking her left hand in mine. "You should get them cleaned more often."

"That requires going to the jeweler," she laughs. "But they look like they did on our wedding day."

"Speaking of our wedding day, I think you should bust out that white lacey thing you wore under your dress?"

"I'll see what I can do." She resituates, hooking one leg over mine.

"Have I told you I love you yet today?"

She beams, tipping her head up to mine "You have, but I wouldn't mind hearing it again."

I put my lips to hers and rest my hand over her stomach. "I love you so fucking much."

"That's more like it."

We stay outside for a bit longer, enjoying the sun and the warm summer air. Then Logan and his family arrives, and it's the typical ten minutes of chaos that always happens before everyone crams around the table.

"Who wants sangria?" Scarlet asks, coming to the table with a pitcher of sangria she made just for tonight. "Besides you, preggers," she says to Charlie with a wink.

"No thanks," Rory tells her and I wait for anyone to raise their suspicions, Rory doesn't drink all that often, so it's not that odd for her to decline any alcohol tonight.

She looks at me, trying not to smile. We planned to wait until dinner to share our news, but I don't think either of us can keep the secret any longer.

"You gonna ask Rory why she doesn't want any sangria?" I ask casually, taking great care to put mustard on my hamburger.

"Oh my God," Quinn squeals, bring her hands up and shaking them excitedly.

"Are you?" Mom asks, eyes going wide.

Rory looks at me and smiles. "Yes. I'm pregnant!"

I take Rory's hand in mine, lacing our fingers together. My heart is so full it might burst, and I look at my wife—at the mother of our child—and couldn't love her any more.

Mom jumps up and runs around, hugging Rory and then me.

"Congrats, man," Archer says, clapping me on the back.

"You didn't know?" Owen asks, throwing his head back in fake shock. "I always thought if there was a way for Dean to carry Archer's baby it would happen."

"Shut up," Quinn and I say at the same time.

Rory laughs and looks down at her stomach. "I can't believe there's a tiny baby in there."

"Enjoy the tiny stage." Charlie pats her stomach and laughs. "I'm so happy for you guys."

"Me too," Quinn says, looking at me from across the table with tears in her eyes. She and Scarlet have been come really close with Rory over the last year and we go out with Wes, Scarlet, Quinn, and Archer at least once a month. Rory and I started trying for a baby the month after we got married, and now, six months later, it finally happened. We found out Tuesday morning that she's expecting, and it's been so hard keeping this a secret until tonight.

Things didn't happen the way I planned, but sitting here, surrounded by my family and the woman I love more than anything in this whole fucking world, I wouldn't have it any other way.

THANK YOU

Thank you so much for taking time out of your busy life to read Rock Bottom! I never actually set out to write Dean a story, but after Kara's character grew into the unlikable you-know-what that she is, I had so many readers beg for me to give Dean a HEA! The more I thought out it, the more I knew I HAD to write this book, and the idea for Rock Bottom came into my head and I couldn't stop thinking about Dean and Rory!

I appreciate so much the time you took to read this book and and would love if you would consider leaving a review. I LOVE connecting with readers and the best place to do so is my fan page and Instagram! I'd love to have you!

www.facebook.com/groups/emilygoodwinbooks
www.instagram.com/authoremilygoodwin

ABOUT THE AUTHOR

Emily Goodwin is the New York Times and USA Today Best-selling author of over a dozen of romantic titles. Emily writes the kind of books she likes to read, and is a sucker for a swoon-worthy bad boy and happily ever afters.

She lives in the midwest with her husband and two daughters. When she's not writing, you can find her riding her horses, hiking, reading, or drinking wine with friends.

Emily is represented by Julie Gwinn of the Seymour Agency.

Stalk me:
www.emilygoodwinbooks.com
emily@emilygoodwinbooks.com

Immortal Night (Thorne Hill Companion Novella)

Dystopian Romance:

Contagious (The Contagium Series Book 1)

Deathly Contagious (The Contagium Series Book 2)

Contagious Chaos (The Contagium Series Book 3)

The Truth is Contagious (The Contagium Series Book 4)

Printed in Great Britain
by Amazon